D0930189

Praise for

WOO-WOO

"Author Joe Coccaro offers an engaging story and interesting characters using charming prose and an intriguing otherworldly plot. *Woo-Woo* delivers both laughs and goosebumps. Get ready to be entertained."

> —**Dr. My Haley, Author of *The Treason of Mary Louvestre* and Collaborator on Pulitzer Prize-winning *Roots***

"Joe Coccaro employs the same quality prose as Richard Russo in telling the story of Carter Rossi's adventures. This is a really great story, and more than that it is a world you are reluctant to leave when you turn the last page."

> —**Amazon Bestselling Author William Hazelgrove, Author of *The Pitcher***

"*Woo-Woo* captures the essence of an isolated beach community and the colorful people who live there. The added elements of a rambling ghost and a bit of romance make for a fun and satisfying read."

> —**Kathy Merlock Jackson, Professor of Communication and Editor of *The Journal of American Culture***

Woo-Woo:
A Cape Charles Novel

by Joe Coccaro

© Copyright 2017 Joe Coccaro

ISBN 978-1-63393-555-6

This is a work of fiction. The characters are both actual and fictitious. With the exception of verified historical events and persons, all incidents, descriptions, dialogue and opinions expressed are the products of the author's imagination and are not to be construed as real.

Published by

◣ köehlerbooks™

210 60th Street
Virginia Beach, VA 23451
800-435-4811
www.koehlerbooks.com

WOO-WOO

a cape charles novel

JOE COCCARO

VIRGINIA BEACH
CAPE CHARLES

You can't depend on your eyes when your imagination is out of focus.

—Mark Twain

AUTHOR'S NOTE

For the free spirits who call Cape Charles home.

CHAPTER 1

CARTER ROSSI EASED the U-Haul onto Tyler Lane, careful to avoid a stray cat leaping over the torrent that flowed into the street gutter. He tapped the brakes to park by the concrete curb and disturbed a stew of leaves and sticks that had fallen from the street's canopy of sycamore and gum trees. The black edge of the thunderhead that had just dumped its load now roiled over the Chesapeake Bay, a few blocks away from where Carter sat. He stared out his window as it flashed and boomed like black-powder cannons at war.

A colorful arc emerged in the storm's wake, teasingly at first with dim shades of orange, yellow, and red, then bursting into a full bloom of greens, blues, and indigo. *A rainbow. How cool.* Carter grinned.

Like most of the other streets in the twenty-seven-block checkerboard of old Cape Charles, Tyler Lane had dips, twists, and gullies that became ponds after downpours. Water needs gravity, and Cape Charles had too much of one and barely enough of the other. The town was as flat as the Bay it bordered, less than ten feet above sea level at its crest and a few inches below in divots. Like rain, wind reigned over this patch of earth, terrorizing and vengeful at times.

Much of the town had been marsh until developers in the '20s and '30s, and the railroad, drained it and then compacted the soupy mud with coal cinders, crushed oyster shells, old bricks, and other debris. That "fill" had compressed over decades, and most of the houses built on it, like Carter's small foursquare, sagged from uneven settling. If human, Carter's old house would be in serious need of a back brace. He had worried about that when he first looked at the 1920s three-bedroom bungalow, but his real estate agent had seemed nonchalant.

"If you were a hundred years old, you'd be leaning and have some cracks too," the agent told Carter weeks ago. "Everything leans 'round here—even the people."

Carter stepped down from the moving van and onto the street, unconcerned about dunking his Keen sandals into the mild torrent. It was almost summer, after all, and the rainwater rivaled the air temperature. If he were a boy, he'd be knee deep with joy, soaking himself and friends. If a teen, he'd be walking hand in hand with his love, splashing in the puddles to wet her shorts and T-shirt, and then figuring some plan to slip them off.

Carter tilted his head a few degrees to level his eyes with his slightly leaning abode. At least the roof was good, and the yard seemed dry. Leaves the size of a catcher's mitt carpeted the approach to his front steps. One cat, then another, sprang from the lilac bush by the front stoop, both looking wet, mangy, and guilty. A dead robin, wings torn off and beak bloodied, lay matted and muddy.

"Get! Go on." Carter motioned at the murderous felines.

About two blocks from where Carter stood, a ten-foot wall of sand dunes pocked with brown grasses provided reassurance. The dunes were like a wall protecting the town from the Bay's angry moods. *They're doing their job,* he thought. Even so, he felt wise to have purchased flood insurance. His old brick home had a basement, and in Cape Charles anything less than sea level got swamped—eventually.

Carter turned and looked in the opposite direction. One block up the street was Oyster Park. His house sat equidistant from the beach and the park—a block and a half in each direction. Kids emerged from the park's covered performance stage, jostling and laughing. Boys got soaked and the girls stayed dry. *Further evidence that girls are smarter than boys,*

Carter quipped to himself. As he stepped onto the sidewalk, he saw two boys hustling toward him, hair matted and looking no better than the dead robin by his feet.

"You Mr. Rossi?"

"You bet," Carter said. "And you are?"

"I'm Jed, and this here is Elroy, but you can call him Roy. Aunt Hattie said you was movin' in today and might could use some help, sir."

Aunt Hattie? "Oh, you mean the real estate lady? Heather Savage?"

"Yes sir. She's my aunt, on my dad's side. Her real name is Heather, but she don't like that cuzin' it sounds too girly. Least that's what she says. My aunt's kinda tough; grew up on a farm out in the county, up the road by Machipongo. Dad says she could chop a chicken's head off with a pen knife and gut a deer in ninety seconds. Skin one in less than thirty minutes too."

"Good thing I didn't ask her to cut her commission," Carter said.

After a few seconds of thinking, the boys laughed. "Nah, she ain't like that—once you get to know 'er," Jed said.

"Well, boys, sounds like you want to make a few bucks. How 'bout sixty each to empty the truck and carry in the furniture and the heavy boxes? It'll save me a trip to the chiropractor."

The boys' eyes swelled, and Jed stuck out his hand for a shake. "Sixty bucks! Thank you, sir. Deal!" He went on, "You know, we got one of those in town."

"One of what?" Carter asked.

"A *chiroproctor,* you know, somebody who fixes backs and stuff. She lives over there." Jed pointed to a blue Victorian across the street. "Aunt Hattie sold 'er that house. Auntie and her company sells just 'bout everything 'round here. Been doing it a long time. Took over the business from her daddy. The Savages go way back 'round here, oldest family in the county, not includin' the Indians, if you know what I mean."

"Good to know your aunt has deep roots and lots of connections in case I get in trouble and need to sell," Carter said. He pointed to the *chiroproctor's* house. "Nice porch. Love the red trim and purple gables. People like their crazy colors in this town. That house doesn't look like it leans much either, at least not as bad as this old girl."

"Yeah, people like their porches 'round here," Jed said. "Yours don't lean too bad. Seen lots worse. Cud use some paint on the trim, if you know what I mean."

"Yeah, she needs lots of cosmetics," Carter said. "You boys been waiting long for me to show up?"

"Kinda. Aunt Hattie said you'd be movin' in today. We was just hangin' round playin' soccer in the park. Roy here is sweet on one of the girls. He was showin' off his muscles when the thunderboomers rolled in. Not much else to do 'round here 'cept chase the girls and fish."

Carter looked from Jed to Roy and noticed Roy eyeing him. But Roy never said a word. He wasn't a talker.

"Chasing girls and fishing. Kinda the same thing, don't you think?" Carter said, winking at Roy. "Everyone make it through the storm okay? Seemed pretty violent and loud."

"Ever'body scattered like flies when the light'nen started," Jed said. "One boy got 'lectracuted in the park last summer. Burned his left ear. He don't hear er speak so good no more. Course, he didn't talk too good before he got 'lectracuted either."

"Sounds like you get some violent storms then," Carter said.

"Sometimes. But the one that came through today weren't nothin' special. Just noisy is all," Jed said. "We get 'em like that a couple times a week in summer. One threw off a tornader that 'bout leveled a campground across the creek last summer. A buncha people got hurt; killed a little Asian boy. Pine trees over there snapped like twigs and fell on the kid's camper. These'ins are pretty sturdy." Jed pointed to a large sycamore in front of Carter's yard. "But you might oughta get some of them branches trimmed. I know somebody with a chainsaw and long ladder."

"Paint the porch and trim the tree. Good advice," Carter said. He eyed the tree's spindly tentacles that looked like the arms and legs of a person with severe arthritis. "You guys ready to get started?"

Carter walked up the nine steps to his covered porch and opened the front door. The boys followed him inside. The house looked smaller than Carter remembered, and bleaker. Only 1,600 square feet, not including the basement. The place was empty, stripped of everything but faded wallpaper and bent curtain rods. The floors were decent, though, except in the kitchen. It was covered with faded and stained linoleum tile from the '80s.

"Place is nice, but looks like it needs some cleanin' up. You know, me and Roy here does some paintin' and yardwork. I'm just sayin'."

"Yeah, this is gonna be a project," Carter said.

It occurred to Carter that the house, on the outside and in, looked sad. It felt that way too—forlorn, like an abandoned child. Hattie had told Carter the demeanor of 205 Tyler Lane was the byproduct of a nasty divorce; the couple had only lived in it a few years. Enthusiastic at first, they had pumped every discretionary cent into support beams in the basement, new plumbing, and upgraded electrical panels. By the time they got to the cosmetic stuff, the marriage had cracked under financial stress and emotional neglect.

"These walls have heard some hate," Hattie had said when first showing Carter the house.

"Well, at least nobody was murdered. At least it isn't haunted." Carter had laughed.

"Hah! They're all haunted." Hattie had smiled and winked. "If you hear footsteps in the night, don't fret. Cape Charles' ghosts mostly keep to themselves. Most just wander 'round like they're lost. Sometimes they taunt ya, I'm guessing 'cause they're bored."

"*Oh great!*" Carter had huffed. "Shouldn't there be some kind of legal disclosure about houses for sale being haunted, kinda like disclosures of asbestos or lead paint?"

"You can prove asbestos and lead is there, but t'aint nobody I know who can prove a house got spirits. Besides, don't take all this woo-woo stuff 'round here too serious."

"Woo-woo?"

"Yeah, spirits, supernatural stuff like that. Anyways, the way I see it, the town must be a pretty nice place, 'cause the dead seems to like stickin' 'round."

"*Touché!* Never thought about it that way. Maybe the town should put that in its tourist brochure: *Cape Charles, a town so great you'll never want to leave.*"

"Dang. That's pretty good, honey. Gil said you was smart."

"*Gil!* You know that SOB, huh?"

"Shoot, everybody knows Gil. His pub *is the town* in the winter. Gil Netters is the only place to get a burger or a beer and be among the living in January, February, and March. Lights off every place else . . . a real ghost town come winter."

"Well, Hattie, don't believe a word Gil says about me."

"Trust me, I don't! Gil's pub is rumor central, and he's the orchestra conductor. Gil trades gossip with customers like penny stocks. Keeps people coming into the pub. He'll pour someone a double shot to get 'em blabbing. Mostly though, people volunteer their thoughts and opinions without much goading, 'specially lately. Been getting nasty with this crazy election."

"Yeah. Seems like this election is bringing out the worst in everyone."

"People is pretty fed up or fired up," Hattie had agreed. "Saw Mr. Grimes from Eastville push old man Standish off his barstool two weeks ago. They was arguing about Obamacare or welfare or something stupid. Mr. Grimes don't like the president 'cause he is, well, you know . . . Anyway, old man Standish called Mr. Grimes an ignorant dirt farmer and a racist. Don't never call Mr. Grimes ignorant. He clocked old man Standish. He went down hard and cracked his hip on Gil's brick floor. Old man Standish lay on his side screaming that he was gonna sue. Gil nearly pissed himself."

"Did he sue?"

"No, not yet anyway. Funny thing is, Mr. Grimes and old man Standish is first cousins; their mommas are sisters. I suspect their mommas will work things out between them in private. I'm guessing old man Standish will be drinking free whiskey at the pub for a while too. People have their own ways of settling things 'round here. These sorts of things make for great entertainment and even better gossip—better than cable TV, right?"

"Much better. So, what was the gossip about the previous owners of my new place?"

"The husband was a merchant mariner and sometimes at sea for months, and his wife was skinny, pretty, and lonely. Catch my drift?"

Hattie had then clicked off a string of rumors like a defense lawyer summing up a case to a jury. Rumor: The crew kept a couple of Russian escorts comfortably on board. Rumor: The wife got lonely and started in with a golf instructor, a guy eight years younger. Rumor: Ex-husband slashed the convertible roof on the golf instructor's Mustang. Rumor: The husband has a child somewhere with a Russian first name. Rumor: The wife made a selfie porn video after the divorce and sent it to the ex-husband.

"A real shame. Nice couple when they first moved here. I sold them the place. But women in their thirties get bored, 'specially 'round here, 'specially with their husbands gone. There weren't nothin' romantic 'bout her messin' with that pimple-face preppy kid teaching golf at the Seabay Club. Boredom and hormones is a raging stew. Women got their needs, same as men. That kid just accommodated her needs, I suppose."

"What about the rumors about the guy? True?"

"Can't prove nothin', so it don't matter, really. My daddy once told me that rumors are what folks believe to be true, and truth is feed corn of all good rumors."

"*Profound!* Was your daddy a philosopher?"

"Nope. Raised pigs and chickens and sold real estate, just like me. Honestly, I think raising pigs for slaughter is cleaner than selling houses. Makes you more philosophical too. You see the world in simple terms."

"You're scaring me, Hattie. A town full of ghosts, hurtful rumors, and pig killers. Not sure I see the charm."

"Nothin' to worry about, honey. Truth is, if you live year-round in Cape Charles and people ain't rumoring about you, then you need some spice in your life. Gil down at the pub will see to it that plenty of folks is rumoring about you. And, if you see a ghost, take a picture. It'll make your property value go up."

* * *

Carter lifted another box from the moving van and smiled as he thought about Hattie's grit and candor—and a rumor mill run amok. *Who needs Twitter in a town like this?*

Inside, he took a water break and a few minutes to take some measurements in the hall entrances and doorways. He spread a few tarps over the golden pine slats, each with waves of grain, groves still tight and straight. Old pine, hard pine. None of that bamboo crap.

"Okay, fellas. What do you say we get the big stuff moved in first upstairs? I want to get my bed set up. I figure we got about three hours before sunset."

After a couple of hours, about half the moving van was emptied and the trio took a break to cool off. The wind had calmed, and the saturated air had expanded in the ninety-degree afternoon sun. Carter removed a Rolling Rock from a small cooler he had set on the porch. Sweat immediately beaded on the green bottle.

"You boys old enough to drink?"

"Yup. We can drink, so long as we don't get caught," Jed piped. "But I ain't so worried about that. Uncle Chip's the police chief in town. And my cousin Smitty's the sergeant. They'd smack us upside the head beforin' they'd arrest us. Dad was a drunk. Dead now, though. They keep warnin' about him and drinkin'."

"So, the top two cops are relatives? Those are pretty good odds of staying out of jail," Carter said. "Okay, take a beer then, but promise not to tell Aunt Hattie—or cousins Chip and Smitty. I don't want to get on their bad side."

The boys each grabbed a beer and grinned at each other.

"Sir, mind if I smoke?" Jed asked.

"I'd advise against it, but that probably wouldn't do any good."

"Well if that's a 'yes,' can I bum a cigarette?" Jed asked.

"Sorry, son. A bad liver is one thing; lung cancer is another. I don't smoke—never did, never will."

"Not even—" Jed started.

"Not gonna answer that," Carter said. "Too many rumors around here."

The boys were careful moving the furniture. They only banged the stairwell walls a couple of times. A few wall scrapes and creases. *Never fails. Nothing ruins furniture like moving it,* Carter thought.

Jed was on the skinny side but had that wiry strength that would surprise a foe in a fight. He had smoky blue eyes, one crossed and filmy. Carter wondered if he could see out of it. Jed's dusty blond hair flowed in wavy knots, and his front teeth were mostly straight but gapped. Braces would have made him almost handsome. He had a long, thin jaw, and his ears were set back. He looked like Tom Petty, overbite included.

Roy, on the other hand, looked like a very young Idris Elba. He had dark skin, arresting facial features, and the bulk of a linebacker—but not the height. His calves were nearly as thick as Hattie's, and his hair was shaved close to the scalp. He had a pierced ear and blue tattoo on his forearm that seemed faded and smudged.

"Looks like your tattoo tried to escape," Carter joked.

Roy spoke up. His words came out with a slight stutter. "My *b*-brother's friend done it. Not sure what it's supposed to be," he said as he looked at his forearm and shrugged.

"Me neither," Carter said. "You need a do-over."

Carter could tell Roy was the smarter of the two, despite his oral impediment. It was Roy who had directed Jed as they tried to figure out the best geometry for getting furniture through narrow doors or up the stairs. His dark-brown eyes were kind, and he never got flustered. Roy had leveraged the weight of furniture and boxes efficiently. While Jed grunted and used his back to lift, Roy had hoisted silently with his thick legs and broad shoulders.

"You're strong," Carter said to Roy during a break. "You play sports?

"*N*-no sir. *N*-no sports to play 'round here 'cept fur *f*-football. Lift weights, though."

"Told ya 'bout his muscles," Jed chimed.

"*G*-go on and stop it, Jed, 'fore I smack you one," Roy blurted. Jed smiled demurely and headed to the U-Haul for another box.

All three were soaked as the sun-steamed humidity stubbornly lingered. Toads and frogs screamed in the drainage ponds at Oyster Park, no doubt gorging on a hatch of insects. Carter had already swatted a few mosquitoes needling his exposed calves and arms, and now he crushed gnats flying suicide missions into his eyes.

"Buggy 'round here," Jed said as he watched Carter scratch and swat. "You'll get eaten 'live 'round this time of day. The town used to spray fur skeeters, but Aunt Hattie says they's run outta money fur sprayin'."

"Hope I don't get malaria or that Zika virus," Carter said as he pointed to a welt on his leg.

"Cats get it," Jed said. "And thar damn sure 'nough of 'um 'round here. Aunt Hattie calls 'em crab bait. Says they're worse than rats, possums, and squirrels. They's kill the birds in the spring, baby ones."

"Yeah, I see. I found a dead robin by the bushes."

"That *m*-makes Aunt Hattie *m*-mad," Roy said.

"Guess I'll have to get a dog to keep the damn cats away. Man, these mosquitoes are bad," Carter said as he slapped his neck.

"My maw says to eat *g*-garlic," Roy piped.

"Eat garlic?"

"Yes sir. Keeps the *sk*-skeeters 'way."

"I guess garlic's good for mosquitoes and vampires . . . and scorned women too," Carter joked. He took a swig of Rolling Rock.

"I don't get it. What's women got to do with skeeters?" Jed asked.

"They's all *b*-blood *s*-suckers, dummy," Roy said.

Carter thanked the boys and pulled six twenty-dollar bills from his wallet and handed them three each. They shoved the bills into their pockets and grinned.

"You fellas need a ride home?"

"Nah. It's just a few *b*-blocks. Just 'bout everything in town justa few *b*-blocks away," Roy said.

"Mr. Rossi, can I ask you somethin?"

"Sure, Jed. Fire away. You want a beer for the walk home?"

"No sir, well, yeah, but that ain't my question. I'm wondering, you gonna be livin' hure alone? I mean, you gotta girl?"

Carter grinned. "Nothing subtle about you, is there. Why do you ask? You trying to fix me up with your Aunt Hattie?"

The boys laughed. "Nah, she's too old for you. 'Sides, she's married to Uncle Wally, and you don't want to get on his bad side. He's a mean drunk. He fought in Vietnam and got some medals. Gets crazy sometimes. I'm only askin', sir, 'cause the pickin's is pretty slim 'round here."

"The pickin's?" Carter said. He looked at Jed's filmy crossed eye and matted hair.

"Yes sir. I mean, they ain't many good-lookin' girls, at least ones 'round your age that ain't married. There's some divorced ones, but they gots kids and is kinda worn out. I'm just sayin' that if you're new here and want a girl, you'd better bring your own."

"Thanks for the advice, Jed." Carter grinned. "I'm guessing from the looks of you two scrubs that the women folk around here probably say the same thing about the local men: *slim pickin's*."

CHAPTER 2

CARTER COULDN'T RECALL ever being in such a quiet place, except maybe when camping out West. He remembered a trip on the outskirts of Moses Lake, in eastern Washington's Columbia River Basin. He and a college buddy had camped for a week in a ravine. They'd eaten peyote buttons and hallucinated, each swearing they saw Indian spirits. Coyotes had howled all night at the star-stuffed blackness. That trip was the first time Carter had ever really seen the Milky Way. Now, standing on his back deck in Cape Charles, there it was again.

By eleven that night, the streets were dry and not even a car passed. No dogs barked, no people talked, no car doors slammed. Just frogs screamed in the park drainage ponds. Even the stray predators that had scurried around earlier were bedded down and out of sight. Carter heard a burst of laughter from two blocks away. *Tourists having fun,* he thought.

Cape Charles wasn't like the crowded resorts of Virginia Beach, Nags Head on the Carolina coast, or even the trendy resort villages farther north along the Delaware/Maryland/Virginia Peninsula. No, this place felt more like a sleepy town from the 1950s than a resort. Locals called it Mayberry. Others said it was like living inside "the bubble." Everyone knew everyone, and everyone smiled, at least on the surface. Beneath the surface was centuries of history as old as the country itself. Carter loved history and had read a couple of books about Virginia's Lower Eastern Shore.

. . .

Everyone thinks about Jamestown and Williamsburg up along the James River as the first American colonies. In fact, the first British settlers claimed land in the Lower Peninsula. Englishmen had traded with Indians and farmed and timbered the seafood-rich Chesapeake Bay, which the indigenous Americans had to themselves until the 1600s. English kings granted the most productive and loyal British colonialists tens of thousands of acres. Direct descendants of those landed gentry still lived on the Shore. They included Hattie Savage's family.

Locals called these fortunate families the "haves." They had owned plantations settled by English traders. Everybody else were "come-heres." There were also generations of "have-nots," mostly the descendants of slaves. Many of the descendants of those poor souls still resided on the Shore, not far from the grave markers of their ancestors. When author Alex Haley was working on *Roots*, he sent a researcher to peruse court records in Northampton County, Cape Charles' home. Northampton didn't send property or other records to the Virginia capital of Richmond. Good thing too. When Richmond was burned after the Civil War, most county records were destroyed. Northampton's survived, including ownership records of slaves and land grants from the king.

"Lots of history here," Hattie had told Carter at his real estate closing. "People 'round here go way back; lots of stuff secret beneath the surface. Lots of people have cousins who don't look nothin' like them, if ya know what I mean. Lots of coffee in the cream. My family has some Indian and probably some African too. My best advice: Be careful about what you say and to who, 'cause they may be kin. Unless you know someone—and their family—you can't be sure who you're talking to. Word gets 'round fast. Easy to make friends here; easier to make enemies."

"Sounds intimidating," Carter had said, "and kind of nasty."

"It's worse than it sounds. Just tradeoffs. Everything's about tradeoffs."

"I suppose. Seems ironic though."

"Forget all that. Sorry I even brought it up. Just enjoy the place. Go with the flow. If you're friendly to Cape Charles, it'll be friendly back. Besides, buying here is a good investment."

"Right. It's always a good time to buy when you're in the real estate business, right, Hattie?"

Hattie had winked. "You betcha! But sometimes is better than others, and now's one of 'em. Where else can you buy a house for a couple hundred thousand dollars two blocks from the beach? We're four hours from ten million people. If this house was near the Bay in Maryland, it'd be 800 grand."

Carter didn't need to be sold. He had done his homework—and he didn't have 800 grand, or even half that. He had recently divorced. This had whacked his savings in half, and his ex-wife had received most of the equity in their house. Cape Charles was affordable. But what he liked most was its eclectic nature. Seemed like there were lots of people rebooting their lives here, creating a melting pot of Northerners, Southerners, haves and have-nots, painters, webpage designers, soybean growers, teachers, divorced folks, trust fund babies on a budget, and a smattering of drunken handymen. Some of the richest people in the county never graduated high school. Some of the poorest had PhDs.

Carter had heard the stories of how watermen with their white rubber boots, or farmers in Carhartts, would often mock Cape Charles' fancy city boys with the pastel-painted houses, plaid shorts, and European convertibles. Some farmers even stopped coming into town, nauseated by the sight of men strolling down Mason Way holding hands or leaning into each other, shoulder to shoulder. But over time, men and women of the land and sea had learned to coexist, each keeping their distance, but remaining respectful.

A massive golf course community and new marina had become the new economic engine of the town. *Southern Living* magazine and *The Washington Post* had hailed tiny Cape Charles as a hidden treasure, an "eco-tourism mecca," a baby St. Michaels, Maryland, of the Lower Eastern Shore. Two syndicated real-estate-reality TV shows had filmed episodes on Cape Charles. The town's two harbors also made it popular with weekend boaters, and it was often cited in boating magazines.

Sometimes an entire yacht club would cross the Bay to party *en masse* here. They'd dock their sailboats and cabin cruisers, rent a golf cart, and ride the streets whooping and laughing and handing out cans of Budweiser. These well-heeled tourists spread lots of money around town, so the town cops practiced restraint.

"You mark my words: In two or three years, you'll make big money on this place," Hattie had told Carter when all the papers were signed at the end of his closing. "I've seen this plenty of times before. The town goes up and then down. But each time it goes up, it rises a little higher, and when it goes down, it's a little lower. We got a lot of new people comin' here, older people with money. This town's on the rise. Trust me."

* * *

In addition to Cape Charles' energy, Carter liked the town because of its name. It sounded exotic—even hoity, like the other famous capes of the East Coast: Cape Ann, Cape Cod, Cape May, Cape Hatteras, Cape Lookout, Cape Fear. A cape is a spit of land jutting into the water and usually at the end of a peninsula. Cape Charles was named after the finger of land where the Delmarva Peninsula ends and fades into the mouth of the Chesapeake Bay.

Cape Charles had provided the Lower Shore with a core. The area had mostly been scattered hamlets and farms until the early 1900s, when railroad barons from Pennsylvania bought 2,650 acres around Cape Charles and carved it into 644 lots with a park at the town's center. The railroad delivered passengers and freight to the town, which was essentially a dead-end street. The only way to get farther south was to cross the Bay by ferryboat or barge.

Railroad workers, boat crews, bankers, builders, and convenience stores had fueled the local economy. Cape Charles' permanent population had peaked at about 5,000. Travelers awaiting passage to the other side had packed hotels, boarding houses, terminals, and taverns. Some days famous actors or musicians had hung out on the piers or in hotel lobbies or walked the streets to admire the architecture of the town's buildings. Benny Goodman and his band had passed through a couple of times, performing free concerts on the pier while waiting for the ferry to

Norfolk. Louis Armstrong too. Wealthy New Yorkers and politicians had strolled the town's main street and stayed in its best hotel suites while awaiting passage south.

The town died a swift death after a twenty-one-mile bridge with two tunnels opened in 1964. It had taken more than three years to build the span, which had used concrete casting made in Cape Charles. When the bridge opened, the plant and the jobs it created closed. Cape Charles had, unwittingly, engineered its own demise.

Economic cancer spread quickly. Trucks and cars no longer needed passage through the tiny town. New Yorkers stopped coming. Boarding houses and hotels emptied, the banks left, department stores closed. And with them went the town's people. Cape Charles shrank to fewer than 1,000 residents.

The flight was so swift that the place became a perfectly preserved ghost town of old Victorians, Gothic Revivals, foursquares, bungalows, and colonials. Since no one was moving in, no one wanted the houses or the forty-foot-wide lots they stood on. So, for three decades, many sat and rotted, slowly sinking into the soft, still settling land. Only the poorest people looking for the cheapest rents moved in. Many of the old buildings became Section 8 federal housing. Cape Charles and surrounding Northampton County became the poorest geographic pocket in Virginia.

Next came gentrification. Upwardly mobile baby boomers from Washington, Richmond, Maryland, Delaware, Philadelphia, New Jersey, and even New York City smelled a bargain by the Bay. They came in droves to snap up cheap summer vacation homes and restore them. This triggered a slow but steady resurgence that ebbed and crested with each real estate bubble in the '80s and '90s. Houses were so cheap, some charged them on credit cards.

"My daddy sold three in one day to these gay boys from up around New York somewhere," Hattie had told Carter. "They got 'em for around $30,000. I think they used a VISA card."

Most bought the houses to use as vacation homes. But some retired in the town. Florida was too damn hot, and the retirees had kids or grandkids they wanted to stay close to. Next came developers who poured tens of millions into the high-end golf community and marina on the edge of town. That lured even retirees and summer vacationers with even bigger money.

Preservations protected old Cape Charles. Most of it was designated a historic district by the town and the state, which meant all but the most decrepit houses would not be bulldozed. That also meant no neon signs or billboards and no buildings taller than four stories. No franchise burger or pizza places were allowed in Cape Charles—not one—and no 7-Eleven, no Walgreens, not even a commercial bank branch or a True Value. Not even a gas station. All of those tacky amenities were up on the highway two miles east of town.

No, all the shops of Cape Charles were decidedly homegrown—for better and for worse. What stores the town did have were strung along five blocks of Mason Way, the town's main street. It featured a coffee shop, a few art galleries, T-shirt shops, a pizza place, Blue Heron Hotel, an ice cream store, a wine shop, Bay Hardware, the old movie theater, a couple of art framing stores, and, of course, the pub and several real estate offices. Savage Realty held the prime spot at the corner of Mason and Harbor.

Of the Mason establishments, no two were as vital as Bay Hardware and Gil Netters. The locals joked that the town had three branches of government: Cape Charles Town Hall, Bay Hardware, and Gil's—the Congress, the executive branch, and the Supreme Court, in that order. The town gavel was the bottom of Gil's beer mug. Carter had experienced the pub owner's rants and proclamations many times over their many years of friendship. In fact, Gil had provoked Carter's move to Cape Charles.

"If this turns out to be a mistake, I'll harass you forever," Carter had told his friend when deciding to make the move.

"Look, moron, your life is already screwed up. You got nothing to lose. Besides, I need more steady customers after the tourist season, so bring your wallet."

* * *

Carter stepped around some unpacked boxes on the kitchen floor and onto the rear deck. The wind had shifted from the south to the west, and he could smell the acridness of the Bay, a brew of seagrasses with hints of marine life. He even caught a whiff of the oyster and clam processing warehouse a mile or so away as the crow flies. He closed his eyes and tried to imagine what flavors he could sense, as if he were blindfolded at a wine tasting. He filled his lungs and held in his breath. The air was heavy but sweet, not the diesel, stale mix of the city or the sulfur pungency of seaside marches during low tide. No, Cape Charles was a more complex brew, more subtle.

Carter thought he heard a door close inside and footsteps. He stepped back into the kitchen and walked the four rooms on the first floor, again, imagining the work ahead. He walked upstairs—nothing. *Just house groans. Probably more settling.*

The house, technically, was more bungalow than house. Though only two stories tall set on a full-raised basement, it looked three stories tall because of an attic dormer and the raised elevation of the foundation walls. Basements in Cape Charles were a mixed blessing. They often flooded, especially during heavy rainfall. But they kept floor joists dry and termite free.

"Just make sure the sump pump in the basement works," Hattie had warned Carter. "She leaks, but she doesn't flood. But make sure you buy flood insurance, just in case."

Carter listened under the twilight of his first night on Tyler Lane as his sump pump pushed water out of the basement and through a drain line emptying into his backyard. It almost sounded like a toilet flushing. A gurgle and swoosh.

Carter's house had three small bedrooms upstairs and a bathroom. Downstairs, it had a family room, dining room, small bathroom, and galley-style kitchen. The house kit had been ordered through a catalog by a boat captain in the 1920s and delivered to town, most likely by barge or by the Eastern Shore Railroad. The house cost $2,078, and the small wooden garage that came with it was $173. It was a mass of brick and plaster, thick pine studs, and thin-slat hard-pine floors—all delivered on large pallets. The floors had prompted Carter's offer to buy.

* * *

Carter laughed to himself as he recalled his chat with Hattie the day she showed him the house for the first time. She was so direct; it was refreshing. She was also sturdy and big, but not unattractive. She had deep-set blue eyes inherited from generations of English who had settled here in the late 1600s. Her family's descendants still owned land here deeded from the King of England. Hattie, though, was unpretentious, and her line of the family had long ago lost whatever Puritan grace it may have once possessed. She walked as fast as she talked, chewed gum with her mouth open, and occasionally blurted a belly laugh. Family members were upset when she refused to answer to her birth name, Heather. The name she preferred, Hattie, was a "black" name, her father had huffed.

"So what," Hattie had fired back. "I think we all know, Daddy, that the Savages are not purebloods. Come on, Daddy, the family secret ain't much of a secret at all."

Hattie spoke her mind and rarely apologized afterward. People like her wither a little or a lot. She was a fixture in town, a wildcard with a big smile and lots of stories, many involving herself. She once saw a schoolboy, a neighbor's kid, mocking an elderly woman walking into the drugstore with a cane. The boy and some friends were loitering by the entrance. The boy called the old woman a "hag" and said she smelled. Hattie was walking out of the store and heard the mocking.

"Excuse me, ma'am," Hattie said to the old woman. "May I borrow your walker for one second?"

Hattie had calmly approached the boy and whacked him three times on his rear end with the walking stick. The others weren't quick enough to escape, and she took a swipe at them too.

"You boys ever disrespect your elders again and I hear 'bout it, I'll tear up your behinds and box your ears—I don't care *who* your parents are!"

One of the boys' parents reported Hattie to the police chief. Hattie's cousin Chip just laughed at the complaining mother.

"Sounds like they deserved a whooping—and more," Police Chief Chip told her. "Go ahead and press charges if you want, but I reckon a complaint won't get too far with Judge Savage."

Hattie was a talker, for sure, which made her such a good real estate agent. She could sell a lawn mower to a hungry goat.

"You can't find floors like this anywhere," she had told Carter during his walk-through of the house. "And this is the best location in town. A block and a half from the beach, a block and a half from the park. Best of all, Gil's is four blocks that way. You can get shit-faced and stumble home. The local cops will even give you a ride. If they give you trouble, call me. My advice: Get a golf cart."

"I'm not worried about getting arrested for being drunk," Carter had said. "But I am worried about flooding. Does it flood here much?" Carter had known the answer, but figured he needed to at least ask.

"In the spring sometimes. We don't get tidal flooding from the Bay in town. Those damn nor'easters can be a pain, but the dunes hold off the water most of the time. Biggest problem 'round here is street flooding from thunderstorms. The water just sits there in the street. The town needs to keep those damn street drains cleaned out. Just make sure your sump pump works."

"I guess it'll all be underwater someday anyway," Carter had said. "Global warming, sea-level rise. Kind of scary. People around here worry about that?"

"That's why they make flood insurance," Hattie had said. "Besides, you'll be dead by the time the Bay reaches this block. I can see you're a worrier."

"Yeah, relaxing isn't my strong suit. I can't seem to figure out how."

"Movin' here is a good start. Trust me. This is a great place, 'specially in the summer. You'll like it. Besides, you're kinda cute. You look a little like that Bradley Cooper fella, you know, *Silver Linings Playbook*, *American Sniper*. The girls 'ull like you. They could use another guy to pass around. Pickin's is slim, 'specially when the tourists leave. You were married, right? Gil's wife's sister, if I recall."

"Yeah, you recall right. No secrets around here, I can see."

"Not many. Gil told me. Got a girlfriend?"

Carter had shuffled nervously.

"Well, if ya don't, there's some fun to be had. There's a few divorcées around who are bored, if ya know what I mean. My advice: If you do any local datin', don't talk about it much—and do it after dark. Everyone knows everything that goes on 'round here. And what they don't know can be found out real fast at Gil's. I'm just sayin'."

"Yeah, that seems to be the case already. Don't worry. I'm not here to find a woman or give anyone anything to talk about. Been there, done that."

"Startin' over can be fun. Depends on your attitude about it."

"Maybe. It's been a rough couple years. I need to dial back on the drama for a while. But I'm sure Gil has already told you—and probably half the town—all about me. No secrets with a bartender, especially one who was your brother-in-law."

"Guess you're right." Hattie had grinned. "Tell one person in this town anything and you might as well told fifty. Tell Gil and you might as well take out a newspaper ad. But hell, better to be gossiped about than ignored, I'd say. What fun's life without drama? I've had plenty. On marriage three. I regret how the first two ended, but I'd damn sure do 'em over. A woman's got needs, if ya know what I'm sayin'."

"Really? No regrets?"

"None, sweetie. I learned long ago that the best-tasting food almost always gives you heartburn or gas. Nice thing 'bout this little town is you can live indigestion free on bread and water—if that's what you really want—or you can burp and fart and dance around, and then have some stories to tell. Depends on what you got a stomach for."

CHAPTER 3

THE SLENDER WOMAN stepped into the pub and took a seat at the bar. She removed her sunglasses and placed them and a cell phone in front of her.

"Welcome to the Island of Misfit Toys. What can I get you, miss?"

"How about a glass of white. What do you recommend?"

"You look like a pinot gris girl. I have a few bottles. Just picked them up this morning. It's chilled and it's light, just like my wife." Gil flashed a toothy smile, winked, and wiped the bar top with a dish towel. "Sound good?"

"Sounds good. Island of Misfit Toys?"

"Stick around here long enough, and you'll see what I mean."

Rose stared into her cell phone, hoping a girlfriend, or maybe her mom, would text. She didn't like sitting at a bar alone but felt immediately comfortable in Gil's.

"Here ya go. I poured it in a chilled glass. It's warm outside." Gil smiled.

"Thanks."

"Menu? We have some decent specials. A lot of people like the crab cake. The lamb burger's good too. It's our special today. Comes with fries or chips."

"No food right now. Thanks, though. You gotta cool place here," Rose said, gazing around.

"Thanks very much. Cost me a small fortune to fix it up. It's a bank building from 1907. See that, it's the old bank vault." Gil pointed to what looked like a small room in the center of the bar with an open vault door at its entrance.

"Pretty cool," Rose said. She slid from her barstool to have a look. A couple of booths stood to one side. She walked through the vault, which led to another dining room on the other side where a few tables pressed against the brick wall.

Rose followed the cavernous room and emerged into yet another small sitting area with booths across from the other end of the bar. She basically had made a *U*. A small metal staircase as steep as a ladder spiraled up to the top of the vault. There were a couple of more tables and two lounge chairs. Rose ascended and stood by the rails rimming the perch. She stared down on the bar and front entrance.

Gil looked up at her and waved.

The ceilings, now just a few feet above her head, were made of ornate tin and were a good twenty feet up. The layout looked like a narrow neighborhood bar plucked right out of Brooklyn.

Just like the owner, she thought.

All the walls were brick. Not the faux brick façade of bars and restaurants designed to look retro. This was the real deal, cracked, worn, and uneven. Even the floors were brick. Gil Netters felt more like a living room than a tavern. The place felt drafty but warm. Gill nets hung like curtains over the cathedral-shaped windows flanking the entrance. When used for their intended purpose, these entanglers reach vertically into water to trap passing fish by the gills.

Rose descended back to her seat with a greater appreciation of the L-shaped bar made of solid yellow pine. She studied the big mirror behind the bar, the pendulum clock from the 1920s that didn't work, the painted mannequin perched on a shelf, and the lines of liquor bottles.

"Do you use those to keep patrons from escaping?" Rose said as she pointed to the draped gill nets.

"You know what they say—drink like a fish. I found those old nets in a dumpster by the pier when I first moved here. They inspired me.

Catching fish, catching customers. Same idea, right?"

"*Gil Netters*. Very clever," Rose said.

"A compliment from the lady. Thank you. And since you're critiquing the place, what'd you think of the loft?" Gil asked as he swabbed a wineglass with a white towel. "Sometimes, when the bar is empty and it's cold out, I go up there and smoke a cigar. What the hell, it's my place, right?"

Rose grinned. "Don't worry. Our secret. I smoke too. Cigarettes sometimes. I shouldn't, but it calms my nerves."

"Where ya from?" Gil asked.

"Born in Ohio, but been living in Pennsylvania the past couple of years."

"So, what brings you here?"

"Good question." Rose sipped her wine. "Smooth. Good choice."

"Thanks. That pinot gris is my wife's favorite, especially this time of the year. That's why I keep it stocked. So, why you here?" Gil pressed.

"Persistent, I see." Rose smirked. "Where's the bathroom?"

"Follow the bar to the end, and make a left."

Gil leaned slightly forward to get a better look as Rose strutted off. *Long legs. Nice ass; sexy sway. And perky tits. 32 C, maybe.* He always made mental notes of new arrivals. Gil was faithful to his wife, Jill, but most of his buddies and patrons were cads. He goaded and enabled them by scouting "new talent" as he liked to say. His mental checklist continued. Sometimes when hot girls were in the bar, he'd text his pals. If nothing else, taunting the locals was good for business. And Gil suspected that the bartender Lil texted girlfriends when a hot guy showed up. So, no double standard.

Real pretty face. Gorgeous oval baby blues. Like the wavy hair. Fake blonde, though. Five four, maybe five five. Nice lips. The boys will like that.

Rose settled back onto her high-back barstool. It swiveled.

"Nice chairs," she said when Gil came back around.

"Yeah. They're pretty popular. Most of the locals would rather sit at the bar than at tables."

"So, where you from? I can tell you're not from here."

"What gave me away?" Gil smiled.

"New York. Right?"

"Yeah, Manhattan."

* * *

Gil Tierney was an Irish-German-Greek Yankee, a tubby, loud Northerner who seemed constantly condescending. His Irish eyes always glittered and smiled, his German contriteness pissed people off, and his Greek sentimentality often made him sappy and temperamental.

His DNA cocktail gave him lots of charm—and balls.

He had stumbled upon Cape Charles in 2001. He and Jill were driving north, heading home after Carter and Jill's sister's wedding in Virginia Beach. Gil's Cadillac had started knocking, forcing him off Highway 13. A service station attendant on the highway, near the entry road to Cape Charles, said he'd need a day to find a part. He offered Gil and Jill a lift.

"You got two choices: The Peacock Inn on the highway a few miles back, or there's a small hotel in town near the harbor. It's more expensive, but at least there is a place to walk and get food. There's a pharmacy in town that serves ice cream and a hardware store. If you're friend to the owner, maybe he'll offer you a drink."

Gil and Jill fell in love that day with the funky town two miles off the highway. But it was Gil who made the case for buying a home there. He turned on his charm and convinced Jill to take the chance. And just like that, they walked into Savage Realty and bought an old Victorian for fifty grand. A week later, after Gil's prodding, they bought the old Harbor Town Bank building on Mason Way, just a couple of blocks west of the hotel and directly across the street from the channel leading into the Cape Charles Harbor.

The old bank's ceilings leaked and were caving in, and the walls were full of pigeon shit. The building would have been condemned in most towns, but its condition was routine for Cape Charles: a *bona fide* dump. Still, Gil and Jill saw great potential in the building and this empty shell of an old railroad town. There were a couple of rathole bars up on the highway, but no one served booze and food under one roof here. The old bank had reminded Gil of a trendy yuppie club where he had worked after college—exposed brick walls, tin ceilings, and walnut window trim.

Back in the present, Gil shot a look at Rose.

"My wife, Jill, quit her job as a pediatric nurse, and I told my bosses in Manhattan to stick it. I was sick of the Wall Street bullshit. They were a bunch of thieves. Ever see the DiCaprio movie *The Wolf of Wall Street*? It was almost that bad. We made money no matter what. It's a bloodsucking business. Jill and I were stressed out; she had a miscarriage and I needed a bypass. I was only forty."

"So, a bar?"

"Yeah. We both tended bar in college. In fact, I was tending bar after college too. That's how I got hired by Lowenstein and Sons. Old man Lowenstein used to come by the club I worked at with his street girls—different ones every week. The place was filled with Mafia guys, crooked cops, tabloid reporters, Hollywood types, and old lechers like Lowenstein. Everybody was snorting coke or drinking martinis. I took great care of that old geezer, and he tipped me big. One day he asked me if I had a college degree. I went to Syracuse and barely graduated."

"So, you're an Orangeman," Rose said.

"No, we're the *Orange* now, not the Orange*men*. The school went PC."

"Is that a lacrosse stick?" Rose pointed to the wall next to the mannequin.

"Yeah, that was my stick. I played for 'Cuse. I twisted my knee when I was a junior, and those pricks took away my scholarship. I started tending bar to pay tuition. Started drinking too much and staying out late and gotta degree in anthropology."

"Anthropology? You seem more like a psychology major, the sensitive type," Rose teased and tossed back her blond and brown locks.

"Anthropology was the easiest major they had with the least amount of math. Anyway, the degree was good enough for old man Lowenstein. He put me in an apprentice broker program, and I wound up selling junk bonds. But my real job was driving the old man and his *goy* bimbos around to bars and hotels. He popped sex pills like breath mints. His eyes were always bloodshot. People thought he smoked pot, but it was the sex pills."

Rose laughed. "Quite a story, Gil."

"Believe me, I got a lot more. I had to fumigate that backseat after I took old man Lowenstein on one of his dates. I kept two towels and a can of Lysol spray in the trunk."

"So, New York City boy comes to Cape Charles. Big change, huh? You like it?"

"Best and worst move I ever made. The bar business is a ballbuster, but I like the people. Well most of them anyway. Lots of smart folks here, but we have a high retard factor too. A lot of morons."

"I can see you don't mince words."

"No, I'm not Mr. Politically Correct. Gets me in trouble on Facebook sometimes with certain groups. But like W.C. Fields said, 'I am free of all prejudice. I hate everyone equally.' "

"Well, I guess that means that you might hate my sister and best friend. They're lesbians, so don't go there." Rose smiled. "Besides, I can tell you're not really a hater. I can tell you like women."

Gil laughed. "I like you . . . and I love lesbians. In fact, if I died and came back as a woman, *I'd* be a lesbian. Sometimes, I wish my wife was a lesbian. If you're a lesbian, maybe I can introduce you to her." Gil winked. "Anything is possible in Cape Charles."

* * *

At about eight that night, long after Rose had left, Gil took a seat on the customer side of the bar, happy to turn the shift over to Lil, and happier to be off his feet. As usual, Jill wasn't here. She was proud of Gil's, but had never been much of a drinker or liked the bar scene. She made it in occasionally to help, but preferred to stay home to sell fish-skin earrings on eBay. Still, everybody teased about Gil, Jill, and Lil. They called them the *Ills,* mostly because all three complained—a lot. Running the tavern was like farming: There was either too much rain or not enough, and patrons either drank too little or too much and were antisocial or obnoxious.

Carter had just finished some wings and was cleaning his fingers with a scented wet wipe when Gil settled onto the barstool next to him.

"Wings were awesome, Gil. I like the bourbon sauce. Messy but good."

"Did you get any in your mouth or just on your hands, you moron?"

"Both," Carter said. "Fingerlicking good."

Gil leaned over and kissed Carter on the cheek. "And you're such a nerd—and a wuss."

"Will ya stop doing that," Carter said as he wiped his cheek. "I swear, Gil."

"Just expressing affections. Jill says I need to be more affectionate, but she didn't say to who. So, there ya go."

"Save it for Jill."

* * *

Gil and Carter had met years ago at a brokers' conference.

Carter was in his early thirties at the time, about ten years Gil's junior. He was working at a small firm based in Norfolk, Hogan and Wynn, finance specialists that orchestrated media company buyouts. The firm essentially hunted for newspapers or TV stations that could be bought and found a buyer and arranged financing for the deal through brokerage firms, like the one Gil had worked for.

Carter was at the conference trolling for seed money for his firm when he and Gil were taking a break, watching Syracuse in the Final Four of the NCAA tournament at a hotel bar. The two alums, cheering on the Orangemen, started talking and drinking. Their team won, and the two newfound friends stayed out all night celebrating. Once a year, they met at Madison Square Garden to watch Syracuse in the Big East Conference.

The two men were diametric opposites. While Gil was a jokester who could make conversation with a snail—and a blend of sarcasm and compliments that was a perfect balance of balsamic vinegar and olive oil—Carter was shy, quiet, thoughtful, and sincere. He could be witty and trade barbs when challenged, but he preferred the sidelines, which made meeting people, especially women, challenging in a bar setting.

When the two first met, Carter had donned a mustache—a wispy patch of light-brown hair that looked more like an eyebrow. One day, while at a New York hotel bar, Carter lost a sports bet and Gil made him down a flaming shot. The blue blaze ignited a few hairs, and Carter was left with a hole in his mustache. The next morning, he shaved it, and Gil nicknamed him Sparky.

"I did you a favor, Sparky. If you kept that thing on your lip, you never would have gotten laid again. You looked like a twelve-year-old. My grandmother had a bigger 'stache than yours."

Carter and Gil's friendship thickened when Jill introduced the shy Carter to her sister, Sophie, on a trip Carter had taken to the Big Apple to catch up with Gil. Sophie liked that Carter came off as mellow, attentive, and a great listener. She saw him as great fatherhood material. Carter liked that Sophie was independent, sassy, and smart. She also seemed to hang on his every word and found time for his calls and text messages.

After about a year of long-distance dating, Sophie moved from her native New York to Virginia to marry Carter. To this day, Gil credited that wedding to his and Jill's discovery of Cape Charles.

"I'm in this shithole because of you," Gil often said when Carter had crossed the Bay to visit his friend.

"Well, I'm divorced because of you—so we're even," Carter had countered each time.

Carter had double majored in journalism and business at Syracuse—and a good thing too. He had tried news reporting for the *Chronicle* paper in Rochester, New York, but hated it. Professors hailed journalism as a noble profession, but Carter quickly discovered newspapers to be glorified factories that churned out content like widgets. The more sensational, the better. The only thing high-minded about daily-grind journalism was the egos of those in the news business.

"They all think they're geniuses or the pope," Carter once told Gil. "One dipshit I worked for told me journalism was his religion. The slimy old fart drank on the job and got fired for bonking an intern."

"If he was a priest, it would have been wine and an altar boy," Gil had said.

Carter had hated the daily news grind. His quota: two full stories a day and at least two news briefs. He worked nine to nine trolling for anything to fill space. He covered cops on weekends—accidents, fires, shootings. He always dreaded calling the parent of some high schooler killed in a car wreck on a Saturday night to ask for a comment. He had to pretend to be empathetic, even supportive. He felt like a whore.

The tipping point came one Friday when a three-year-old drowned in a neighbor's pool. A storm had blown over a section of the fence two neighbors shared, and the toddler had wandered into the neighbor's backyard.

Carter's boss, the lecherous weekend city editor, insisted he go to the house and interview the parents and neighbor. Carter tried calling first, hoping to avoid a face to face. But no one answered in either household, so he went out. He knocked on the door, and the two parents answered, hysterical. The father, tears in his eyes, his voice cracking with emotion, ordered Carter to leave. As Carter retreated to the sidewalk, a TV news truck pulled up.

"Great!" the father said. "Isn't it enough that my daughter is dead? You people."

Carter hustled next door and knocked. No answer. Through the front window he saw people sitting inside a dark den, the TV blaring. Perhaps they hadn't heard him knock. Carter went around back to see the pool and take a picture with his newsroom-issued Nikon. At least he'd have something to show the city editor.

The neighbors saw the intruder pointing his camera at their pool and unleashed their Rottweiler from the back door. The dog bolted over the fallen fence and charged. Carter received three stitches on his arm and then a summons for trespassing. The newspaper got the charges dropped by offering an apology and a small settlement.

Carter was sick of the "blood beat," as he called it. Profiting from other people's pain seemed exploitative and undignified. He had noticed that the guys and gals from the advertising department seemed happier. They left work by six each day and had weekends off. They drove BMWs. People in the news department drove Toyotas. The ad people wore pressed suits; newsies wore wrinkled khakis. So Carter made the switch. He tried selling advertising for a year, but sucking up to furniture store owners and car dealers seemed as prurient as writing about drowned children.

Carter read in the Syracuse alum magazine about an apprentice program for a small media firm in Norfolk. The owner was a Syracuse grad and school benefactor. Norfolk was the South, but South-lite, not redneck country. Plus, it was warmer, and Carter was sick of upstate's long, gray, cold winters. He'd had enough of lake-effect snow, frozen fingers, and sliding on ice. He had skidded and crashed his Corolla twice.

Sidney Hogan liked the kid from Rochester; sharp, good-looking, Northern, but not Yankee. Polite, sensible. Hogan knew the upstate market well; he had sold a few small newspapers to the owner of the *Chronicle*. The Rochester people spoke highly of Carter and would be sorry to lose him. One of the business school professors whom Hogan admired provided Carter a four-star reference. That was good enough for Hogan.

What Hogan especially liked was having someone in the firm he could call a *journalist*. That gave the firm street credibility with the family-owned small newspaper owners who worried that selling out would sully the journalistic heritage of their forebearers. Hogan himself couldn't have cared less about journalistic and blueblood traditions. Newspapers and TV stations were commodities to be bought and traded like pork belly futures and fast-food franchises. The Fourth Estate and First Amendment stuff—nothing but sentimentality.

"These are businesses, and we keep them alive with fresh blood and money. Nostalgia doesn't pay bills," Hogan would say. "No margin, no mission."

At least Sidney Hogan is honest, Carter had thought, *and probably right.*

* * *

Carter had been lonely in Norfolk and started inviting down his buddy Gil and his wife. They liked the city, especially in the fall. And after Carter's wedding, when they found themselves stranded in Cape Charles, Gil and Jill opened Gil Netters right after 9/11.

Gil was a conservative, and in Cape Charles, this played well. Whites on the rural Eastern Shore were mostly farmers, real estate agents, watermen, or lucky spermers—the offspring of old families with land and money like the Savages. They reviled taxes and loved guns. Blacks were okay to them as long as they were polite and didn't complain or date whites. Hispanics were necessary for harvesting crops and roofing houses. Come-heres like Gil and Jill were tolerated as long as they respected the established order. As long as Gil understood his place as a server, he'd be fine.

* * *

"There was a cute one in here today," Gil piped to Carter while sipping his second whiskey. "Just your type: skinny ass, perky tits, pretty eyes. I'm guessing thirty-six, maybe thirty-eight. I was gonna text you."

"Little young for me. Besides, I'm not lookin'," Carter said. He finished his draft. "Last time you hooked me up resulted in a disaster. Remember Sophie?"

"Quit being a wuss. You're forty-six, and I presume your johnson still works. Use it or lose it. Get over it, for Christ's sake. It's no fun living vicariously through you."

"*Vicariously*. Big word. Learn that in anthropology class?"

"Moron. At least I'm not afraid of girls."

"Go home, see Jill, and excavate your backyard. Go study some jawbones," Carter chided.

Gil laughed. "I love this guy," he called to Lil.

Lil rolled her green eyes. "You're both so freakin' immature. Want another Blue Moon, Carter?"

"Give him one and another Maker's Mark for me." Gil gave Carter another kiss on the cheek.

"Will ya stop that Mafia boss kissy shit! You're not my brother-in-law anymore." Carter wiped his cheek. "They'll be calling this place *Gay's* instead of Gil's."

Lil laughed and handed Gil his whiskey.

"Gay bashing is non-PC, my friend. Come on," Gil said. He sipped his bourbon. "I'm the politically incorrect one, remember? And you're the Hillary pantywaist liberal."

"I wasn't gay bashing, and slobbering on my cheek isn't PC either, you Trump Nazi," Carter said. "I'm going home to take a shower."

CHAPTER 4

CARTER GRABBED HIS coffee mug, stirred in creamer, and settled in his recliner with his Kindle to read the morning news. He then checked for overnight messages. The morning looked calm and sunny, so he headed for the back deck.

Carter, please call me when you're up, a text read.

Sophie. Shit! This can't be good, Carter thought. He dialed his ex-wife.

"Thanks for calling. You up?" Sophie asked.

"Of course I'm up. I called, didn't I? Either that or this is a bad dream. What's the matter, Sophie?"

Carter had spoken those four words thousands of times, because something always seemed to be the matter with his now ex-wife. Sophie was dramatic and pushy, a drama queen in spades. There were no easy problems or lighthearted conversations between them. She had expectations, and when troubled she needed to be heard.

Carter braced himself, gulping coffee so that his mind wouldn't be trampled by the ensuing assault at dawn. *I've only been in Cape Charles a few weeks, and Sophie's still hassling me with her drama.*

"Carter, I'm leaving Virginia Beach. There's nothing here for me anymore. In fact, I hate it here."

"Moving? Okay, sounds good to me. Where?"

"Do you really care where? And you should know where. Christ, Carter, we were together fifteen years."

"Okay, Sophie, how many guesses do I get?"

"Screw you, Carter."

"Enough with the love taps. Tell me what you need."

"I'm moving back to New York, and I'm moving in with a friend."

"A friend. And who might that be?"

"Carter, it's serious. I just wanted you to hear it from me before big-mouthed Gil or my sister tell you. I owe you at least that."

"I appreciate the courtesy, Sophie, and I hope Mr. Whomever makes you happy."

"Carter, it's *Miss* Whomever. My college roommate."

Carter almost dropped his phone. After a few seconds, he recovered. "Great. You're a lesbo. Perfect. Just perfect, Sophie. Gil will never let me live this down."

* * *

Sophie and Carter's marriage had bobbed on stormy seas for many years. Then it capsized after Sophie caught Carter *in flagrante delicto* with a hooker in their home on a weekend she was supposed to be away. Sophie had suspected something was amiss for a while. For several months, about $500 had been going unaccounted for in their checking account. And she'd found wads of cash stuffed in an athletic sock in Carter's dresser. At first she thought her husband might have a drug habit, most likely cocaine. This was worse—*hookers*.

Sophie viewed men as little more than hormonal apes, and now her anthropologic hypothesis seemed unassailable. "Of the ten most important things to men, sex takes up the first nine spaces," she would tell Jill. When they'd first met, Carter had seemed more civilized to Sophie. He actually read books, subscribed to *National Geographic*, and genuinely strived to make sex mutually inclusive. She liked receiving oral sex, and he was very accommodating.

"Sometimes, in the middle of the night, he would wake up and stroke my hair," Sophie told Jill toward the end of her marriage. "That got me hotter than a pistol. On Sunday mornings, he'd bring me orange juice, coffee, and turn on the news. Then he'd rub my feet. Now, all I get is slippers for Christmas."

Carter could take a punch in his verbal spars with Sophie and gently return one. Sophie had liked that too. She had also liked Carter's body. He stayed in shape, hitting the gym several times a week, running, playing beach volleyball, skiing, always active.

Not long after they were married, Sophie and Carter bought a townhouse in Virginia Beach. She'd quit her guidance counselor job in New York and didn't look for another, figuring she'd get pregnant. They tried almost every night for more than a year. They tried so much, in fact, that intercourse became revolting. Sophie decided, unilaterally, to undergo *in vitro* fertilization. She paid $15,000 to a local fertility clinic.

"No way," Carter had insisted. "People who do that wind up with a litter. The kids are born premature and wind up with all sorts of health problems. No way, Sophie!"

"Selfish bastard! Just give me your sperm. I already cut the check."

After two brief pregnancies that terminated naturally, Sophie gave up and started visiting friends in New York. She hated Virginia Beach even more.

Carter was swaying in that direction too. He had become bored with suburbia and his seemingly mundane life as a broker of small-market media deals. His bosses were nice enough, but they were culturally conservative and far too pretentious for their mediocre social status. *Big fish in small ponds are really just medium-sized fish everywhere else,* Carter often thought.

Once they quit trying to procreate, Sophie saw no point in having sex. Carter's penis was useless as an empty revolver—inert and hard. Carter still had needs, hence, the hooker and the ensuing generous divorce settlement.

* * *

"Damn you, Carter, you really don't give a shit about me, do you?" Sophie huffed over the phone.

"Well, I thought we established a mutual disinterest years ago," he quipped.

"Asshole. I say I'm moving back to the city to live with a woman, and you act like I'm calling you with a grocery list to fill before coming home."

"Well, those grocery lists were sort of a pain," Carter said.

"Asshole!"

"I *am* an asshole. Point taken. Sorry. Look, I am happy for you, Sophie. You should move on. I have. It doesn't matter that it's with a woman. Whatever floats your boat. I obviously didn't. The only question is whether I tell Gil and Jill that you're a lesbian or do you?"

"They already know, asshole. They've known for years."

CHAPTER 5

CARTER'S BACK WAS as tight as a banjo string after weeks of unpacking, moving furniture, and painting. No amount of stretching or squats at the gym had prepared his hips and lower spine for the grinding and twisting of painting ceilings and moving queen-sized beds. His small foursquare was starting to feel like a reality-show fixer-upper house project, one where the new owners discover that minor problems are major and structural catastrophes lurk beneath the floors and between the walls. Crevices crept along the plaster walls like veins on the back of a painter's hand. The kitchen looked World War II vintage from a bombed out French village. Bathroom crud and mold made Carter wear flip-flops when he showered, and the pine floors he loved so much bowed and creaked. Sure, the house had a lot of *charm* and *potential*. But it was now clear those sales buzzwords the real estate agent had bombarded him with were euphemisms for *money pit*. It was going to take patience, cash, and lots of Advil to make this 1925 hag a beauty.

* * *

The morning was warm but with a south breeze just brisk enough to keep the bugs down. Carter sat on his front steps drinking coffee and chewing on a breakfast bar as he listened to the leaves rustle on the massive sycamore.

"Dammit!" he yelled. "Get!" A tabby with a tail as thick as a raccoon's and hateful green eyes scurried across the street and under a porch.

Another dead bird—this time a goldfinch in full yellow and black plumage on his front steps. Carter cradled the victim in his palm, its eyes closed and a speck of blood on its orange beak, no doubt from a fang puncture wound.

"Damn cats!"

Carter caressed the bird, the size of a computer mouse, and admired its sheen and elegance. *Such a waste.* He wondered if anyone had heard his outburst. He looked to his left and saw several people with dogs in the park—old folks with little dogs, mostly. One person caught his eye. She wore athletic tights, a tank top, and sandals, and walked at a decent clip. From the back she looked trim and athletic. Her hair was short, blondish, and her arms looked thin but firm.

Perky tits, nice ass. At least the cats won't ruin her.

Carter always considered himself an assman, and these glutes were impressive. Nicer than Sophie's. This woman was built like a dancer. She had what he thought of as a Goldie Hawn apple rump, lifted and round. Carter felt himself stir slightly thinking about how he had loved to pleasure Sophie when they first dated and how she always wanted to be taken from the back.

Carter hadn't been with a woman in months, and he was getting lonely. He looked at the dead goldfinch and stroked its feathers.

"You deserve a dignified resting place. How 'bout under the sycamore?"

* * *

"Howdy there, good lookin'." The boisterous voice was unmistakably Hattie's. "I was drivin' by and saw you sittin' out here."

"Just burying a bird. Can I get you some coffee?"

"No, honey. I'm showin' a house down the street in ten minutes. It needs some work, but they all do 'round here. What's ya got there?"

"Goldfinch. Cat got it."

"Those stinkin' varmints. Town needs to do somethin' 'bout that. Evil creatures. They kill for the fun of it. They piss all over everything. Worse smell in the world."

"Yeah, kinda like ex-wives." Carter smirked. "Piss all over everything."

"Speakin' of ex-wives, I hear your ex is a lesbian."

"Christ! Who told you that, Hattie? Oh, let me guess—Gil."

"Close. Jill. Saw her at church. I told ya, no secrets."

"Secrets in Cape Charles? An oxymoron."

"Yep, lots of morons 'round here, for sure, just like Gil says all the time. Gotta run, honey. Oh, for that cat problem, mix some vinegar and pepper and spread it around your bushes. That'll help keep them stinkin' vermin away. If that don't work, I got some traps we can set. Cats make good bait for crab traps. See ya 'round, honey."

"Right. Good to see you, Hattie. I guess."

* * *

The day whizzed by just like the last month had, and Carter decided to venture out. He popped a couple of Advil, shaved, shampooed, and slipped on his fancy shorts, Keens, and a black Punch Brothers concert T-shirt, his favorite. He had been working out a lot with free weights, and it showed in his pectorals, biceps, and calves.

"Hey, where you been, Sparky?" Gil called when Carter walked into the pub.

"Stayin' out of trouble, which means stayin' away from you. Hear about Sophie?"

"Of course I did. I've known for weeks."

"Yeah, and Jill's already talking about it to the locals." Carter shook his head. "I just moved here, and my reputation is already shot. Guy loses wife to another woman. Great!"

"Quit whining. This is a good thing. Jill and I discussed it. We think that having been married to a lesbian improves your reputation. We did you a favor by spreading the news."

"Whatever, Gil. You're a dick."

"Well, I have a reputation to protect too."

"Well, by the time I found out, it was already all over town. Hattie the real estate lady knows. Christ, Gil!"

"Come on, Carter. You know Sophie doesn't put on lipstick without calling Jill first to ask which color to wear. She's been thinking about moving to New York since last summer. She and her old roommate have been diddling each other for years. How could you not know that?"

"I didn't, and thanks a lot for the heads-up. I thought guys were supposed to stick together. It's the bro-code."

"Dude, I love ya, but my wife can be a ballbuster. She ordered me to keep my mouth shut. Said I'd be in deep shit if I told you. You know Jill, she's a woman of her word. And, honestly, I don't want to end up divorced and destitute like you."

"Whatever. Truth is, I don't give a shit. I'm glad Sophie's moving back to the city. She should have never left. She hated Virginia Beach, and she resents me for moving there. So, good riddance."

"Well, she was one sweet piece of ass, you gotta give her that much."

"Jesus Christ, Gil, that's your sister-in-law—my ex-wife."

"I know, good damn thing she's a lesbo too. If she wasn't, I'd divorce Jill."

"Gil, you're an animal."

"Yes, I am, and you should be more of one too, you wuss. Now is the perfect time to strike. Act smitten and hurt, and maybe you'll get sympathy sex from some stranger. I'm telling you, seize the opportunity here. Get your head screwed on straight."

* * *

Until moving to Cape Charles, Carter had felt pathetically predictable. He suffered the same symptoms as so many unfulfilled middle-agers. His feelings were stupidly American: self-absorbed, impatient, never satisfied. Boredom—not cheating or abuse—was why half of all marriages failed, he figured. At least that's what he'd read during his Internet research on the topic. His ruptured wedlock was no doubt a casualty of the condition *taedium vitae.*

At the tail end of his time at Hogan and Wynn, Carter had been depressed. His unhappiness had been apparent to just about everyone at work, including Sidney Hogan. Then Sidney sold the firm, which sent Carter into a steeper mental tailspin. Technically, Carter hadn't been a partner, but old Sidney treated him like one. The day after the sale, he handed Carter a check for $165,000 and another $75,000 for six months' pay. Since Carter and Sophie had already divorced, the bonus and pay were all his, enough to buy a cheap house and to modestly live on for a while. Carter knew that at some point he'd have to find work again. But the severance would give him about a year to reboot.

The day Carter was cleaning out his office, old Sidney walked in and handed him a business card.

"Carter, this is my niece. She's a therapist, first-rate. She's helped lots of friends. Go see her."

"Therapist? Like physical therapist? I'm not hurt."

"Yes you are, my boy. Between your ears. Go see her."

About two months later, Carter dialed the number handwritten on the back of the business card. The shrink picked up on the third ring. She told him to come by her office Saturday morning, which Carter thought odd.

The parking lot in the two-story office building was empty, except for a green convertible Jaguar parked near the entrance. The Virginia license plate read UVA91. The only name on the building entrance was Freemason Associates. The door was open, and the lights were on in the reception room. An electronic bell dinged when Carter entered.

A woman came bounding from a hallway behind the reception area. "You must be Carter Rossi. Hi, I'm Kate Lee-Capps."

Carter reached for her hand, and they shook. Her skin was soft, but her grip was firm.

"Come on back to my office. My uncle said lots of nice things about you."

"He seems to like you too," Carter said. "I appreciate your time— *I think.*"

Kate's waist was thin, her butt lifted and round, her hair thick but supple. Carter stared at her ass as he followed. *Damn near perfect.* Her age? *Maybe thirty-eight.* Her office was sparsely decorated and desk uncluttered. No couch, just three cushioned leather chairs in a circle with a round coffee table in the middle. Copies of *Southern Living*, *Psychology Today*, and *Sports Illustrated* were spread like a peacock's tail feathers on the tabletop.

"Have a seat, Carter, and let's jump right in."

"Did anyone ever tell you that you're a dead ringer for—"

"Kate Hudson. I know," Kate finished. "I hear it all the time."

"No, I was thinking more of Teri Garr."

"Don't get on my bad side." Kate laughed. "I'll give you rotten advice that will ruin your life."

"Don't worry. Someone has already beat you to it." Carter smiled.

He was glad to be seeing a woman therapist—especially a hot, sassy one that would give him shit. That's one reason he showed up for the appointment. He wanted a harsh female perspective, not the sympathetic ear of another guy allaying the guilt he felt for sleeping with hookers and wrecking his marriage. Carter wanted to be bitch-slapped, or at the very least spanked like a misbehaving child. He needed a sobering bucket of ice dumped over his shoulder. Otherwise, his guilt would flourish.

"So, Carter, I hear you've been through rough stuff," Kate began. "Uncle Sid told me you're a newly minted divorcé. Welcome to the club. I'm a veteran. Tell me why you think your marriage failed."

* * *

As her name suggested, Kate Lee-Capps was Southern, hailing from a long lineage of Richmonders. She was attractive and had a hint of the aristocracy in her voice. She was relaxed, dressed casually in jeans and a white V-neck shirt. Her mouth curled up on the ends, making it seem like she always smiled. She even had a dimple in her left cheek.

A doctorate diploma from the University of Virginia hung on her office wall, with a field hockey stick painted UVA blue beside it.

"You were a jock, I see," Carter said.

"Was, kinda. Played softball and field hockey. Ran cross-country too."

"I can tell. You're in great shape."

Kate grinned. "You look fit too. Work out?"

"Yeah, gym rat, and run, mostly."

Carter had Googled Kate before the appointment and learned that she had been a marriage counselor while pursuing a PhD. With credentials in hand, she now specialized in treating teens and young adults with self-esteem disorders.

"Running helps with stress and boredom. Running is so boring it makes everything else seem exciting," Carter said. "I get bored easily. Always have. Even as a kid, I'd get excited about buying some toy, and after having it a few days, I wanted something new. Same thing with cars when I got older. I get hyped up, buy something, and I'm ready for something else. Six months seems to be my threshold for just about everything."

"Women too?"

"Well, now that I think of it, probably. The longest I dated before marrying Sophie was about eight months. It was like that all through high school and college. A different date for every dance."

"So, you were excited about getting married to Sophie, but then the magic disappeared. Classic. You were married a long time. I'm guessing at least ten years."

"Pretty close."

"Why do you think it lasted?"

"I guess I thought it's what I was supposed to do," Carter said. He felt his neck stiffen. "You know, all of your buddies get married. You get tired of showing up at Thanksgiving and Christmas alone. I guess I just settled in and focused on my career."

"Honestly, Carter, this is all pretty cliché. There's been about a million B movies made around this theme, entire sitcoms even. So, you were feeling guilt for not being a grownup and you went and got yourself a wife. Is that what you're saying?"

"Yeah, I guess. I don't know. Maybe. She wanted kids. It didn't happen, and the magic died."

"Did you want kids?"

"I don't know. I guess I would have liked being a dad, but, honestly, I was pretty happy just being me."

"Tragic, selfish, sophomoric, but pretty normal, Carter. Indifference is one of the curses of the human condition. Dispassion makes us feel inadequate. It's that conflict between what we *should* want versus what truly makes us happy. Look, not everybody is emotionally wired to be a parent or a spouse. If you don't like applesauce, eating more of it isn't going to make it taste better. You get what I'm saying?"

"Not what I expected to hear, Kate, but I'm following you. I thought you'd prosecute me for being a narcissistic slob."

"No. I'm saving that rage for our next president," Kate said. "Donald Trump significantly raised the bar for narcissism."

"What a legacy, and not even in office yet," Carter said.

"Look, Carter. Human beings are fairly simple creatures. We always seem to want what we don't have, right? So, when we don't get what we want, the spoiled brat in us comes roaring to the surface. We get spiteful and petulant when forced to do things that we don't like. It's all the same web of emotion. Very primal."

"I'd say that sums me up pretty concisely. Guess that makes me an ape."

"Sort of. Human beings really aren't all that complicated. We don't like being told what to do, and most of us always want more, unless you're a Zen Buddhist. And I'll bet they even fake it. People who learn to want what they have seem a lot happier. Unfortunately, there is only one person to achieve that: the Dalai Lama."

"Thanks, I feel better now. I'm in good company. We're all greedy slobs, I guess."

"That's harsh, but probably not too far from the truth. But I think the real issue is that you're getting *monotony* confused with something else."

"With what, doc? Don't keep me guessing here."

"It seems to me, Carter, that you've spent most of your professional life trying to make others happy. My uncle Sid, your former wife, your parents. Am I right?"

Carter nodded like a contrite Catholic fourth-grade student scolded by a nun for looking up a girl's skirt.

"You worked hard, made some money, and treated others well. You remained loyal and in a rotten marriage for a long time because you thought that was the responsible thing to do, correct?"

"Well, no affairs, if that constitutes being responsible."

"But you cheated?"

"A couple times, yes, when I was traveling. And maybe a couple more times."

"That it?" Kate asked indignantly.

"You sound disappointed."

"I am, sort of. Cute guy, no kids, cold marriage. Come on, Carter, fess up. No affairs?"

"I've said enough already. I plead the fifth."

Kate laughed. "You want me to cuff you?"

"Jeez, what kind of doctor are you? You gonna throttle me with your field hockey stick?"

"Maybe, if you ask nicely."

"Sid didn't tell me I'd have to be your submissive."

"For now, I am just a friend. Look, Carter, from what I gather you're a decent guy; you've been loyal to my uncle Sid, to your ex-wife, to family members. You work for charities and raise money for the arts. Sounds to me like you've checked all of the boxes. And it sounds like maybe you haven't been selfish enough."

"What about the hookers?"

"I don't advocate paying for sex, Carter. It's sleazy and probably not safe. Plus, it's illegal. But it's temporary. Seems to me that a full-blown affair with emotional commitment is much more incendiary and, frankly, deceitful."

Carter's head snapped back as if being slapped. "You have my attention."

"Look, Carter, you've compromised and sacrificed. You've subordinated and even repressed what makes you happy. Having kids didn't happen, and that's not your fault. You're getting boredom and guilt confused with a loss of freedom to pursue what makes you happy. Willing subjugation manifests as boredom, and over time that turns into resentment. An unfulfilling job, or marriage, or environment can feel like simple boredom, but it's really about resentment."

"What about the responsibility of making a relationship work? I did take vows, you know."

"Carter, I have been doing this a long time, and I can tell you with a large degree of certainty that the best predictor of the future is the past. People do not fundamentally change their behavior; feelings do not radically shift. Your wife didn't get her way, and she shut you down. The magic was gone after that. Once it vanishes, it is very difficult to resurrect. Taking a romantic cruise to rekindle the spark is a waste of money."

"That sounds like a pretty cynical view of people and relationships, doc. You're basically saying people don't change, at least not enough to matter.

You're saying mistakes can't be fixed or circumstances can't be improved. Wow! I wouldn't put that on a billboard if I was in your profession."

"Neither would I if I were a marriage counselor. But I'm not—at least not technically. But I do like to think I have a pretty good bead on human behavior."

"I wonder what you would have told me if I'd said you look like Kate Hudson."

Dr. Kate Lee-Capps laughed. "I warned you."

"So, seriously, you're saying that my relationship with my ex was pretty much doomed and the breakup inevitable."

"That's close. What I am saying is that when it comes to troubled relationships and feelings, there is a high rate of recidivism—both good and bad. Happy relationships tend to stay happy. Sad ones, unfortunately, get stuck in the mud and sink. Spouse beaters tend to remain abusive. Victims tend to stay victims. If you're not happy with someone now, you won't be happy in the future. That's my point. You may learn to accept a poor relationship, which is a form of capitulation. Or you may gut it out to protect the kids or out of guilt. Better to cut the cord. There's no glory in being a martyr. Life is too damn short, Carter."

"Wow. I really expected to be guilt-tripped. Instead, I almost feel good about myself. I thought I needed at least a couple more sessions before feeling emancipated. Kinda disappointing that you're letting me off the hook."

"No, Carter. You need to let yourself off the hook. Stop being a wuss."

"*Wuss!* Is that an official medical term? That's what my ex-brother-in-law calls me. Christ!"

"Maybe you should listen to him . . . and to me. The only one beating up on you is yourself."

Coach Kate stood and motioned Carter to do the same. She was about five feet ten in heels, two inches taller than Carter.

"Come here," she said. She opened her arms and gave Carter a hug. "You're a good guy, Carter Rossi, and you're cute. A little short for me, but cute. And I'm guessing you're a bit of a romantic. Stop being so damn morose, and go have some fun. Starting over ain't so bad. I've done it twice."

"Two-time loser, huh?"

"Two-time winner, Carter. I knew when to move on. No martyr here."

"The real estate lady I'm buying my house from in Cape Charles said almost the same thing. I guess I should have paid her a higher commission. So, how much do I owe for your wisdom?"

"Give me another hug, and when you see Uncle Sid, tell him he owes me dinner and a very good Oregon pinot noir."

* * *

When Carter got home that night, he thought more about Kate than Sophie. In the morning, he sent roses to Kate's office with a note attached:

Kate,

You're right. I'm a wuss. And you were wearing heels. No fair! Call if you ever get bored or want to share that bottle of pinot. And if you visit, bring the field hockey stick and handcuffs.

Carter

CHAPTER 6

CARTER DECIDED TO spend a few hours Saturday on the beach. He never could stand the idleness of sitting in the sun. He was constantly up and down, walking, or wading in the water or going for a run. It was that stupid boredom thing. It had driven Sophie crazy. She could lie idly on the beach for hours. Carter lasted fifteen minutes, tops.

It was sunny and dry. Not much wind either, which was unusual for this tiny patch of land by the sea. Carter sat with his darkest sunglasses, a pair of Oakleys he had bought at an outlet mall. Out of the corner of his eye he glimpsed that perfect ass again—the one from the park. Carter had spotted it as soon as he crossed over the path between the sand dunes. The woman was standing and stretching, facing the Bay. Her legs were slender and long; her firm arms dangled, slightly curved at the elbows. Her yellow-striped bikini bottom cut along her pube line. This had to be the woman Gil had described, the one he had seen in the bar. Carter needed to make sure. He quick-dialed his iPhone.

"Gil, it's Carter. I'm at the beach. You working?"

"Of course I'm working, moron. It's the weekend. It's summer. We can't all lie around whacking off all day like you. Some of us have responsibilities. What do you need?"

"That girl you told me about, the pretty one with the nice ass—what was her name?"

"Rosie, or maybe Rose. Can't remember."

"What color was her hair again? How long?"

"Shoulder length. Blondish-brownish."

"Long legs, right?"

"Yeah, and nice lips. Why you asking? She there?"

"I'm at the beach, and I think I see her. You said she's cool, right?"

"Yeah, but she may be a lesbo."

"Christ! Another lesbo!"

"Well, one way to find out, moron: Grow some balls, and go for it."

"What does she drink?" Carter asked.

"She likes pinot gris, the same stuff Jill likes. You want a bottle? Stop by the back of the pub, and I'll slip you one. But I'm charging you double."

It only took Carter five minutes to walk from the beach to Gil Netters. Waiting by the back door in a brown bag was a chilled bottle of the white wine and two glasses. A note was inside.

Bring back the glasses, and if you don't get laid you had better lie and say you did. Grow a pair, and good luck, moron.

* * *

Technically, there was no drinking on the beach. But it was tourist season, and if the cops clamped down, the beach would be empty and the town fathers would go nuts. As long as people were discreet, everything was cool.

Carter plodded through the sand. He spotted her chair. Beside it was a pink and green umbrella, a book, a small cooler, and a beach towel. *Perfect.* Carter craned his neck to see what the woman was reading: *The Book of the Damned* by Charles Fort. She also had a copy of *Psychology Today* magazine in her lap, the same magazine that had sat on top of Dr. Kate's coffee table.

I need to get a subscription. Great chick magnet.

"Can I help you?"

Carter startled. *Caught gawking. Dammit!*

"Sorry, I was just—"

"Being nosy, that's what," the woman said.

"Yeah, I guess I was. I apologize. Want me to move? This is the spot where I usually sit. I just didn't want to plop without asking first."

"You don't need permission. The beach is free. Can't stop you from sitting on *your* spot."

"I'm sorry, I think."

"Take it easy. Just messin' with you. What's your name?"

The woman eased into her beach chair and covered her legs with her towel.

"Carter Rossi. You?"

"Rose Portman. Nice to meet you." She reached to shake Carter's hand. "You a local?"

"I am now, I guess. Just moved here last month. You?"

"Just visiting."

"How long?"

"Not sure yet," Rose answered.

Carter started feeling relaxed and even welcomed. Rose seemed nonchalant, but not disinterested. Her blue eyes seemed to smile. They had the same sharpness as the cat that murdered the goldfinch. When Carter stared into them, her pupils pulsed and dilated. He had read once in *National Geographic* that dilating pupils were a sign of attraction.

"Want a glass of wine?" Carter offered. He pulled the pinot gris from the brown bag and two small wineglasses. He showed her the label.

"Interesting. You always come to the beach by yourself with a perfect bottle of wine and two glasses?"

"What if I said yes?"

"Then I'd say you're exceedingly optimistic, or you're lying."

"Then you'd be right about both."

Carter figured that if he had any shot with Rose, he'd better fess up. He told her about Gil and how he texts the locals. And Carter admitted to seeing Rose in the park.

"So, this was a setup?"

"Kinda. A spontaneous one. Obviously ill-conceived. Gil has been riding me about meeting people, specifically girls, so I figured I'd try."

"Girls? So you prefer boys?"

"Christ no!"

"So, how did you know it was me on the beach?"

"Honestly, your ass."

"Stand up," Rose said. Carter did, reluctantly. "Now turn around . . . Yours isn't so bad either."

They laughed and toasted.

＊ ＊ ＊

The next couple of hours passed quickly. The Bay breeze swept away the summer humidity and cooled their skin. They sipped the wine, talked some, and paused to stare over the water, watching parents and kids splash around in the shallow tide. Rose asked Carter to rub sunscreen onto the back of her shoulders, and she did the same for him.

Her skin felt like a wedding veil, his like oak veneer.

Rose and Carter didn't talk about anything serious or pry too much into each other's resumes. They chatted mostly about Gil Netters, the town, its characters, and its charm. Carter mentioned his ex once or twice, just to signal that he wasn't married. Rose didn't hint at her status, but she wasn't wearing a ring. She was also coy about where she was staying, saying only that she was on a friend's boat.

"You at the jellybean piers or the old town harbor?" Carter asked.

"The jelly what?"

"The old harbor or the new one?"

"Oh, the new one," Rose answered. "The one with all of the orange, purple, and yellow houses."

"Right, the jellybean houses," Carter said. "That's what the locals call them. It's all that faux West Indies architecture, the stuff all over golf courses in Florida. Kinda tacky, I think."

"Not so bad," Rose said. "Nice facilities at the pier, clean. I like the Oyster Reef restaurant there too. Gorgeous view of the Bay. But don't tell your friend Gil I said that. His place is cool too, but in a gritty, old-school way."

"Gil knows all and sees all. He's like the Wizard of Oz. He probably knows what you had for dinner last night and how much you tipped the waitress."

"Small town," Rose said.

"In every way," Carter said. "I like the historic district. Lots of funky old houses. You into old stuff?"

"If you mean old houses, yes. If you mean old men, not really."

"Yes, houses." Carter laughed. "You know, old architecture, gables, cupolas, stained glass, creepy attics, and leaky basements."

"I like them, but I have to be careful around them."

"Careful of what? Why?"

"Old buildings. Never mind," Rose said.

The sun began its final daily descent over the Bay, an orange fireball seemingly rebelling and gasping, throwing off deep reds and then purples as the horizon doused its glowing embers. At dusk this time of year, cars lined Bay Avenue to watch the orange ball fade into the sea. The sunsets were a blaze of deep hues, a magnificence captured all over town in photographs and paintings hanging in shops and art galleries. This was one of the only places on the East Coast to see the sun set over water.

"Have you seen the sunsets here?" Carter asked.

"This was my first on the beach. Spectacular," Rose said. "Getting chilly fast, though. Want a ride home? I've rented a golf cart. Beats walking."

"I'm only a couple blocks away, but, yeah, I'll take a lift."

A few minutes later, Rose pulled up in front of Carter's place and eyed his house.

"Cute," she said. "I need to get a better look during daylight."

"Yeah, anytime," Carter perked. "Love to show her off. She has *potential*, as they say around here. She sags a bit and needs a facelift."

"We all will, eventually."

Carter wanted desperately to kiss Rose, at least on the cheek, and invite her inside. *Get some balls. Grow a pair, Sparky!* He could hear Gil's voice in his head.

"Nice meeting you, Rose." He stuck out his hand for a shake. "Maybe I'll see you around?"

Rose pushed his hand away, leaned over, and gave Carter a hug and a peck on the lips. Her pupils pulsed.

"Hope you didn't lose any bets with your buddy at the bar. See you around—maybe."

* * *

A couple of hours later, Carter's phone rang.

"How'd it go, Sparky? You get laid?"

"Thanks for the wine, Gil, and no, I didn't. We hung out, but nothing happened."

"Sounds like you blew it, moron. She's in here now with some dorky old dude with a Scottish accent named Malcolm. He's holding her hand and keeps kissing her on the cheek. Pathetic! You can't even compete with a shriveled up seventy-year-old. Seems like the only way you're getting laid is if I hire another hooker. I'll start taking up a collection with the boys."

"Appreciate the thought, Gil, but no hookers, okay? And thanks again for the wine."

"Don't mention it. I put it on your tab, moron, and don't forget my wineglasses."

CHAPTER 7

CARTER HAD BEEN taping, sanding, and patching drywall cracks for nearly six weeks. He decided it was time to get some fresh paint on the walls. He strolled into Bay Hardware, past the wooden Indian statue in the doorway and the Trump/Pence sign in the window. The store owner, Cyril Brown, made no secret of his political predilections. Each day, almost every day rain or shine, Cyril and a group of equally strident old-timers sat together cracking jokes or ogling pretty girls passing by on the sidewalk or hot moms in tight shorts stopping in for a paintbrush or furniture polish.

Bay Hardware had been passed down through three generations of Browns. Cyril, now in his seventies, started working there after serving in Vietnam as a first lieutenant. The store had changed very little in the past fifty years. The aisles were narrow and stuffed on each side with an array of paints, polishes, PVC piping, hinges, nails, and electrical wiring and boxes. The wood-slat floors creaked and moaned, and old decals and signs from the 1940s, advertising tobacco, oysters, whiskey, hammers, nuts, screws, and varnish, were randomly scattered around the old shelves, cases, and windows.

The store looked more like a hoarder's garage than a place of business. Rubber boots and waders, mostly bought by watermen, were on racks. Ball caps and jars of local honey were stuffed in bins around the counter. Cyril and his store attendants wrote down every item sold on a piece of paper by the cash register. He preferred to keep track of inventory the way his father had and his grandfather before him—stress free and low tech. Old oval aisle mirrors were strategically placed so Cyril could monitor the entrance and cluttered aisles from his chair by the register.

In the midst of this hodgepodge of a store was a Fisher wood stove. A couch and two chairs faced its black iron doors. On nice days, "the boys" sat in wicker rocking chairs in front of the store. Cyril's chair bore his name, carved into a white wooden tag attached to the back of the headrest. He kept a bungee cord stretched from arm to arm to keep anyone else from sitting on his throne when unattended. Cyril's court jesters all had arranged seating as well, each flanking Cyril at the center. Guests and passersby could take an empty seat, but only by invitation from the king.

When it was cold or wet, Cyril's court huddled around by the stove. It was raining this morning, so Cyril and a buddy settled inside and commented on stories they read in a local newspaper.

"Mornin', Carter, can I help you?" Cyril asked.

"Hey, Cyril, looking for some interior latex."

"Gettin' ready to paint, are you?"

"Yes sir. Gonna be a long process."

Carter had been introduced to Cyril a couple of times, first by Hattie Savage when she was showing him the town, and once by Gil when they were having breakfast in the coffee shop, just a few doors down from the hardware store.

"Pull up a chair," Cyril said. "This here is Belford MacIntosh. We just call him Mac. He's kinda hard of hearing, so you have to speak up."

Carter reached over and shook Mac's hand. Mac looked like a skinny version of Andy Rooney, with eyebrows as thick as cordgrass and matted gray hair to match. You'd need a weed-whacker to thin the hair in his ears and nose. He chewed on an unlit cigar, the slurry staining his teeth a dark tea.

"We was gonna have a drink. Care to join us?" Cyril invited.

"You mean coffee?" Carter asked.

"No, too late in the morning for that." Cyril reached behind his chair and lifted a bottle of Inver House Scotch. Cyril usually wore a collared shirt and khakis, and today was no exception. On Sundays, he clipped on a bowtie for church.

"Thanks, but I don't drink before noon," Carter said. "It's only eleven."

"Eleven eighteen to be exact," Cyril said as he glanced at a Pittsburgh Paint advertising clock above the entrance. He poured a splash into a red plastic cup. "Go on and take it. It'll make the paintin' go faster. Go on," he prodded Carter.

"So, did you boys read in the paper about that Bruce Jenner fella changing his sex?" Mac said.

Cyril's eyes lit up. He leaned over toward Carter and whispered, "This is gonna be good."

"That's old news, Mac. You got a problem with Mr. Jenner—or is it Miss Jenner?" Cyril provoked.

"Nope, no problem here. Let me tell you somethin'. When I was young, I lived up in Northern Virginia by Alexandria. I had me two or three girlfriends all the time. I had needs, you know, and I liked girls, all colors and shapes. Anyways, I had this one girlfriend, part Asian I think, who liked to do certain things. She weren't the prettiest—kinda tall and hairy arms. Wore lots of makeup too. But she had a talent. Well, one day *Roberta*—that was her name—tells me that she's really a *Robert*."

Cyril smiled. "So, you were dating somebody named Bob, and you didn't know it? What did ya do about it, Mac?"

"Can't hear ya, Cyril. Speak up."

"I said, what'd ya do about your girlfriend Bob? You break up?"

"Nothin.' I didn't do nothin'."

"You mean you kept seeing Bob?" Cyril asked.

"You bet. Roberta was doing a fine job—real fine."

Two elderly women standing at the checkout register to buy umbrellas heard Mac's booming voice and Cyril and Carter laughing. They both set down their umbrellas and walked out.

"Guess they won't be comin' back," Cyril said, a glint in his blue eyes. "Don't get wet!"

Carter raised his plastic cup in cheers and swallowed its contents. "I wouldn't expect repeat business from them, Cyril. Thanks for the drink. Nice to meet you, Mac."

"Say what?"

"I said, 'It's nice to meet you, Mac.' Not everyone has such an open mind," Carter said.

"Hold on there, Carter. That Scotch was for sipping," Cyril said. "You need to have another. Hand me your cup."

* * *

Nobody knew more about Cape Charles, past or present, than Cyril Holmer-Brown. He was the de facto mayor, the godfather of wheelin' and dealin', a repository of information, gossip, insults, and compliments. Before Hattie Savage's dad started selling real estate, the Browns matched buyers and sellers. They'd sell you the house and everything needed to fix it. It was like the California merchants who sold shovels to prospectors during the Gold Rush.

If the Browns didn't like you, finding a house could be tough in Cape Charles. The Savages and Browns made an easy truce, forging a symbiosis of mutual trust and interests. The Savages sold newcomers hope, and the Browns sold the shovels.

In modern Cape Charles, rumors fanned by Gil and confirmed by Cyril were gospel. If Cyril didn't know about something, it must not be true. If he wasn't sure, Hattie Savage would find out.

Cyril had an ornery streak, some said hateful. But to Carter he seemed affable, funny, and one hell of a lot smarter than he pretended. He was thin, tall, and had a bad back from years of lifting store inventory. In his younger years, he looked like Charlton Heston. He spoke with a hint of Old World New England blueblood and the accent of a Delmarva waterman. In his office he kept a picture on the wall of his Vietnam buddies, including then-Corporal Mac, and next to it a portrait of the late Supreme Court Associate Justice Antonin Scalia.

"Carter, I heard there was a spooky lady in town," Cyril said.

"*Spook* lady? It ain't right using that word," Mac huffed. "Cyril, this ain't the '50s no more. I don't appreciate talkin' like that. You is supposed to say colored or black."

"Not *spook,*" Cyril said more loudly. "*Spooky,* like ghosts."

"Oh . . . I see." Mac laughed. "Ain't all that surprisin'. We got those damn things all over town. Just like stray cats—ever'where. I ignore 'em. And if I think I see somethin', I just shoo 'em away, just like if I see a cat sittin' on my porch or shittin' in my flower bed."

Cyril shook his head and sipped Scotch from his red plastic cup. "I haven't seen any ghosts, except maybe Natalie Wood in my dreams, but plenty folk around here say they have experienced something. You just heard old Mac here."

"I know you fellas are just yankin' my chain," Carter said.

"Not really," Cyril said. "Folks around here call it *woo-woo.*"

There goes that word again, Carter thought.

"Woo-woo. Look it up," Cyril said. "Real word."

Carter recalled how Hattie had described it, but he did a search on his iPhone to humor Cyril. There it was, the definition of woo-woo in Merriam-Webster: *dubiously or outlandishly mystical, supernatural, or unscientific.* Hattie had pretty much nailed it.

"Okay, I'll bite," Carter said. "So where have people seen ghosts?" He'd heard Hattie's take; he might as well hear Cyril's.

"Oh hell. The old Royal Palace movie house; the old schoolhouse down the street; at least a couple dozen houses in town; a couple of the B&Bs," Cyril said. "People say the ghost in the coffee house tosses forks, knives, and spoons around. They just jump off the table. Even Gil's supposedly got one in the pub."

"Really? Gil never said anything to me," Carter said.

"Not something people really talk about. Probably not good for business. People will think you're crazy, or at the very least a liberal," Cyril said. "Same people who believe in ghosts believe in global warming. It's all in their heads."

Carter laughed. "The Donald would be proud of you, Cyril. I'm surprised your Trump sign by the door isn't bigger. Is this his campaign headquarters for Cape Charles?"

"Trump?" Mac piped. "Did you say Trump? Nothin' but a loudmouth maniac who thinks he's God's gift to women. *National Enquirer* says he can't get it up. That's why his first two wives left him. That's why he had to go to Russia to find a third. Ask me, his new wife, Mel . . . innia, whatever, looks like a man. Bony face and thick eyes. I bet he got her through one of those Internet dating sites. A limp dick, that's what Donald Trump is."

"At least Trump *has* a dick," Cyril countered. "That's why I'm for 'em. We're too damn soft in this country. The Chinese are pissing all over us. We got Muslims running around with bombs. Our boys are dying in Afghanistan. We need someone in that job with balls, not some liberal lesbian who's gonna keep getting our boys overseas killed."

Mac rose from his chair and hobbled over to the counter. He opened one of the umbrellas left there by the women. "Made in China. See that, Cyril. You're a damn hypocrite."

"You guys are brutal," Carter said. "I don't know how you remain friends."

"No one said we was *friends*. Weez just Army drinkin' buddies," Mac said as he slid back into his chair.

Cyril smiled, leaned forward, and the two clicked their plastic cups in a toast.

"I'll drink to that," Cyril said, grinning. "Cheers, you liberal fruitcake."

"Back at ya, you mean old Nazi."

"You two need marriage counseling," Carter said. "I know someone who can help." The two old guys laughed. "So how about we avoid politics, at least until I leave. Tell me about this ghost lady."

"I don't know her name," Cyril said. "But she was in here a few weeks ago asking about historical records, and she bought a couple flashlights, a beach umbrella, and sunscreen. She paid cash. She was with some old guy with an accent. Irish or Scottish I think. Says they was doing some genealogy research. The old guy said somethin' about them being *para* . . . psychologists from some Scottish university. Edinburgh, I think."

"Parapsychologists! What'd she look like?" Carter asked, alarmed.

"Pretty sandy blonde. Nice ass and mouth."

"Yeah, her lips was nice," Mac piped, "but not as nice as Roberta's."

CHAPTER 8

THREE SHOTS OF Scotch before noon were hard to shake off. Carter hated Scotch. In fact, about the only hard booze he could stomach was vodka mixed with either fruit juice or tonic. He was more of a wine guy, which only added to Gil's insults.

Carter left the hardware store with paint cans in hand and headed to Gil Netters for lunch. He didn't want to be harassed by Gil, but he was hungry and curious about the girl and the ghosts and the old dude she was with. When he arrived, Gil was behind the bar with Lil.

"Hey there, Sparky," Gil bellowed. "What can I do ya for?"

"You seem cheery. Hell, you're even smiling. What's up with that?" Carter said.

"He's always cheerful," Lil said, "just sometimes less so than others."

Lil looked good today. Her breasts bulged beneath her black Gil Netters T-shirt, and she had pulled her black hair back into a ponytail. Gil, as usual, wore a clover-green collared golf shirt large enough to hide his midriff bulge. Despite the poundage, he looked solidly built, with broad, thick shoulders and a barrel chest.

"So, tell me about *not* getting laid, moron," Gil said.

"I will. But first, tell me about the Gil Netters ghost." Carter figured he'd start with that first. A part of him didn't want Rose's identity as the ghost lady confirmed. She seemed too sophisticated for that type of thing.

"Who told you about *that*?" Lil said.

"Doesn't matter. I heard, that's all."

"I don't like talking about that stuff," Gil said.

"Well, I will," said Lil. "I've seen it and felt it. Don't know what it is, but I don't like it."

Lil's wide green eyes bulged, and she leaned over the bar close to Carter so nobody could hear. She stood on her tiptoes. The tattoos on her arms' cleavage rippled.

"We call the ghost 'Gina.' She's definitely a woman, maybe in her twenties or thirties. Kinda hard to say."

"So, you've seen her?" Carter asked.

"Well, kinda," Lil said. "I was facin' the mirror behind the bar one night, looked up, and saw the reflection of a woman walkin' into the dining area in the vault. She looked well dressed. I figured she'd seated herself, so I went in there with a menu. I looked around, and no one was there. A minute later, our cook, Frier, comes running out the back yellin', 'A lady just walked into the pantry area, and when I walked in there to see who it was she disappeared!' Frier was pretty freaked out. He's superstitious to begin with and didn't come to work for a week.

"Another time I was leaning over cleaning bar glasses, and I felt someone tap my shoulder," Lil continued. "I looked up, and no one was there. The same thing happened to Gil a couple nights later, right, Gil?"

"I guess so, yeah," Gil said. "There's been lots of stuff like that over the years. Pretty much everyone who has worked here awhile meets Gina. It's usually the same kind of thing. They get a glimpse of some lady who disappears, or they feel someone tapping their back or pushing them. I felt it a couple times. It's weird. It's like a white glowy thing with people features."

"Who came up with the name Gina?" Carter asked.

"I did," said Lil. "That was my aunt's name. She and my mom used to hold séances when they was kids in North Carolina. My mom didn't believe in that stuff, but Aunt Gina did. She used to tell me scary stories all the time. She made my brother cry once, and I peed on myself in bed 'cause I thought somethin' evil was tryin' to get me. My grandma made Aunt Gina go talk to the minister. He told her the devil would take over her body if she kept messin' 'round with spirits."

"Interesting," Carter said. "But it doesn't exactly sound like you have proof of anything here at Gil Netters."

"I'm not saying I have proof, Mister Smartass," Lil said. "And I sure as hell don't know for sure what I saw. But I saw something, and I felt something. That I *am* sure of. And I know Mr. Frier, our cook, and some of the others will tell you they're sure too. I ain't sayin' what it is running 'round here. But it's something, and I damn sure don't like it."

A group of tourists walked into the pub and sat at the bar.

"Enough of this crazy stuff," Gil said in a low voice. "So, Sparky. What about the girl? Couldn't make it happen, huh? You owe me twenty-six bucks for that bottle of wine. And where are my glasses, moron?"

* * *

Every old town has its stories, and most are just that—folklore, fairy tales, imagination run amok, some devious twist of history unexplained. No surprise Cape Charles has some of that woven into its fabric of abandoned train stations, lighthouses, and old Victorians. *Imaginations could easily become unhinged here*, Carter thought as he headed home after lunch. *This would be a good place to stage one of those ghost "reality" TV shows.*

Carter took a slight detour and turned onto Bay Avenue in hopes of seeing Rose's purple golf cart. The sun was now up, the breeze gentle, and the Bay nearly still. A perfect beach day. There it was, parked by the Tyler Lane beach entrance like before.

Carter walked the sand path between the dunes and spotted Rose's pink and green umbrella. She was alone, wading knee deep in the water. Her yellow bikini bottoms rode low on her hips, making her legs seem even longer than Carter had remembered. A gust coming in from the south pushed the hair off her neck. Carter removed his Keens and looked at his size ten feet imprinting the sand. *Get some balls*, he told himself.

Carter set his sandals and paint cans by Rose's chair, then walked over to the water and waded toward her. The water was flat, barely a ripple, and at least seventy-five degrees.

"Hey there, pretty lady."

Rose pivoted. "Well, well. Don't tell me. I'm in *your* wading spot."

"Yup. But I'm happy to share," Carter said with a smile. "Friends share, right?"

"Oh, we've graduated to friend status." She smiled and adjusted her shoulder straps.

"Afraid I'm getting sunburned."

Back at her chair, Rose handed Carter sunscreen. As he massaged it onto the back of her neck, he fought the urge to kiss below her hairline. He then moved to her shoulder blades and the backs of her arms.

"You burn easy?" Carter asked as he stepped away.

"Usually my first or second time at the beach. After that I brown up like a rotisserie chicken. Probably the Portuguese blood in me, from my mother's side."

"Portuguese roots! What about the rest of you," Carter asked as he sat on the beach towel beside Rose's chair.

"I'm a mutt. The name Portman is Eastern European on Daddy's side, a mishmash of Polish, Austrian, and Hungarian, best I can tell. What about you, Carter? Are you a melting-pot baby too? Anything exotic in those veins?"

"Nothin' royal about my people from what I can tell. Dad's people are from Rome."

"Italian. Yeah, I can see it," Rose said. She ran her fingers through Carter's slightly wavy, dark hair.

"Last name is Rossi, which my dad shortened from Rossellini to sound more American. Dad designed display windows in fancy New York City department stores."

"*Rossellini.* Wasn't there a famous Italian film director by that name?"

"Impressive," Carter said. "You'd clean up on *Jeopardy*. Yup. That's the one. Roberto Rossellini made films in the '40s and had a fling with Ingrid Bergman and apparently lots of other actresses. He was the notorious family playboy. My grandfather's first cousin. I have photos of them together as kids in Rome."

Rose smiled and stroked Carter's hair again. "The descendant of one of Italy's most notorious playboys. That's a lot to live up to."

"I think I'd rather be related to the Queen of England," Carter said. "More dignified . . . and lucrative."

"Yes, but far more boring. Italian playboy—I like that. What about the rest of you, you know, your mother's side?"

"Like I said, more mysterious. She died when I was two. Her family name seems to be Austrian, or Romanian, or somewhere ending in *ian*— like you I guess. She had blond hair and light eyes. Her maiden name was Booth, like John Wilkes, the guy who shot Lincoln. I've never taken the time to find a birth record. I tried Ancestry.com, but it was a dead end. Kind of frustrating, actually."

"I know what you mean about Ancestry," Rose said. "They tease you with a few tidbits of free information and then make you pay up for the good stuff. I got pretty frustrated too."

"So, your trip here is all about exploring your family tree?" Carter couldn't work up the nerve to ask her about the ghost stuff; he hoped his guess about Rose being the ghost lady was wrong.

"Kind of. There is one relative I'm interested in learning more about, a great aunt on my mother's side: Luzia Rosa Douro."

"Is that where you get Rose from?"

"Very observant, Carter. Gold star. Yes. My mom named me after her. From what my mom says, several members of the family fled Portugal around 1916. They were afraid of a German invasion. So, her aunt Luzia and a couple of other family members fled to France. Apparently, Luzia met an American sailor there."

Rose told Carter pretty much all she had been able to find out about her great aunt from Google searches, some old letters, and recollections of family members. The American sailor Luzia met had served as an officer aboard a Navy cruiser assigned to escort convoys bringing supplies to the British, French, and Italians. German U-boats were a constant threat, torpedoing supply ships. The Kaiser's Navy even targeted passenger liners, sinking the British Lusitania and killing almost 1,200 civilians.

Luzia met the young officer, Ensign Douglas Kinard III, while she was in a dress shop in France. Luzia was a dancer by night back in Portugal and a milliner by day. Her hats had become quite fashionable.

She had trained in ballet and the classics and had hoped to perform in dance companies in Italy or France. She was stunning, with a face like Greta Garbo's but with a harder body and more grace—shoulders back, chin up, and a gait more even and light than a Tennessee Walker. Douglas Kinard III had stood breathless when he saw her through the window of the dress shop as she measured a customer's hat size. He stared for minutes until she finally noticed him and smiled coyly.

Kinard was a handsome man, regal even, with a square jaw, deep-set eyes, and blond hair that glistened white when stroked by the sun; Rose had found online a family portrait of the Norfolk Kinards, a well-to-do family that had owned a small fleet of barges that hauled timber between Cape Charles, Richmond, and Norfolk. Douglas was the oldest of three brothers and by far the most handsome. His father was friends with a couple of Norfolk admirals and parlayed his son's pedigreed education—he'd attended a private boarding school—into a Navy commission. Better to enlist as an officer than be drafted into what certainly appeared to be an unavoidable clash with the Germans, the admirals confided to their rich friend.

Young Douglas, just twenty-two, asked Luzia to be his wife, jumbling Spanish and French phrases he had learned while at school. Luzia, who had been a virgin before enveloping the debonair ensign, accepted the proposal on a drizzly evening the night before his warship deployed. That night, filled with lust and his heart aching, Douglas slipped onto her finger a gold ring set with a ruby the size of a pinky fingernail. He had received the heirloom from his grandfather for luck and had worn it on a neck chain. The ruby, Grandfather Kinard had claimed, had come from a gypsy who had foreseen a bright future and good fortune for Douglas' father, the senior Kinard, a prophecy fulfilled.

Luzia used money Douglas had given her for passage to America. He had written on a postcard an address in Cape Charles, Virginia. From New York, she could ride a train to the small coastal town. On a map, he circled the spot in the shape of a heart.

Douglas worried about Luzia making it to Ellis Island safely. He told his bride-to-be which passenger liners would have Navy escorts—a fortuitous tip. Luzia made it to New York about two months after she departed France and then boarded a train south to the spot on the map circled with a heart. She wasn't sure when she and Douglas would rendezvous, only that she would wait there until they did.

Luzia hadn't realized that while she was in New York being processed at Ellis Island, her beloved Douglas had been heading toward the Hudson Harbor aboard the *USS San Diego*. Ensign Kinard was no hero and longed for his bride-to-be, so he had written his father, who, once again, had used his pull. Kinard had been reassigned to shore duty, instead of being sent back across the Atlantic. The cruiser was being sent to New York to guard a convoy of cargo ships heading to supply France with weapons and ammunition. He was to ride it to the Hudson Harbor, get off the ship, and take a train ride back to Norfolk.

A German U-boat had been prowling the US coastline, looking for easy targets. It had come across two on the same afternoon: a Navy cruiser and a French passenger boat. Douglas Kinard had been on one and Luzia Rosa Douro on the other. The benevolent U-boat captain had passed on the civilian ship and, instead, stalked bigger prey. He torpedoed the *San Diego* near Fire Island just hours before Douglas Kinard was to disembark and report back to Norfolk. News about the U-boat attack exploded onto front pages. Shipping and ferry passage in deep harbors, like the Chesapeake Bay, or in open waters, was suspended while the Navy scattered ships to hunt down the ruthless German submariners.

Luzia arrived in Cape Charles a few days later, still unaware that Douglas had been aboard the *San Diego*. She had used the money Douglas had given her and a stash provided by her father before leaving Portugal to rent a room in a boarding house owned by the Kinard family, a Victorian with six bedrooms on Harbor Street, just a block in from the beach. It was the address Douglas had provided. He had sent word ahead that the family inn was to reserve its best room for his special guest and that she was to be pampered. The innkeepers obliged.

Instead of arriving at a quaint summer resort, Luzia stumbled into a chaotic mess. Cape Charles had become constipated with stranded travelers seeking passage to Norfolk and angry barge crews stuck in port. The Navy had suspended all commerce and passenger ferry transport until it could deploy patrol boats to chase off German U-boats now lurking off the coast. Studebakers, Model T's, and Packards awaiting ferry passage lined roads into town, their cloth tops baking in the sun.

Unsavory boat crew members, stranded and frustrated, plied the town for opportunities to replenish their dwindling cash reserves needed for booze, loose women, and lodging. Packs of thieves worked the area. They pickpocketed and stole from boarding houses, stores, or unoccupied cars. Local police were overwhelmed. Luzia had only been in Cape Charles a week and twice found her room broken into. So, she took her money and what jewelry she had and put it all in a safety-deposit box at Colonial Savings and Loan, one of the town's local banks, one with armed guards by the door. That deposit was the last known record of Luzia Rosa Douro's life.

* * *

Carter listened mesmerized, like a four-year-old being read *Green Eggs and Ham* by Dr. Seuss.

"Wow. So, your great aunt Luzia was here in Cape Charles. Did she ever hook up with her Navy guy, Douglas?"

"No. Aunt Luzia died here, or at least that's my guess. I'm trying to figure out exactly how and where. What I know for sure is that the bank she put her money in burned up really bad. What I don't know for sure is if the fire had anything to do with her death, but I'm guessing there's a connection. She was never again heard from. Two people died in the fire: a bank security watchman and a woman. Newspaper accounts said the fire probably was an arson and that the body of the woman was found in the vault and couldn't be identified."

"Seems strange. You'd think someone in a small town like this would know the identity of someone who was killed," Carter said.

"You would think so," Rose said. "But remember, little Cape Charles was bustling back then and had a lot of strangers hanging around. Transients held up here waiting to get passage to Norfolk."

"Still strikes me as odd. A woman turns up dead in a bank vault, and no one knows who she is."

"Carter, you're thinking like a twenty-first century man. Lots of people in the early 1900s were undocumented. There are gravesites around this country filled with people who died anonymously. I think that's what happened to my mother's aunt. There was no record of Luzia in this country—no birth certificate, Social Security number, nothing I could find other than her passage through Ellis Island. I think the woman who died in the bank was her. What I can't figure out is why she was in the building at night when it was burning."

"What about the Navy guy, that Douglas character? Did he come for her?"

"He died too. I found some old news stories online about the *USS San Diego*. Just about everyone abandoned ship. Douglas Kinard III of Norfolk, Virginia, and four or five others died on board."

"What the hell," Carter said. "Sounds like a 1940s melodrama."

"It was, Carter. And I need to write the ending. That's why I'm here. I need to find out what happened to Luzia. The worst part is, she may still be among us, stuck."

"What do you mean by *among us*?"

"Meet me at C Pier at seven. I'm on the *Topp Kat*, third boat from the end. It's a cabin cruiser with a dark blue hull. And bring a couple bottles of that pinot gris Gil serves. I'll grill some tuna steaks. Oh, and one more thing, Carter. We'll have company."

CHAPTER 9

CARTER WAS HAPPY for the invite, but disappointed he'd be a third wheel. He walked from the beach to Gil's to bum a couple of more bottles from his friend, knowing he wouldn't escape unscathed.

"So, Sparky, the little hottie invites you over but says you'll have company. Interesting play. She's either lying to keep you off guard, or she's yanking your chain for grins. Or maybe she's into kinky stuff."

"Come on, Gil. Always with the weird sex stuff. You're watching too much porn, or you had a weird childhood. Jill needs to cut off the cable and find you a shrink. In fact, I know one."

"Don't need cable for porn. There's plenty on the Internet. And you should know."

"Sorry to disappoint you, but it's not my thing."

"Bullshit, Sparky. We all look at the stuff. Keeps the juices flowing, and it keeps us all sane when we're not getting any. Maybe if I strapped you into a chair and made you watch for a few hours, you'd grow some balls. Anyway, here's a couple bottles of pinot gris. I'm charging double."

"Don't you always."

"Throw the other person overboard and try to get laid, moron. Maybe some weed will improve your chances. Ask Lil. She usually has some."

"No thanks, Gil. The stuff makes me dumb and paranoid."

"Try it. You might like yourself better that way, moron."

* * *

Carter took a little longer than normal getting ready. He put a new blade in his Trac II razor, plucked a few nose hairs, lathered on a scented hair conditioner, and spritzed his chest with a musky cologne his ex had given him on their last Christmas together. The final touch: hair-styling cream. A dark-blue collared shirt with the tail out over pleated shorts. Leather sandals.

Hope this isn't overkill. I feel like a freakin' teenager on a first date.

Carter knew the *Topp Kat* well. It was a charter boat used to go offshore for billfish and finfish. When the fishing was lousy, as it had been throughout most of June, Captain Neally would rent the forty-six footer to those looking for a place to have a private party. Rumor was that discreet out-of-town businesswomen who were regular fishing clients sometimes rendezvoused on the *Topp Kat* with boys for hire. The boat had two berths, a head, one room with couchlike benches, a wet bar, and a flat screen that rose from a cabinet with the touch of a button.

"Permission to come aboard," Carter called out.

The glass door to the cabin slid open. "Come on in, and watch your step," boomed a man's voice with a heavy accent.

Carter shook hands with the old guy, quickly figuring it was the same person Gil had described slobbering all over Rose at the pub.

"Nice to meet you. Carter, is it?"

"It is. And you are?

"My birth name is Malcolm Dunbar."

"Make that Dr. Dunbar," Rose interrupted as she stepped from the berth below into the main cabin. "Nice to see you, Carter."

Carter handed her the two bottles of pinot gris.

"These are for us," Rose said. "Malcolm wouldn't touch the stuff. He only drinks—"

"Brandy," Carter interjected. "Very old brandy."

"Quite right, my boy. What gave it away?"

"Well, you kind of look like John Houseman, you know, the actor in *The Paper Chase*. You have that air of sophistication."

"I'll take that as a compliment. I've worked decades to appear pretentious. Tried snobbery, but it didn't feel quite right."

"Well, now that you boys have been properly introduced," Rose said, "how about a toast to newfound friends?"

The three verbally danced for the next twenty minutes, making small talk while Rose seared tuna steaks on a propane grill on the stern.

"Spring asparagus and fresh tuna caught this morning. A full moon and calm summer night. Here's to perfection," Rose toasted.

After dinner, the three settled into deck chairs on the bow. They watched other boaters come and go on the pier, some quietly holding hands, others swaying and loud from too much beer or pot. Music and partying echoed over the water from other boats moored along the pier. A squawking heron flew overhead and Canada geese followed, honking with necks stretched looking for a landing strip.

"Quite an eclectic crowd you have here," Malcolm said.

"Yes, this sleepy town wakes up in the summer. Tourists and retirees have been pouring into this place the past couple years," Carter said. "Some of the locals worry it's turning into another hoity hangout for Northerners. Some of the old Virginia families are even spreading rumors that the Italian mob has been buying up waterfront land to drive out the locals and build a hotel."

"Think it's true?" Rose asked.

"Fact and fantasy seem to mingle comfortably around here," Carter said. "If you tell a lie enough times and enough people repeat it, then it's no longer a lie. Cyril at the hardware store says the mob rumor is BS. No Mafia, no hotel. Just some Jersey guys thinking they've found Shangri-La."

"Shangri-La. Very clever my boy, very clever," Malcolm said. "He's a smart one, Rose. Excuse me for a moment while I refresh and refill."

By now Carter was on his third glass of wine and feeling bold. It was his first moment alone with Rose since arriving an hour earlier.

"So, what's the deal with you two? Are you involved?"

"Involved? With Malcolm? Just what do you mean?" Rose teased. "Do you mean romantically? Jealous type, I see."

"Yes . . . and no, I'm not." Carter blushed.

"Malcolm is a dear friend and mentor. I was his graduate studies assistant at the University of Edinburgh. He visits when he's in the US, and we still do some research together from time to time. He's like an uncle to me."

"Well, he must be a dirty old uncle because Gil says he was slobbering all over you at dinner the other night."

"Gil. The eyes and ears of Cape Charles. You had better find more reliable sources for information. Malcolm wasn't slobbering. He does get kissy when he's been drinking, but never gropey. I hope *you* know the difference, Carter."

"Yes I do, and no, I don't get gropey either."

"Did I hear something about groping," Malcolm said as he slid the cabin door closed behind him. "In Italy and Spain, that's a fine art."

"It's apparently been elevated to a fine art in this country too," Rose said. "Donald Trump has been practicing the art for decades, if you believe the tabloids. He brags about grabbing women by the crotch."

"Vulgar man," Malcolm said. "Repulsive. I saw him once at a golf event in Edinburgh. He was dressed like a New York pimp—gold watches and rings, blue silk suit, three tall blondes at his side. His Trump jet. He kept reminding everyone he was 'very rich.' All the markings of a man with a small penis and really bad hair."

"I'd rather not discuss the next president's penis size or shape. We've been through that before with Hillary's husband," Rose said. "No more dicks in the White House, please!"

"Agreed," Carter said. "So, Luzia brings you two to Cape Charles."

Rose and Malcolm smirked at each other.

"The honor of explaining ourselves and our work is all yours, my dear. This old man has had too much libation and not enough sleep. I shall retire to my berth and let the waves rock me into a blissful slumber. Carter, the pleasure has been all mine."

Malcolm puckered his lips and smooshed them on Rose's cheek. "Goodnight, my beautiful dear."

"Goodnight, dirty old man."

* * *

"Quite a character," Carter said. "Very charming."

"Charming, cunning, and a daring intellectual. He is regarded as the grandfather of our field around the world."

"And your field is?"

"Parapsychology."

Rose is *the ghost lady!* "What do you mean, like the study of poltergeists?"

"No, not exactly. Let me explain."

Rose talked for the next twenty minutes almost nonstop. Carter felt like a newspaper reporter again, nodding to show attentiveness and interest, asking short follow-up questions, and never interrupting. The best reporters were great listeners. If only he had a notebook and pen.

Rose explained that parapsychology is a branch of psychology that uses the scientific method to study psychic phenomena—reincarnation, religious miracles, levitation, psychokinesis, telepathy, clairvoyance, extrasensory perception, and, most commonly, apparitions, the meanest of which are poltergeists.

"So, you prove, or disprove, the existence of ghosts."

"Well, not exactly, Carter. We use very strict scientific criteria to evaluate and understand what people think they saw and, more importantly, why."

"No offense, Rose, but it sounds squishy to me. How can you prove something that may not exist or that is a figment of someone's imagination?"

"Physicists do it all the time. Using quantum mechanics, they imagine worlds based on mathematical equations. On the other end of the spectrum, priests and shamans and rabbis and imams extrapolate from ancient stories to create alternative worlds too. No one has seen Heaven or Jannah, but tens of millions of people believe both places exist."

"I get all of that. But religion is a belief system that denies science, and physics is at least something tangible that can be tested and duplicated."

"You sure you want to drill deeper here?" Rose said as she filled her wineglass. "This stuff can make your head explode."

"I'm good. My brain hasn't felt this alive in months. Stories about ghosts and mind reading are far better than listening to Gil wax on about his glory days at Syracuse and me deflecting his insults."

"You really need to get a life, Carter, or some new friends."

"I thought I just did. That's one reason I'm here, Rose."

Carter sat stiffly beside Rose on the small cabin "couch"—mahogany wooden storage boxes covered with vinyl seat cushions and backrests. Rose's summer dress slid higher as she curled her legs beneath her to better face Carter. He could see her blue underwear. The dress strap slid slightly down her right shoulder and exposed a tan line. Her shoulders and legs were bronze. Carter could smell perfume, or maybe it was shampoo. Either way, the lavender bouquet filled his head. So *what* that she was the ghost lady! He imagined sliding his face under her skirt so he could inhale her more fully.

Kiss her, you fool. NOW!

"So, you were saying that you try and figure out why people think they see what they saw—or something like that."

"Right, something like that." Rose giggled. "For something to be considered a science, you need to have a provable hypothesis. You remember that from grammar school?"

"No, I must have skipped the sixth grade," Carter said. "But go on."

"The problem with my field is that we can't conduct experiments or duplicate our findings in a laboratory. If a ghost shows up someplace and is seen by a few people, we cannot tell when it might appear again—if ever. So, we can't verify or measure."

"So, it's not a science then."

"Well, that's what the traditional scientific community would say. But that doesn't prove or disprove paranormal activity. It only proves it's not science by conventional standards."

"You were right, Rose. This is making my head hurt. Maybe Gil's rants aren't so bad after all."

"You asked for it, and now that you got me revved up, I can't stop. So, pay attention."

Carter stared at Rose's full lips, trying to concentrate on her words, but imagining her locked on him.

"People claim they can have a premonition that something is going to happen, and then it does. You're thinking about your mother, and then suddenly the phone rings. You have a vision of a car accident, and you find out a cousin died in a wreck. Happens all the time, but not on a recurring basis to the same person in any predictable way."

"So, then none of this stuff is science, which means it's not considered *real*. That's the bottom line, right?"

"No, not *real* by conventional terms, because science has been defined in a very narrow way. Like I said, you have to be able to replicate your findings so they can be tested by others. Under that definition, parapsychology will never be accepted as science, and, by extension, its subject matter will never be considered real."

"So, where does Malcolm fit into all of this nonscience stuff?"

"What Malcolm, me, and hundreds of others are trying to do is come up with a scientific method for our field. We're trying to figure out how to reliably predict and measure."

"So, you really haven't answered the million-dollar question, Rose. Are ghosts real? Are people reincarnated? Do we have extrasensory perceptions?"

"I don't know, Carter, and I won't until we have measuring sticks that work. But here is what I think: The truth is what we believe it to be. If someone believes they saw a ghost, then that thought is tangible. It exists in their mind. It is real to them. Maybe we have to first believe that ghosts exist before we are able to sense their presence. Maybe you can't get to Heaven unless you believe it's there in the first place.

"I am a scientific agnostic, Carter," Rose continued. "I believe that our minds are far more complex and sensitive than we can imagine. There are psychological powers occurring within us that we barely sense. We have abilities of perception that we can't comprehend. I believe evolution will fix that; but for now we're still monkeys afraid of the unexplainable."

"So, if ghosts are real then there would have to be some form of life after death. Correct?"

"Maybe. Or maybe our bodies leave a sort of carbon footprint that can be sensed by some of the living. Maybe we live in parallel universes. Maybe people on the other side see us cross from time to time into their universe and think we're ghosts. Is that a mindblower?"

"Damn, Rose. I feel like I've stepped into *The Twilight Zone*."

"You asked for it, my dear. Welcome to my mixed-up world. Pour me another."

"No kidding. I should have brought three bottles. I'm gonna have trouble getting to sleep tonight. Unless . . ." Carter glared into Rose's eyes and flashed a wry smile.

"Not a chance, big boy. Not tonight. Not here with Malcolm on board."

"Gil said to toss him overboard."

"Yes. I'm sure he did, and I'm sure you could. But then we'd have another ghost to deal with, and I think Malcolm would be one mighty pissed off poltergeist. Time to go. You want a ride home on the golf cart?"

"Only if you park it at my place and spend the night."

"Persistent . . . and I thought you were the bashful type. Your buddy Gil was wrong about that too."

CHAPTER 10

CARTER OPENED THE front door and flicked on the hallway light. Rose stepped gingerly behind him, almost tiptoeing. She stopped in the entrance hall, stared upward, and listened. In silence, she removed her sandals and ran her fingers through her hair to tame the frizz that had been riled by the damp night.

"You okay?" Carter asked. He wondered if she was too woozy to climb the stairs to his bedroom.

"Yes," she whispered. "Just give me a moment."

"A moment. Okay. I'm going into the kitchen to get us a couple of bottled waters, or would you prefer more wine?"

"Water's good. How 'bout both?"

Carter stepped down the hall, past a bathroom and into the galley-style kitchen. He flipped on the light and rooted around in the fridge for a bottle of Dasani and some chilled chardonnay.

Rose rubbed her feet on the old pinewood floors. She closed her eyes for a moment as she tried feeling the wood grain between her toes.

"I love the floors," she called out.

She walked through the living room and into the dining area off the kitchen, rubbing her hands along the old plaster, pressing her fingertips as if feeling for a pulse. She stepped into the kitchen just as Carter finished pouring the wine. He handed her a glass.

"Cheers," he said as they clinked. "I stole these from Gil. Look familiar?"

"Our beach glasses. You're such a romantic, Carter Rossellini."

"So, what do you think?" Carter hoped for at least an empty compliment about his house.

"Cute, like you. And it's happy."

"Happy? What do you mean?"

"No bad energy. Nothing lurking."

"Like ghosts?"

"Yes, Carter. No evil spirits. I told you, I have to be careful with old houses. I see things, and those things know I see them. They can't hide from me, and sometimes they get angry or playful. It can get weird or even scary if you're not use to it."

"Holy shit, Rose. I think I believe you, and you're freaking me out."

Rose put her hand up to silence Carter. She placed her wineglass on the kitchen counter and walked down the hall toward the stairs.

"What is it, Rose? Do you hear something or see something?" Carter whispered.

Rose put her index finger over her lips. "*Shh!*" She placed her hand on the banister and stepped lightly and slowly up the wooden stairs. She walked gracefully on her toes like a ballerina, her calf muscles bulging and her shoulders back and straight. Despite his fright, Carter couldn't help but swallow her ass with his eyes. He tucked in one step down from her as they ascended.

Rose stopped on the landing before taking the *L* three steps to the top. "Hear that?"

"What? Hear what?" Carter asked.

"Which is the master bedroom?" she asked in a whisper.

"Straight ahead."

"Why is the door closed? Did you close it, Carter?"

"I don't know. I don't remember," he said, his voice cracking.

"Oh my God! Wait here," Rose said.

Carter suddenly had to piss really bad. But he froze, crunching his shoulder against the wall. The hall light was on, and Rose placed her hand on the doorknob, brass and original to the house. She turned it slightly, cracked the door open, and peered in.

"Oh God! Oh my God! Carter, wait there."

"What is it?" he whispered, eyes bulging.

"Don't move." Rose took a deep breath, stepped into the room, and gently clicked the door closed. Carter could hear the floorboards creak. He heard his closet door open and then close. He heard the window slide open, and then he heard Rose's voice.

"Be gone . . . be gone."

Carter was too scared to move. He knew he should crash into the bedroom to battle whatever it was Rose had confronted. But he couldn't. He felt emasculated, like someone whose swim trunks have come off in the ocean surf and has to walk to his towel naked and shriveled.

"Carter, it's okay now. You can come in."

Carter softly eased open the door and stuck his head in. The room lights were off. Sitting on his queen-sized bed with the blue sheets drawn down was Rose, naked and on her side.

"It was stuffy in here, so I had to open the windows." She giggled. "Got ya!"

"Damn you! I gotta pee."

"So, Carter, was your fear real or imagined?"

* * *

Carter buried his face into Rose that night with the unbridled intensity of a starving man being served a full meal. Rose groaned in ecstasy again and again, exhausted from the torrent flowing from her and the boil within.

When Carter finally mounted her chest to breast, he teased, entering and then exiting until she grabbed him from behind and pulled him in, their hips clashing and then locked. Both of them dripped with sweat, their stomachs like Teflon, sliding back and forth without friction or delay. He collapsed on her, heart pounding. She lay breathless, wondering if what she had just experienced was real or imagined. The heat, the moisture, the night air—it was all too perfect, the stuff of the Harlequin novels she had read as a teen.

Carter lay wondering if it had ever been better or more intense. He did what most guys do: He rated this experience against past encounters. Only one came close, a July night in the hills of North Carolina in a hotel overlooking a mountain lake during a drizzle. He had been with his college sweetheart, a dancer, a Southerner whose words covered him like molasses, sticky and sweet, whose perfectly tight orbs were rock hard but inviting. They were in their twenties and knotted in ecstasy until they collapsed from dehydration. They slept ten hours in each other's arms, their limbs entangled, him sliding into her over and over, then sleeping some more to recharge. His life had been worth living, just for that moment.

Rose lay wondering why such lustful bliss hadn't happened more often in her life. She was stunning, and she knew it. But was she too cerebral, too demanding, too preoccupied. She thought about her ex, his ribbed abdominals, biceps, and calves. His calloused hands that felt like fine-grit sandpaper when stroking her thighs and shoulders. His thickness. His length. His broad shoulders elevating him like a drawbridge over a river. If only he wasn't so superficial. If only he had made it beyond trade school. If only he had understood more than bricklaying and hockey.

Rose and Carter lay speechless in thought, both on their backs listening to the whir of the ceiling fan, moistening their throats with Dasani. Carter looked at Rose's navel, a perfect dimple, and felt himself harden again.

"I need to know if that was real," he said. "I need to duplicate and verify."

Rose giggled and pulled him into her arms, whispering, "Yes, Carter, this is real."

CHAPTER 11

CARTER EXPECTED ROSE to be gone when he awoke in the morning. Instead, her calf pinned his leg and her head rested heavy on his shoulder. The ceiling fan swirled the morning air oozing in through the windows Rose had opened. Sometime during the night, exhausted and damp with sweat, they had pulled the blue sheets over them.

Carter's mouth felt pasty, and his head filled with a dull throb from last night's wine. The dead weight of Rose's leg surprised him too. He struggled to escape without waking her, hoping she would remain unconscious while he showered and perked morning brew. Carter was nearly zombielike in the morning and needed a java jolt to become approachable and conversant. Without it, he'd drag his feet and his mind would be in a haze so dense his eyes would need fog lights to see through it. It took a few minutes, but he successfully extracted himself, inch by inch, and slipped quietly away, sighing with relief in the bathroom and again as he tiptoed down the stairs.

While listening to the electric pot hiss and chug, it occurred to Carter that he hadn't spent a full night with a woman since his rendezvous with the hooker. He had been laid a couple of times—once by a woman celebrating her final divorce decree at a Norfolk bar across from the courthouse and the other time by a blind date arranged by a coworker at Sid's firm. In both cases, the women had hit and run before midnight, stealing away with only a peck on the forehead and then a text the next day. Carter didn't care. Recreational sex left no casualties. Wear a condom, find their G-spot, and everyone wins.

Shit! No latex with Rose.

After a second mug and a slice of peanut butter toast, Carter checked in on his guest. Still asleep, peaceful. He didn't want to disturb her. He threw on some shorts and a clean T-shirt.

Back downstairs, Carter scribbled a note and left it by the electric percolator. *Coffee's made. Fridge is stocked. Help yourself. I enjoyed last night, and hope we'll see each other again soon.* He headed to Gil's. It was almost eleven, and he couldn't wait to let his ex-brother-in-law and abrasive best friend know about his success. And he had questions, a lot of them, about the pub's past.

* * *

In the warm months, Gil and his regular customers often congregated around three patio tables on the sidewalk in front of the pub. A steady Bay breeze agitated flies just enough to keep them in hiding. During low tides and still nights, the insects waged revenge. This late morning was windy but warm as the sun hooked south and exhaled on Mason Way.

Carter rounded the corner and heard a ruckus. Gil and a few other locals were watching an argument between two men. Carter stepped into the semicircle next to Gil.

"What's going on?"

"Oh man. Mr. Frier and his cousin Nate are throwing down."

"Over what?"

"A snake," Gil said. "A goddamn pet snake."

From what Carter could discern, Nate had bought an albino snake and named it Walter, after Ben Frier's dad. Ben and Nate were first cousins from a black family whose roots reached deep into Eastern Shore soil. They lived next to each other on the same farm owned by their fathers. Ben, a retired Navy chef and Gil's head cook, was lighter-skinned than his cousin Nate, but besides that they looked like brothers, both handsome with high cheekbones, thick chests, piercing brown eyes, size thirty-four inseams, and size thirteen feet. In high school, Ben had played middle linebacker and Nate had played defensive end. When games got tight, they'd loosen up teammates by goading each other in the huddle with predictable one-liners.

"You getting fat, Nate," Ben would say, pointing at his cousin's distended belly.

Nate would grab his crotch and say, "When you got tools as valuable as these, you need to put a shed over 'em."

Ben and Nate were two of the smartest kids in their high school, each graduating with honors. Ben had opted for the Navy after graduating, and Nate had studied business administration at a state college. Both loved the Shore and had returned to raise families and be near kin. Ben chose to work at Gil's because he loved to cook. Many said his culinary skills were five-star.

"This place gets into your blood and never leaves your mind," Ben would often say.

Ben was fond of just about all things living—except for lizards. He never liked snakes growing up, and Nate used that as ammo. Naming a snake Walter after Ben's father was a stick in the eye, an insult plain and simple, but harmless like most of the haranguing between them.

"Damn you, Nate. You're disrespecting my kin, which means you're disrespecting me. You're calling my daddy a snake. That's what you're doing, and you know I've hated those evil things ever since you put one in my bed when we were growing up."

"Damn, Benny. Hold your shorts. Walter is my pet. If I named my dog after Walter, you wouldn't be riled like this. I named 'em Walter because he's light-skinned like your yo' daddy—and handsome. That's all."

"A snake ain't a dog. A snake ain't no damn pet either. And your snake is white as those clouds up there, not brown. You just wanted to rile me, and you did, I'll give you that. Good thing we're cousins because I'd crack your head with an iron skillet if we weren't."

Carter couldn't tell whether Ben Frier was mad or just fooling around. He hadn't lived in Cape Charles long enough to know the difference.

He knew Nate was a jokester, though. And he'd been in Gil's enough times to know the dueling cousins each reveled in holding court and exaggerating. It was classic one-upmanship.

"Snakes make great pets," Nate countered. He bounced on his toes and waved his thick arms as if preparing for a wrestling match. "I carry Walter around with me. He curls 'round my neck. I feed him twice every day. He likes mice and beetles."

"Nothing wrong with eating mice, but snakes aren't pets, pure and simple," Ben crowed. "Pets come when you call 'em. Does a snake? *Never!* Snakes don't even have ears. Does the snake let you pet 'em? *Shee-it.*"

"Yes, Benny, I pet Walter when I feed him and when he crawls on my neck," Nate said, arms raised. "Sometimes I let him get in the bed with me."

"*Damn,* Nate. You're a fool then. What you should do is put 'em inside your pants leg to make it look like you gotta dick."

"I'd be downsizing by putting Walter in *my* pants. My snake's already longer."

Gil had just taken a swig of beer and spit it out laughing just as two older women walked by on the sidewalk.

Ben eyed the passersby and continued, "Tell you what, Nate. Go home and get Walter, and then set 'em down about a hundred feet over there in the grass, then come back over here. If you call Walter by his name and he comes, I'll suck your dick right here in broad daylight on Mason Way."

Carter, Gil, and the others laughed so hard that they had to sit. Gil was doubled over. Nate and Ben finally busted up too. Lil stood in the doorway watching the ruckus. She shook her head and smirked like a college-dorm-room monitor who had caught coeds in the act. Gil sent Lil back inside for two drafts of summer ale, one each for Nate and Ben and another stout for him.

Ben and Nate high-fived each other and went inside. Gil, Carter, and a couple of the local boys sat around a sidewalk table, laughing and repeating some of Ben's and Nate's lines.

"Oh shit," Gil said a few minutes later while sipping his chocolaty brew. "Here comes Smitty."

The police sergeant stopped his unmarked cruiser in front of the pub and finger-waved at Gil, who wiped his sudsy mouth on his sleeve and walked to the patrol car. Smitty leaned out of the window. *Looks like a male version of his cousin Hattie,* Carter thought. He had deep-set eyes, heavy, round cheeks, and a proud, upturned nose.

"Gotta couple calls about a disturbance. Little early in the day for bar fights, ain't it, Gil?"

"We're okay here, Smitty." Gil chuckled. "Just Mr. Frier and Cousin Nate having fun."

"Yeah, I know. But a couple tourists came into the station a few minutes ago and said there was a fight and lots of swearing. Said two black men were beatin' on each other, and hecklers were cheering them on."

"I wouldn't say lots of cursin', and nobody was beatin' on anybody." Gil smirked.

"Okay, Gil, but it's summer. We got bird watchers and moms who drive Mercedes SUVs with young kids in tow. They ain't like the locals," Smitty said. "I got a complaint that Cyril and Mac were telling obscene stories in the hardware store. Somethin' about blow jobs and Trump and gay men."

Gil busted a laugh. "You know Cyril ain't shy about his views. And he's too old to care about customer satisfaction. Cyril will admit to that. He'll wear his bowtie and repent for his insults on Sunday, but he'll be hitting the Scotch and instigating again on Monday."

"Probably so, Gil. But you boys need to tone it down. I got my orders. The mayor and the chief want us to be family friendly. 'Good for tourism,' they say. Just try to keep things under control, okay, Gil, especially on a public street during the day when people are walking around. You and the boys can cut loose in the fall when the place clears out. Hell, I'll join ya."

"Gotcha. No worries. Thanks, Smitty. By the way, I could use some more of that summer flounder you been catching. Tourists love it."

* * *

Carter and Gil slid into a booth inside the pub's vault, both limp from laughter.

"Only in Cape Charles," Gil said. "Hungry?"

"Yeah, I could eat something. Long night."

"Do tell, Sparky. I'm guessing you were either up whacking off all night or maybe, by the grace of God, you finally grew a pair and scored with a *real* woman."

"You have such a way with words, Gil. I'm always ready to slit my wrist after I talk to you."

"You know I love you, moron. Now tell me how it went with Little Miss Tight Butt."

"Well, very well. She spent the night. In fact, she may still be there. I slipped away."

"You got her back to your place, and she didn't run away? How many bottles did you drink?"

"Three, but we had some help. Her friend, the old guy," Carter said.

"Don't tell me—three-way?"

"Stop being ridiculous," Carter huffed. "No, the old guy is her college professor. Friends and colleagues, that's all. They're staying on Neally's boat at C Pier. We had some dinner and drinks there, and then she came back to my place after he went to sleep." Carter flashed a grin wider than the painted smile on a circus clown's face.

"So, it was pretty hot, huh?" Gil said as he leaned forward and did his best Groucho Marx bouncy eyebrow.

"Let me just say that I'm worn out—and hungry."

"How 'bout an early lunch—a lamb burger with extra bar fries and a Guinness, on me. The wine you never paid me for is on me too, but I still want my wineglasses back, you moron."

"You're the nicest prick I know," Carter said. "And don't tell Jill about the girl, okay? I don't want Sophie to know about my personal life, or anyone else for that matter."

"Jill's gonna find out anyway, Sparky. She knows everyone on your block. By the sound of it, you and Little Miss Hot Ass probably kept the neighbors awake last night with your screams of ecstasy."

"I hope not, but we did have the windows open," Carter said. "And she left her golf cart parked out front."

"Oh shit, Sparky. You'll be reading about it in the newspaper by tomorrow. Guaranteed. I can see the headline now: *Town Numbnuts*

Finally Grows a Pair."

"Good thing you make a great martini and own a bar, because you sure as hell ain't a poet, my friend."

"You're right. I was always better at chemistry than English."

* * *

Carter felt revived after the burger and fries hit his bloodstream. Lil cleared the booth and brought her boss and his best friend two spiked coffees. Lil looked thinner than Carter remembered—maybe because he usually only saw her from the waist up when standing behind the bar. Today, she looked less like a biker chick with buff arms and tattoos and more like a preppy college girl with a ponytail and thick-rimmed glasses. Or maybe a sultry librarian hiding beneath prudish clothes, a sexy ball of fire aching to be unleashed. She wore a navel-high, deep V-neck white T-shirt and blue jeans that hugged her hips without forming a crotch line.

Carter always liked Lil's North Carolina drawl and the contrast of her green eyes and black hair. She reminded him of his college sweetheart, the dancer with the perfect ass who had forever branded his psyche like a hot iron that marathon night of entangled bliss by the mountain lake. Privately, he and Gil called Lil "Wonder Woman" because she resembled actress Lynda Carter—tough yet inviting, a dominatrix.

"Wonder Woman is looking good," Carter said.

"You noticed, huh?" Gil huffed. "She's taking hot yoga and working out—all for you, dipshit. She swoons every time you come into the bar. She practically squirts when she talks to Jill about you."

"Get out of here, Gil. I'm like twenty years older than her."

"And that's a problem? What are you, stupid? How many guys have a superhero lusting for them?"

"You're just messin' with me. Lil is hot. She could have any guy in town."

"I know," Gil said. "That's what I told Jill. Damned if I know what she sees in you. Maybe she wants to spank you or hold you upside down or something. Probably likes you because there's not a lot of options around here, I'm guessing. You're fresh meat. *Carpe diem,* Sparky."

"And *baciami il culo*, Gil. I hope you and Jill have a good laugh, but not at my expense. Look, I got to ask you about the bar and this ghost stuff. Rose told me why she's in town and what she does. It's pretty weird. She thinks that a family member, a great aunt I think, died here and that the woman's ghost is still hanging around. I'm connecting some dots, but I'm wondering if it's the same ghost Lil was talking about."

"I told you I don't like talking about that stuff," Gil said, his mood getting tense. He lowered his voice. "Look, there is some weird stuff that happens around here, like I told you. I looked into it awhile back. I talked to the town historian, who said that this building burned up pretty bad back when it was a bank in 1920 or so. All but one bank employee got out, and two bodies were found in the vault—supposedly a man and a woman—but no one could identify the remains. The only other thing I heard was that the bank had been in Cyril's family or that they were part owners. That's all I know, and all I care to know."

"Well, that's pretty close to what Rose already knew. But the confirmation will help. Would you mind talking to her about this?"

"If it will help get you laid again," Gil said. "But keep your mouth shut. I don't want the staff freaking out, or the town. Mr. Frier will quit. He's very superstitious. That's why he hates snakes. And you heard Lil."

"I won't say a word about the Gil Netters ghost if you don't tell Jill about Rose and me. Deal?"

"You drive a hard bargain, Sparky. You finally get a girlfriend, and she turns out to be some kind of freako. That's just perfect. Another crazy bird lands in Cape Charles."

"Just keep an open mind. This ghost stuff could be good for business, Gil. Maybe we can conjure the spirit every Wednesday night and you could charge admission and sell T-shirts."

"I'm tellin' ya, don't mess with this stuff. Better to leave it alone. You've heard the saying about letting sleeping dogs lie, right?"

"Well, well. Who's the wuss now? Maybe *you* need to grow a pair."

"I have a pair, and I like them just where they are—not slashed off and jammed down my throat. I'm telling you, be careful with this shit."

CHAPTER 12

HATTIE SAVAGE SAT at her desk in the bay window of Savage Realty, just a few steps from Gil Netters and Bay Hardware on Mason Way. Like Gil Netters, Savage Realty was in a building that over its ninety years had had several incarnations. It had been a dress boutique, a bistro, a shoe repair store, and a dentist's office. The Savage family had bought the building for next to nothing. One of the local banks was pulling up stakes after Cape Charles' economy collapsed in the 1970s and unloaded its assets at fire-sale prices. Hattie's uncle was on the bank board, and her daddy had scooped up about a half-dozen commercial properties for about twenty cents on the dollar.

Hattie had a perfect vantage point from the bay window. She could see who was coming, going, and who had lunch with whom. She'd always pretend to be on the phone looking busy, but as soon as someone stepped through the office door her conversation would conveniently end. Men were "honey" and women "dear." Her smile was as big as her voice, inviting, commanding, and joyful. She was a mixed breed—half-used car salesman and half-church deacon. And that's how she dressed—bright pastels but below-the-knee conservative and always flat sandals—even in the winter. Her double-E wide feet had plenty of natural insulation.

Hattie's handshake was firm and reserved for people she had just been introduced to. Everyone else got a hug, except for Cyril, because he didn't hug anyone. No hugs for his sidekick, Mac, either because he had once grabbed Hattie's ass. She had spun like a professional wrestler and back-armed Mac into a rack of rubber waders and hip boots that cushioned the dirty old man's fall. He'd been scared of her ever since, stepping off the sidewalk when he saw her coming. Privately, he called her "Momma Brahma."

"What brings you in here, stranger? Ready to sell already?" Hattie said, rising from her desk to give Carter a hug.

"Let me guess. Today is a great day to sell a house," Carter said.

"Unless you're buying. Cape Charles is hot right now," Hattie said, followed by a belly laugh. "Come visit with me. Coffee?"

"No, I'm good. Just had some lunch and an Irish coffee with Gil. People sure do start drinking early around here."

"Some consider it our national pastime." Hattie laughed. "Not me. Not anymore. Got into trouble too many times. Alcohol makes you speak the truth, and nothing good can come from that. So what can I do ya for, honey?"

"It's about a girl, the one in town doing research about a lost family member."

"You mean that skinny chickie stayin' on Neally's boat with the old man. Cute girl. Him too. You have good taste. Heard you two had some fun last night."

"Christ! Already? Unbelievable."

"Don't worry, honey. We was all rootin' for you. Glad you found your stride." Hattie leaned over her desk and gave Carter a congratulatory tap on the shoulder. "So, how can I help you impress this young gal? Sounds like you rang her bell pretty good last night."

Carter spent the next ten minutes telling Hattie about Rose, Malcolm, their parascience, and Rose's missing relative. Hattie sat expressionless, nodding and mumbling "uh-huh" as Carter tried to make sense of it all. She was as serious and sincere as a school guidance counselor listening to a sophomore confessing to unprotected sex.

"So, I guess what I'm really wondering is whether all of this ghost stuff is real. People seem to joke about it on the surface, but when you start to ask serious questions, they get nervous. Gil nearly shit himself, told me not to mess around with the supernatural."

Hattie stiffened and sat upright in her swivel desk chair. She folded her hands on the desktop and fixed her green eyes on Carter's pupils.

"First off, I've never seen a ghost," Hattie said. "Now, that may be because I don't want to see one and because I'm agnostic about all of this woo-woo stuff—even religion. My daddy said that when we die, that's it, we're dead. If there's some kind of life after death, then that's a bonus. I subscribe to that notion, Carter. Takes the worrying out of life. I believe in doin' all your livin' while you're vertical, with feet on the ground."

"Well, then how do you explain all the people who say they have seen spirits, or heard voices, or seen the Virgin Mary appear, or had a premonition about a relative being sick, or that they were reincarnated?"

"Like I said, honey, I don't dispute what people *think* they saw or heard, but I don't claim it to be true either. When I talk about ghosts bein' in town, I'm just makin' conversation. The way I see it is that if you believe somethin' happened, then it happened to you. Period. That simple. Sounds to me like this Rose lady has your mind in a knot—and maybe another part of you too. You seem pretty levelheaded. What did you two do last night, besides you know? Did you have a séance?"

"It's not like that, Hattie. She's more of a scientist. I like her, and I want to help. She's got my curiosity up, and, besides, I'm getting tired of patching plaster and painting all day. This is a nice distraction. Maybe the paint fumes are getting to my head."

"Okay, honey. There's a fella who lives across the creek on one of the oldest farms in Northampton County. About ten to fifteen years ago, we had scientists from all over the place crawlin' 'round here, drilling holes in the ground and using fancy boats with all these electronic gadgets. Some of them were from South Africa and Europe. A few stayed in the old Cape Charles Hotel.

"Anyway, they was here trying to figure out the Bay crater. You know about the crater, right? They did lots of exploring around Greyson Plantation over on Kings Creek. That's Jessep Greyson's place. Jessep is, shall we say, a believer in the past. He thinks he was reincarnated, and he'll swear that the past ain't really the past at all. He was really happy to let the scientists crawl around his land and punch holes in the ground. He said maybe they'd find out why so many curious things seem to happen at Greyson Plantation.

"One of these nerdy science guys stayin' at the hotel told me that the center of the giant crater is smack-dab under Jessep's 757-acre farm. He said there's a magnetic field around parts of the crater stronger than most anything he ever saw. He used some fancy word to describe it: *anomaly,* that's what he called it. The way I heard it, the magnetic waves from whatever is down there would make the hair on a donkey's ass stand up straight and chickens sit backwards on their eggs."

Hattie scratched her chin. "We got a fella named Major who used to be bipolar—you know, depressed or angry, couldn't sleep, just a god-awful mess. Moved here 'bout eight years ago with his huntin' dog named Minor. He started feelin' better after a few years. Don't take lithium or Prozac or any head-meds no more; just smokes weed every now and again and drinks Miller Lite. Says it's the best he's ever felt. Doctors can't explain it. Says his brainwaves is different. That boy's happy all the time, always whistling and smiling at the sky."

"Damn, Hattie, I need to get some of what Major has. I had no idea all of this weird stuff happens around here." Carter scratched his head.

"No, not *around* here," Hattie blurted. "*Here!* This place is ground zero for the biggest crater ever to smash into North America. That outer space rock left a hole about a mile deep right over there." She pointed southwest over the Bay. "Right goddamn there! When you walk down the street, you're standing on it. Coordinates 37.2679 – 76.0174." Hattie pointed to a map on her wall of a longitude-latitude grid of Cape Charles. "Head out a ways by boat, and the Bay floor drops down 600 feet. Watermen call it the ledge. Damn straight, honey. Livin' here is like walkin' on the moon."

Carter sat quiet for a few seconds to absorb the geography lesson. He had seen the signs about the Chesapeake Bay Crater over the beach, next to other informational plaques about Bay critters and birds. Carter, like most, had glanced at the graphic of the comet strike but never thought more of it. Things that happened millions of years ago seemed to him like more myth than fact, nothing more than grist for sci-fi flicks. It was hard enough trying to imagine life pre-1800s. After listening to Hattie, though, a fiery ball of hot iron from outer space punching a mile-deep hole in the earth felt more real at that moment than mastodons or Jesus of Nazareth.

"So how do you know Jessep?" Carter asked.

"Fourth cousin on my momma's side."

"I should have known." Carter chuckled.

"I'll give him a call."

"That'd be great, Hattie. Is Cousin Jessep friendly?"

"He's a curious fella. Likes reading poetry and drinking port wine and sherry. Thinks he lived in the 1800s. If you want to get on his good side, bring a good bottle and share a poem. He likes that Longfellow and pretty girls too. Had a couple of wives. One left him years ago, and the other died on the farm—natural causes. Had the cancer from smoking. She's buried in the family plot on the farm, not too far from where those geologists was drillin'."

* * *

Hattie held up her finger for Carter to stay quiet while she dialed her cell phone. "Cousin Jess. It's Cousin Hattie. Been awhile. Momma says thanks for the bushel of snap beans and the flounder fillets. Says she'll send you over some fried chicken and a sweet potato pie. Jessep, I got a small favor to ask. There's a fella who lives in town here—nice fella—interested in the crater. I told him about the scientists at Greyson Plantation. This fella, name's Carter, has a girlfriend who's a scientist. Young, good lookin' too. They have open minds about things and they's smart to talk to . . . Well, that'll be just fine. Let's break bread soon, cousin."

Hattie hung up and said that Jessep Greyson would be happy to meet with Carter and his friends the next day—if it rained as forecast. If the sun was up, he'd be busy in the field cutting orchard grass to feed to his Tennessee Walkers and a few other horses he boarded. He said to stop by in the morning around nine—if it was raining or wet. Hattie drew Carter directions on a napkin and told him not to be late.

"Jessep's got some Dutch-German blood in him from his daddy's side. He's punctual and don't like to be kept waitin'. He's left the dock to go fishin' many times without me because I was runnin' late. He carries a railroad pocket watch everywhere. Even sleeps with it, I hear.

"When you get to Greyson Plantation, drive past the main house. You'll see a dirt lane. It takes you to the old guest cottage by the creek. Jessep stays there most of the time now. Says the main house is too run-down. Good luck, honey, and be patient with him. Jessep's a talker. I ain't promising he'll answer your questions, but it will be entertaining listening to his stories, I can promise you that. Visitors leave Jessep's scratchin' their heads or reachin' for their Bible."

Hattie wrapped her heavy arms around Carter and wished him luck. Just as he stepped onto Mason Way, he heard thunderheads relieving themselves to the south. A few minutes later, it started to drizzle.

*　*　*

Greyson Plantation was an Eastern Shore landmark for a few reasons. Besides being at the epicenter of the asteroid strike, it was among the oldest contiguous working farms in Virginia and the US, first planted by white settlers in 1640. The plantation house and cottage were also on the National Historic Registry. Notable industrialists and politicians like colonialist John Mason, Supreme Court Justice John Marshall, and President William H. Taft had stayed as houseguests. Confederate officers had used the Greyson house as an encampment several times, with Major Quincy Greyson, an ancestor Jessep Greyson held in high esteem, hosting the man he considered to be Virginia's greatest warrior, General Robert E. Lee. As for Jessep, he rode an American Saddlebred that looked remarkably similar to Lee's famed horse, Traveller. And Jessep swore he had served in Lee's army.

The Greysons had kept a few slaves during the plantation's heyday, mostly for domestic chores and tending to livestock. Mature young men had worked the fields, some of them free men who traded their backs and shoulders for shelter and a patch of land to grow vegetables. Quincy Greyson and his sons had not been above breaking a sweat, often working side by side with "the help" to haul firewood, till the ground, or clean tack.

Quincy Greyson, as his daddy before him and sons afterward, didn't practice corporal punishment. The Bible actually meant something to him. Instead of whippings or backhands, he applied economic sanctions to rule in the ornery or disrespectful.

"A hungry stomach hurts more than a bloody back," Quincy would tell his sons. "Beatings will ruin a man's spirit just like they do a horse's. Once you beat them, they can never be trusted again. They'll buck or kick when you least expect it. Horses and men are vengeful creatures—remember that. And never strike a woman or child unless they is coming at you with a knife. They is tender, like God intended, and meant to be protected. Anyone who strikes a woman or child on this farm will feel the wrath of God, which will be mild compared to the wrath delivered by me."

The Greyson slave girls were treated warmly, according to oral history at least. So warmly, in fact, that slave descendants still living in Northampton County claimed to be of Greyson lineage. Just like the six children created by the couplings of enslaved concubine Sally Hemings and Thomas Jefferson at Monticello, the illegitimate Greyson offspring were never given the family name. Hattie forgot to mention this widely known, but seldom discussed, tidbit to Carter when he was at the real estate office earlier in the day. So, she called him that evening and warned him not to talk to Jessep about the Civil War or slavery.

"Sore subjects," she said. "Jessep is still in denial that the South was defeated in what he calls 'The War of Northern Aggression.' Even worse, like I mentioned before, our family line strayed. Don't bother me none. I know we have darker blood cousins in the county with Greyson blood in their veins. I know who they are, and I swear one of them is the spittin' image of Jessep, just not as pale. If Jessep mentions the war, just zip it and nod politely."

* * *

On the *Topp Kat* that night, Rose and Malcolm were inside sipping beverages and staying dry. The rain came steady, but with more warm summer kisses than cold slaps. The inlet by C Pier and the Bay were mirror still—not a ripple or bending reed; not a cackle from red-winged blackbirds nor squawk from a hungry egret, just the gentle tap of summer drops hitting the placid surface. Not even gulls patrolling for scraps. Not even a bloodlusting feline lurking by the dock for fish scraps or a disoriented mallard chick. Everyone and everything seemed hunkered down in a dreamy state, sedentary and calm. The earth's rhythm was a lullaby here, a wispy swoon.

"You recover from last night, my dearest?" Malcolm always called Rose "my dearest." He was friend, brother, father, confessor, and coach to Rose, a bedrock of emotion, a safe landing when life's waters tossed her around like a toy boat on a choppy lake. He looked chipper tonight, which wasn't unusual. Malcolm always seemed chipper even when annoyed. He relished life, and now seven decades into it, he coveted it more than ever. Time was now Malcolm's currency. Time was more valuable to him than academic admiration or the British pound.

"Money is in infinite supply, and fame is fleeting. Time, oh sweet time, is the rarest commodity. Spend it wisely," he once wrote Rose in a birthday card.

Malcolm was still a handsome man, thick legged, only a slight paunch, and with a trimmed gray beard and full head of hair to match. He wore tweed jackets, long-sleeve shirts year-round, and alternated between the music of Yanni and Yo-Yo Ma. His Scottish was brogue-lite, not in the muffled, dense rolling vowels and trembling like Scotty on *Star Trek*. He was an educated man, a PhD who prided himself on articulation and could easily have held his own in the British Parliament. Mostly, Malcolm was a joyous man, though never married and without children. Perhaps, Rose often thought, that was the secret to his demeanor. He avoided the inevitable head-on collisions that come when two people nest and procreate. "Monogamy," he would say to Rose, "works for swans because they only live for twenty years. If they lived much longer, there would most certainly be a swan divorce court."

Malcolm provided Rose with thinking points, not dictates. He was wise, but not perfect, and sometimes a bit too cynical.

"Well, my dearest, is the young Carter a suitor or a mere plaything?"

"Oh Malcolm, why always so crass? Can't he be a mere distraction, or an innocent interlude? He's cute and a tad low on self-esteem, which makes him irresistible. He can drink without getting sloppy or sleepy, and he has a college-boy naïveté. Let's just call him entertainment for now. Plus, he's smart and used to be a newspaper journalist. He knows the locals, and I think he can help us." Almost as if hearing an alarm in her head, Rose turned. "There's Carter now."

Carter had hopped from the pier onto the deck and was now lightly knocking on the cabin door.

"Enter at your own peril," Malcolm chortled. "Were your ears burning? My dearest here was just gushing about you."

"And a good evening to you," Carter said as he slid the door closed behind him.

Rose stood and greeted him with a kiss on the cheek. "Wine?"

"Please," Carter said. "Chardonnay if you have it."

"One white coming up." Rose smiled, and her eyes bubbled like freshly uncorked champagne. Malcolm noticed her buoyancy.

"So, what brings you here, besides the obvious?" Malcolm started.

Carter locked eyes with Rose and smiled, feeling the heat in his cheeks. "I did some poking around town today, and I think I have something—or should I say someone and some place—lined up for tomorrow morning that you may find fascinating and helpful. We're going a couple miles south of here to a farm on the next creek over. It's called Greyson Plantation, and it's the epicenter of the greatest geologic calamity ever in North America."

"Do tell, young knight," Malcolm piped.

"Have you heard of the Chesapeake Bay Crater? If not, I'd suggest you boot up your PCs tonight and put Google to work. Once you've done that, see what you can learn about magnetic anomalies. It may be the source of the woo-woo around here."

"*Woo-woo?* I thought that was a sound trains make," Malcolm chortled again. "I am not sure I've encountered such profundity before. Sounds quintessentially American, like Cheerios."

"Sounds like a Saturday morning kiddie cartoon to me." Rose chuckled. "But we're very familiar with the term. Some people use it to mock our work."

"Bring your Ouija board and a couple notebooks," Carter said. "I'll pick you up at eight forty, sharp. Oh, and professor, bring a bottle of your best sherry and a poem if you have one. If not, Rose needs to wear a short skirt and tight top. Our host has discriminating tastes from what I'm told. He likes his wine and women sweet."

CHAPTER 13

CARTER ARRIVED HOME worried about the poetry thing. Hattie had made it sound important to impress Jessep with sherry and poetry. *Why poetry?* He wasn't sure. Seemed odd, but so many things around Cape Charles seemed about twenty degrees off-center. Malcolm would cover the sherry, but even that high-minded Scot likely didn't have Keats or Byron by his bedside.

Carter booted up his PC and opened a file he called "Musings." It was mostly a list of rhymes and limericks he had jotted over the years when bored at work or when sick of watching TV at home. He wasn't a poet, not even close, but he deeply admired the poetry of American author Jim Harrison and always loved song lyrics. None were better than Bob Dylan's, Joni Mitchell's, and Notorious B.I.G's.

As a teen, he read lyrics on album covers or song sheets as he listened repeatedly. Ultimately, Carter concluded that he had neither the courage nor imaginative dexterity to write music for public consumption. He remained artistically closeted out of practicality. Writing newspaper articles, he'd found, was a vulgar substitute for real creativity—lifeless, stagnant, and pedantic. But chasing and typing facts and arranging them in a reverse pyramid of importance was steady work that had paid the rent. At least he could call himself a writer.

"Newspaper work is cleaner than the Ford plant and pays more than Walmart," he'd joke.

Carter scrolled through his list of musings, wincing at the idiocy of some. But there was one that seemed to fit his quest with Rose, an aborted effort inspired by a Dylan song and penned by Carter after his session back in late spring with Kate Lee-Capps, the psychologist. Carter had thought about sending the rhyme to Kate as a cathartic admission that he was moving on with life. But Carter being Carter, he'd chickened out. He had dwelled on Kate a lot and feared she would think the poem clumsy or juvenile and dismiss him as morose. Carter had felt like a hormonal eighth grader with a hard-on for his just-out-of-college sexy English teacher. Acting on such impulse would leave a wake of foreboding, he'd reasoned, and shatter the sexual fantasy of Kate visiting him at night.

The poem, Carter had decided, would remain his undisclosed tribute to Dylan. He always considered Dylan America's greatest poet, not a mere folk singer. He would celebrate mightily when the aged rocker received the Nobel Prize for Literature. Stockholm would provide Carter and the world with a moment of sanity by celebrating Dylan, a peacemonger, and by so doing snub headlining hatemongers like Putin, Netanyahu, Trump, and Kim Jong-un.

Carter pulled up the rhyme and printed out a copy:

Trust What You See

Streets fill with water, the beach with blowing sand
Here comes the wind, I'm taking a stand
The howls and hollers, the screams don't scare me
Legs stuck in the mud, please leave me be

Look to the right, then look to the left
I'm crossing to the other side, with some distress
I worry that something big will run over me
You can't hide from what you can't see

Please think with your mind, not with your heart
That's the only way to get a real fresh start
If you don't believe in yourself, you can't trust what you see
Walkin' in the dark scares the hell out of me

Sometimes I care, most times I don't
I'm not often right, so I don't often gloat
Honesty gets you more, and is easier spoke
Please accept the truth, so I can stay afloat

Bobby Dylan says all the truth adds to one big lie
That the person who you love's not the apple of your eye
Love that starts hot, runs out of steam
At first I was confused, now I see what Bob means

He means open your mind and close your heart
That's the only way to get a fresh start
Believe in yourself, so you can trust what you see
Imagination lights the dark sea

Carter winced when he finished reading. *Christ! Maybe not such a good idea.* He decided to take the copy with him anyway, but hold it in reserve and reveal it only if relations with Jessep needed thawing. *God, I hope old Malcolm comes through with the sherry and Rose shows some cleavage.*

* * *

Hattie's napkin instructions were spot-on, and the next day, Carter and his cargo ambled down a paved road flanked on both sides by century-old oaks and sycamores. If only they were draped with Spanish moss, the entrance to Greyson Plantation would feel antebellum. The paved top turned to gravel, which crunched under the tires of Carter's SUV. Puddles formed in ruts bludgeoned by tractor and truck tires, and the wind blew droplets from tree leaves on his windshield. Gray clouds, careening out to sea like a surfer on a wave, made it feel more like five in the morning than nearly nine.

The gravel turned to dirt as the trio passed the main house, a red brick structure three stories high with thick, white porch columns and windows that were at least eight feet tall. The roof was slate, with patches exposed where the heavy shingles unhinged during storms and slid crashing to the ground. Hitching posts by the front porch sat rusted and peeling along the circular driveway, making it easy to imagine horses and carriages staged like taxicabs waiting by the grand entrance.

"Magnificent, absolutely magnificent," Malcolm piped from the backseat. He craned his neck sideways as they rolled past the tired structure.

The house sat on the bank of a tidal creek, the view obstructed by willows as thick as a horse's mane but as light on the wind as gosling down. The branches swayed like ghostly arms with the slightest breeze. About twenty yards behind the main house stood a dock on pilings battered by storms and bowed with age. Next in line was a round building with two thick brick chimneys jutting like smokestacks from a refinery. Carter slowed to give Rose and Malcolm a better look.

"I believe that is an oyster house," Malcolm said. "Inside, I believe you'll find two large fire pits used to roast oysters and probably other tasty bivalves like mussels and clams. I've read about such places. They were venues for social gatherings, a place where families and friends gathered to celebrate and feast. Some of these old oyster houses were big enough to host dances and weddings. This one must have been grand in its day."

Rose rolled down her window and snapped a few pictures with her iPhone.

"I'll text them to you, Malcolm."

The dashboard clock registered one minute until nine. And, at that second, Carter spotted a man standing on the narrowed path leading to the next building down the line.

"That must be the guest cottage, and standing next to it must be Jessep Greyson," Carter said. He rolled the car forward the last few hundred feet, and a large brown dog stormed it. Malcolm's eyes widened.

"Hunter, heel!" a stern voice commanded. The brown Labrador retreated and sat, its block head even with Jessep's right hip. "Come on out. He's friendly. Just don't want him jumping on you. It's a low tide, and he's been chasing muskrats by the boat dock. He's caked with mud."

Rose stepped from the SUV, and just as Carter had hoped, she exposed just enough skin in the right places to magnify her beauty without appearing sultry. Jessep's eyes froze on her like a deer staring into a poacher's spotlight.

"Good morning, my fine lady, and welcome to Greyson Plantation. I'm Jessep Greyson."

"And good day to you, sir." Rose blushed and felt like she should curtsy as Jessep tipped the brim of his summer-weight homburg and gently cupped her hand and kissed it behind her knuckles. Jessep's eyes locked on hers; his were kind, but with a playful deceit of Rhett Butler. He looked like Clark Gable too, minus the mustache.

Jessep turned toward Malcolm and Carter and tipped his hat again. He wore a long-sleeve, collared white cotton shirt, gray slacks, and square-toed boots—practically the same attire he wore year-round. In cooler months, he layered on a vest, coat, or scarf.

"Good day, gentlemen. So nice to have visitors. Cousin Hattie speaks very highly of y'all, and I trust her judgment implicitly. It appears as though the morning showers have relented, so perhaps we can take a stroll in a bit. But first, may I interest you in coffee, perhaps with a splash of libation as sweetener?"

"I believe I can help you with that," Malcolm offered. He handed Jessep a bottle of sherry.

"Why thank you, fine sir," Jessep said. He examined the label and looked pleased. "A Napoleon Hidalgo. Very nice. A classic Sanlúcar, nutty, and delightful with morning coffee. Shall we?" Jessep extended his arm toward the cottage. He held open the door and motioned to Rose to pass through first. She wore a tight denim skirt, which Jessep eyed intently as she stepped past him. Carter winked at Malcolm, optimistic that they had made a positive first impression.

* * *

If it were 1860 or thereabouts, Jessep Greyson would be magazine-cover worthy. He was a handsome man of well over six feet three, thin but not frail. At fiftysomething, he had a full head of slightly wavy Dutch hair, more black than gray. His mutton chops flared almost to his square jawline. They gave him the appearance of an Amish man, but with more refined features and better clothes. He had long legs and leaned ever-so slightly forward when walking, as if using gravity to propel himself. Each stride seemed to cover twice the length of the average man. A child could never keep up.

Most striking were his bluish-gray eyes that glowed as if powered by a battery. Some said the color mirrored Jessep's Confederate soul.

Jessep was a Virginia gentleman. A strict chivalric code incubated in his DNA. He never raised his voice, rarely cursed, and always treated women like porcelain objects that would easily chip or break. When greeting an attractive woman, he would take her hand in his large, calloused palm and hold it gently as if cupping an egg. He would remove his brimmed hat, bow his head, and lightly kiss the back of a maiden's hand. Young girls or prudish females would get the same greeting, minus the hand kiss. Jessep respected one's personal space and, unlike Cousin Hattie, he was no hugger, unless in the privacy of his bedroom with a lover.

Jessep largely kept to himself on Greyson Plantation and never shied from its name. The words *farm* or *estate* had become the politically correct euphemisms for Southern plantations, as if to disinfect American history. But make no mistake, Greyson Plantation was a *plantation*, a designation Jessep, his father, his grandfather, and the Greysons before them fully embraced.

Despite his Southern heritage, Jessep was no barbarian—and certainly no Trump supporter. Jessep rejected Trump for one unassailable fact: Trump was a Yankee. In fact, he was the worst kind: a vulgar, ostentatious New Yorker who mistreated women and bloviated with the vocabulary of a fifth grader. He was also an uncultured liar and brute who held no appreciation for fine liquor or literature. The only paintings Trump liked were oil portraits of himself, a man with unsurpassed vanity.

Jessep found Mrs. Clinton less of a pill, but one too bitter to swallow. He detested her pro-gay agenda and racial demagoguery. She hated guns, and he loved them. But it was her sense of entitlement he found most revolting—a condescending heir apparent to the throne of democracy.

He abhorred politicians who squandered tax dollars to curry voter favor, and he thought redistributing wealth through taxation was stealing. In fact, he hated nothing more than paying taxes—not to the county, the state, and by no means to the illegitimate IRS. To reduce his property tax bill, he allowed the exteriors of the buildings on Greyson Plantation to deteriorate. Inside, the buildings were tidy and maintained, but he refused to let tax assessors, or any public official, enter uninvited.

Jessep read lots of books on political philosophy. He squarely embraced the small-government convictions of Jefferson, but acknowledged the nation-building aspirations of Hamilton. He liked constructive debate moderated by facts and reason. What he despised was lurid shouting and schoolyardlike name calling of current candidates and the pandering, empty-headed TV commentators and their networks. Facebook? Twitter? Jessep had no use for them.

He had grown exhausted by the lack of civility or substantive debate in the Trump-Clinton war, so by early summer he had decided to vote for neither of the front-runners, a stealthy sentiment building across the Eastern Shore of Virginia, rural America, and the Rust Belt. Jessep thought he might never vote in a national election again. Nearly every contemporary American president had been a major disappointment: Nixon the thief; Carter the incompetent; Reagan the senile spendthrift; Clinton the impeached whoremonger; W. Bush the doltish warmonger. As for Obama, well at least he was dignified and intelligent, but his political stripes were decidedly blue-black, polarizing those like Jessep, who were decidedly red-white.

* * *

Rose nearly gasped when she stepped inside Jessep's home. Hand-carved bookcases covered the entire wall in the cottage's small sitting area. At its center was a stone hearth big enough for a small boy to stand in. A leather sofa, a wooden rocker, and a reading chair and ottoman faced it. This was a man cave, a sanctuary of leather-bound books, old family photos, and heavily grained woods.

On the opposite side was a bar top milled from yellow knotty pine and a set of eight matching barstools. Jessep's great-great grandfather had rescued the bar from a Richmond tavern burned and looted in 1865 by conquering Yankees. The pub had been owned by a relative killed by drunken bluecoats. Sherry, port, and cognac sifters were stocked behind the bar's wooden shelves.

"This place is amazing, just amazing," Rose said as her eyes soaked in the scene. The cottage was one large room with a billiard table at the far end, more shelves with books, and a wall of portraits and photographs, a visual anthology of the Greyson lineage.

The cottage's magnificence had resulted from Jessep Greyson's frugality. Stubbornly self-sufficient and pennywise, he had built a sawmill from old tractor parts and other mechanical odds and ends and had salvaged an old blade from a nearby abandoned farm. He had milled cottonwood, pecan, dying walnut, and a few white oaks and used it all to make new cabinets, a dining table, end tables, and ceiling-to-floor bookshelves for the cottage.

"Who is that?" Rose asked Jessep as she, Malcolm, and Carter followed a few steps behind. "That person looks exactly like you. I mean *exactly!*" She stared in amazement at a photograph of a Confederate sergeant, three large stripes pointing down on each sleeve.

"Well, that man is William Benjamin Greyson, brother of my great-great grandfather."

"I swear he could be you," Rose said. She bounced between studying the portrait and looking at the live version standing beside her.

Jessep smiled. "Perhaps that is me. Please excuse me while I get the coffee heated."

After a bit more gawking, the trio settled in the sitting area by the great stone fireplace. They looked at each other, stunned. The place felt like a museum of photos and artifacts. But most impressive, especially to Malcolm, were the books. While Rose and Carter absorbed the family portraits and photos of the plantation, Malcolm's eyes wandered down row after row of literary classics, philosophy, and poetry, and books on ornithology, climate, soil sciences, and entomology. The breadth of Jessep's library would have rivaled Thomas Jefferson's. Malcolm wondered where Mr. Jessep Greyson had attended university and how far he had advanced.

"So, let me guess," Carter said, "you're a College of William and Mary graduate. Or, perhaps Washington and Lee University in Lexington."

"Neither, sir." Jessep chuckled. "Why spend tens of thousands of dollars on something that you can get for free with a library card. Knowledge is absorbed, not bestowed."

Rose immediately noticed that the focal point of most modern man caves was missing: a large, wall-mounted flat screen.

"No TV, Jessep?" Rose asked.

Jessep scratched his chin and measured his words. "I mean no offense, but TV atrophies the mind. I kept a TV for exactly sixteen months and found that period to be my most depressing and least productive. The programs I witnessed were vulgar, superficial, and, in my view, pandered to banality and egotism. They made our world seem unattractive and filled with despair. My time on this earth is precious. I prefer to use it constructively and to feel optimistic."

"Jessep, if you don't mind, may I ask you something personal?"

"Please do, Rose. More coffee?"

"Jessep, you said that the person in the picture on the wall, your ancestor the sergeant, perhaps *is* you. You laughed, but I sensed that you weren't teasing."

"Cousin Hattie told me that you and your distinguished colleagues have open minds. Well, let's see just how open. I believe, without an ounce of reservation, that I lived before as William Benjamin Greyson, sergeant in the First Virginia Calvary Regiment. I was killed on the third day in the Battle of Fredericksburg in December 1862. I remember everything about that day and the years leading up to my enlistment and death."

"So, you believe in reincarnation?" Malcolm piped.

"Reincarnation is, as I am sure you know, an imprecise term. In general, yes, I hold that some form of transmigration occurs. But whether it's a spirit returning, as Hinduism prescribes, or memories and imprints passed biologically through our DNA, I cannot say with certainty. But I can say without reservation or reluctance that I have experienced the life of Benjamin Greyson."

"Quite remarkable," Malcolm said. "We've done considerable research at Edinburgh, and of the paranormal fields those experiencing transmigration seem to have the most precise and vivid recollections. The biological connection in a case like this, with a direct DNA chain, seems profound."

"It certainly explains my predilections," Jessep said. "Why else would a man who dwells in the twenty-first century prefer the medium of old books, solitude, and less than fashionable attire? I have two siblings nothing like me. My younger brother left the farm after high school and works for Microsoft in Seattle. My little sister is a pediatric surgeon in Raleigh. Neither have these links to the past, yet they live within me."

Jessep spent the next hour recounting story after story about the visions, dreams, and wide-awake revelations he experienced through the eyes of his fallen kin. Each encounter was rich with detail and precision. There was nothing ambiguous or contradictory. He remembered full conversations with Sergeant Greyson's family, wife, children, parents, neighbors, scenes from family picnics, the time he was kicked in the chest when trimming his horse's hooves. He remembered the smell of his wife's apple cobbler, honeysuckle in the spring, the first time he fired a rifle, and hunting deer with his brothers. He spoke of these things as if they had just happened.

"If you believe in an afterlife," Jessep said, "then isn't it conceivable that a *beforelife* exists too? Nothing in this world is linear. I believe Einstein proved that."

"So right you are," Malcolm said. "After a lifetime of study and research, I'm agnostic. It's impossible to understand what we don't comprehend."

CHAPTER 14

BY NOON, THE clouds had cleared and the sun lit the sky a brilliant blue. The air was so clean you could taste it on your tongue. Jessep had served his guests oyster sandwiches, green beans, and tea, and, as was his daily practice, had sought out a bit of inspiration before setting out to the fields.

"So, do any of you admire poetry? Nothing like the wit of words to stimulate curiosity and put one in the right frame of mind. Can anyone cite a favorite rhyme?"

Carter's throat tightened. Malcolm and Rose hunched their shoulders and looked away. Carter knew it was his turn to ante. He nervously cleared his throat.

"Jessep, I have on occasion made some effort at writing lyrics and happen to have with me a recent attempt. I'm not good at this—terrible actually—but writing relaxes me. I find it cathartic. Hattie says you love poetry, which is why I brought this along. I'd very much appreciate feedback. Would you mind? And please be honest."

Jessep accepted the printout, stared at it briefly, and without a hint of reaction said, "I would be honored. Now, may I show you three the plantation and what I think you really came here to see?"

* * *

They walked by a hayfield and followed a worn deer trail through a narrow patch of woods. They emerged into a mowed parcel a few acres wide. Near its center was a concrete slab about the size of a manhole cover.

"In 2005, a group of geologists drilled down nearly 700 feet. This was one of about a dozen bore sites on the Shore and across the Bay. I recall that they spent nearly one and a half million dollars on this project. Scientists came from Austria, South Africa, Japan, and from throughout the United States to participate. A few lived on Greyson Planation and stayed in the main house while here.

"They were doing hydrology and sediment studies to determine how the crater affects the water table in Southeastern Virginia. I'm assuming you know about the asteroid strike, correct?" Jessep paced around the sealed hole capped with concrete. Pointing down at it, he said, "They determined that this is ground zero, a two-mile-wide swath that stretches from where we are standing to Cape Charles. Yes sir, right here, about a mile below us, is the core of the comet that created the land we stand on. It must have been a magnificent sight."

* * *

Indeed. Thirty-five million years ago, the asteroid blazed in from outer space at 76,000 miles an hour, a bolt of light that would have blinded anything seeing it. The iron fireball pulverized the earth, launching debris sixty miles into the sky and evaporating millions of tons of water instantly. The space rock ripped through a mile of sand and sediment until it smashed into bedrock granite. The dislodged ground rippled into a concentric circle, like a rock thrown into a pool of water. It created what looked like an upside-down sombrero with an upturned rim.

A firestorm of boulders from the impact rained hundreds of miles away as the earth fractured and quaked. Tsunamis crashed into the Blue Ridge Mountains, submerging under water more than two-thirds of what is currently Virginia. Eventually, that water rushed back into the center of the sombrero, a hole as deep as the Grand Canyon, sweeping up everything in its path.

"There are 170 known craters made by asteroids on earth, and this one is ranked the sixth largest," Jessep said with pride. "Good thing the dinosaurs died about thirty million years earlier, because the Bay crater would have annihilated them."

"Unfathomable," Malcolm said. "The human mind is incapable of grasping the enormity of such events. Our worlds are so micro."

"Indeed, sir. There is so much we're incapable of comprehending," Jessep said.

"Jessep, your cousin Hattie mentioned that there are unusually strong magnetic readings attributed to the comet. Is there anything you can tell us about that?" Carter asked. "Is there any truth to that?"

"It's a difficult science to understand, but here is what I've discerned from reading academic papers from the research: Yes, there are what have been described as magnetic anomalies here. Scientists have found elevated readings right here and beneath Cape Charles."

Malcolm and Rose grew excited and quickly exchanged nods. Their research, and that of other parapsychologists, had correctly correlated the intensity of magnetic fields with paranormal experiences. Dr. Malcolm Dunbar himself had written a paper mapping paranormal hot spots. He and graduate assistants, including Rose, had combed data on magnetic field readings from oil companies and academic geologists worldwide who were exploring for oil, gas, water, and fault lines.

"We're quite familiar with the magnetic force here and anecdotal reports about apparitions," Malcolm said. "That's principally why we're here. We're looking for manifestations, or at least people experiencing them. Plus, Rose has a personal interest as well—a family member who decades ago vanished in Cape Charles."

Standing in the field on that sunny afternoon, Rose and Malcolm elaborated on their hypothesis. They explained that, in theory, strong magnetic waves stimulate interaction between the right and left lobes of the brain. The increased mental friction heightens sensitivities and, for some, receptivity to otherwise invisible forces and energies.

"It wakes up parts of the brain that are dormant or disconnected. At least that is the hypothesis," Malcolm said. "Introducing strong magnetic waves essentially increases the polarity between lobes. It's like letting light into a dark closet. It's like massaging a muscle to improve blood flow."

"Your cousin Hattie told me about a local fella—I think his name is Major—who had bipolar syndrome," Carter said. "After living here a few years, he seems cured."

"Major, yes, of course," Jessep said. "We hunt geese together on occasion. His dog Minor is one of the best retrievers in the county. He'll swim 100 yards to fetch a crippled bird. Major is a splendid chap. Always upbeat. Very bright and generous toward others. That's why I like sharing a duck blind with him. Indeed, on one of our outings he told about his recovery from disambiguation. Neurologists performed magnetic resonance scans and found enhanced activity in his hippocampus. They had no explanation why. I can only surmise that the elevated magnetism from the crater played some role. Moving to Cape Charles was the only variable in Major's life that had changed."

Rose looked under the brim of Jessep's homburg and into his shaded gray eyes. "Perhaps, Jessep, this explains your special gift. Perhaps living here has enabled your perceptions. Perhaps, as you theorize, there is a nexus between the past and the present that you are able to experience because of your proximity to this magnetic anomaly. And Malcolm and I surmise it's why Cape Charles has such a high concentration of apparitions. It's one of the hot spots discovered in Malcolm's research."

"You mean the woo-woo," Jessep said with a grin.

"Precisely," Rose said, "the woo-woo."

* * *

The quartet returned to the cottage, mostly in silence as each tried to connect the dots plotted by real science and pseudoscience. At the bar, Jessep poured each of them a glass of the sherry Malcolm had brought.

"I'd very much appreciate a copy of your research about hot spots and magnetism," Jessep told Rose. "And I think I might be of further assistance regarding manifestations. There is more to what I have encountered than re-experiencing a past life. Greyson Plantation has several apparitions who appear quite frequently—at least to me. That's why I live in the cottage. The main house is, how shall I say, inhabited. It drove away my first wife and chased off my brother and sister. They wanted no part of that legacy and fought mightily to deny what their eyes witnessed.

'It's just young minds playing tricks,' they used to say. Both of them, by the way, hated Halloween."

Jessep refreshed his glass and continued.

"What's odd is that some houseguests over the years have seen the inhabitants while others were oblivious. Two of the geologists who stayed here, for example, were happy and perfectly comfortable. The third, a sedimentologist from South Africa, left after a few nights and rented a hotel room in town. He never told his colleagues why, but I was suspicious, so I sought him out. He said he woke up twice and saw a black man and black lady leaning over his bed smiling at him. He described Cecil and Whinny, former house servants. Both died on the plantation in the late 1800s and are buried in the family plot down the road. There are pictures of them in the family photo album. If I brought a lady friend home, and she spent the evening, they would toss her clothes out the window. One lady friend was drying her hair after a bath and saw Whinny holding a towel and staring at her in the mirror. As you can imagine, that puts a crimp in one's love life."

"Are there other apparitions on the plantation?" Rose asked.

"Yes. There's Mr. Henry. He took care of the horses and livestock here for decades. Every morning at sunrise he would walk around the farm, listening to the birds and smelling the morning air, especially in the spring. He was a big fella, with a full, thick beard—a mulatto, you know, high yellow. At least a few dozen times a year I see Mr. Henry walking in the field. He died fifty-three years ago, when I was a boy."

Carter and Malcolm sat silent and mesmerized, as if in a movie theater.

"Who are the others?" Rose asked. "Former servants or family members too?"

"Sometimes I see other people walking around here, but I can't be sure who they are. They seem to just be going about their business, carrying a basket with vegetables, or walking down the stairs in the house, or standing in a dark corner in the barn or next to a horse in the stables. Sometimes I even see animals—cats mostly—just perched somewhere and leering. I've seen Hunter, my rude chocolate Lab, barking at them. The people I see don't bother me none, but those cats do. They're evil in death just as in life. I do my best to keep the feral ones thinned out. They're destructive and full of disease."

"Jessep, I believe you, every word," Rose said like a convert at a Baptist revival. Her eyes glazed. "I haven't experienced these types of things, but I do have a heightened perception. It's hard to explain, but sometimes I feel the presence of things or have premonitions. I've felt more sensitive, more aware, since we arrived. Would you mind if we work together?"

"Surely," Jessep said. "However I can be of service, my lady."

Jessep's eyes lit up as if he had hit triple bars on an Atlantic City slot machine. Carter, on the other hand, felt like he had gone bust.

"I can think of nothing more enticing or invigorating," Jessep said. He lifted Rose's hand across the bar and gently kissed it. "When would you like to perform this . . . research?"

"Soon, very soon," Rose said.

* * *

"You seem smitten," Malcolm teased after he, Rose, and Carter had strapped on their seatbelts in the SUV. "I thought you might swoon and faint."

"All in a day's work," Rose countered. She stared at the tree-lined avenue as they exited Greyson Plantation. "You boys told me to turn on the charm, remember?"

Carter said nothing, jaw clenched as they ambled onto the highway and then left onto the road leading into Cape Charles. He wondered if Malcolm was teasing Rose or merely pointing out fact. *Smitten?* Jessep Greyson was, Carter had to admit, eerily charming, unpretentiously smart, and flawlessly dignified. Carter reasoned that he should resist showing any contempt for or jealousy of Jessep because Rose would interpret that as a lack of self-confidence. And why should he feel threatened? Jessep was nearly twice Rose's age, fit and charming, but with all of the physical limitations that come with seniority. Surely Carter could compete with that, at least sexually. He'd already tamed Rose's lust.

"So, Rose, what's your plan for Jessep?" Carter asked.

"For starters, he is charming," Rose said. She smiled at Carter and batted her curled eyelashes as if to taunt. "Beyond his peculiar charm, he makes for an interesting case study. Who can say whether his paranormal experiences are intentional fabrications or real manifestations? There seems to be substance here—a lot of it."

"Hard to compete with that," Carter blurted. "But I think I can help you as well."

"Oh my sweet Romeo, so you're *competing* with Jessep?" Malcolm snorted a laugh from the backseat, and Carter winced.

"I just mean that I know a little about the town and can do some investigating. I told you I was a newspaper reporter in a previous life."

"What do you have in mind?" Rose perked.

"Cyril Brown down at the hardware store. Gil told me that Cyril's family were owners or key investors in Colonial Savings and Loan, the bank that used to be located in the old pub. Remember the vault inside Gil Netters? I'm guessing Cyril would know something about it. Cyril and I get along great. He's crotchety but very smart and a font of knowledge about this place. I'll go have a chat with him in the morning."

Rose leaned her mouth close to Carter's ear and whispered, "And what about tonight, boy toy? Want to have a chat with me? I feel stimulated after being around all of you manly men today."

"Sounds like I need to defend my turf," Carter whispered back. "But do me a favor: Make sure we remember to close the bedroom windows and draw the shades. Either that, or we need to charge admission."

CHAPTER 15

CARTER SLIPPED FROM under the covers, stepped lightly into the bathroom, and took a shower to wash away lovemaking residue. Rose lay asleep, lightly breathing and curled on her side, her hair strewn over her face and legs splayed like a pair of scissors. She was a bed hog. She had pushed Carter to the outer rim of his queen mattress. As the warm water poured over his head, Carter wished he could sleep as soundly as Rose, the way he had as a boy after playing outside all day, his body exhausted and mind unencumbered. He could sleep twelve hours straight back then, without a twitch.

* * *

The morning was bright and warm, and, as expected, Carter found Cyril rocking in his wicker-back chair, jawing with Mac and a couple of other locals with front-row seats to the Cyril-Mac morning diatribe. The sparring duo split the cost of a newspaper subscription and shared it each morning during the week, critiquing the headlines—rarely with compliments—and almost always taking opposite views.

"I'm tellin' you, Mac, my boy Trump could win this thing if the damn Republicans would just shut up and go with it. They're worse on him than the Democrats. And this anti-Muslim, white supremacist stuff is a bunch of hooey," he said and pointed to a headline. "It's the damn liberal media peddling poison and fake news. But I'll tell you what, the only people being faked out are those liberal pollsters. Mark my words. Everybody I know is voting Trump. Look around the county—there are twice as many Trump signs in yards."

"What's that you said, Cyril? Somethin' about *white supermarkets*? Can't do that no more, and it's wrong," Mac huffed. "People should be able to buy food where they want. Blacks and Mexicans gotta eat too." Mac had raised his voice and tilted his ear toward Cyril.

"White *supremacists*, not *supermarkets*." Cyril snickered. Mac and Cyril's fan club about spit out its coffee.

"Mean! That's what Trump and his hooligans are," Mac roiled. "He's a hateful man who's going to hell. *White supermarkets!* That's discrimination! That's unconstitutional."

"Drink some more coffee, you ol' fool," Cyril said. "Trump ain't no racist. He's just a tough sombitch. Someone needs to be. Working people are getting screwed paying for all these programs that let people eat without workin'. I worked every day of my life. No one paid me to sit at home."

"*Work!* You call this work?" Mac said. "Cyril, you don't do nothin' 'cept sit around squawking all day and selling stuff in your store made in China."

Carter waited for a pause in the banter before stepping into the arena. "Mornin', gentlemen. Do I need to get an ambulance? Sounds like someone's gonna have a heart attack."

The boys laughed.

"So, what you up to, Carter? Ready for a drink?" Cyril asked.

"Too early, but thanks. Cyril, I do have something to ask . . . about your family."

"Be careful there, lad," Mac warned. "Old blueblood Cyril here will challenge you to a duel if you insult his kin. The Browns is fightin' people."

"Pistols at twenty paces? No thanks." Carter laughed. "No, this has to do with the old Colonial Savings bank, the building that Gil Netters is in."

"What about it? My granddaddy was treasurer of the bank board for about fifteen years. The place was destroyed in a fire back around 1920 or '21, I think. Did you know that, Carter?"

"Yes, that's what Gil said. You aware of any records or information about what happened, besides the newspaper article about the fire."

"Not much survived," Cyril said. "Two people died. Place was pretty much gutted from what I was told, except for stuff stored in the vault. Someone had the good sense to lock it down before they ran out of there. But two people got locked inside and suffocated in the heat. A bank teller tried to save 'em but the smoke got 'em. I'm guessing there was lots of cash and deeds and safety-deposit boxes. We used to have some of them around, but antique stores bought 'em. The bank closed after the fire, but most depositors recovered their savings and valuables, at least that's what my grandfather said."

"Any records left, or were they destroyed?"

"Most of that stuff is long gone." Cyril thought a moment. "Come to think of it, there are a few footlockers and boxes in the attic here from the old bank. My daddy made me carry them up there when I was a kid. He said they were in the basement of Granddaddy's house in Eastville. I'm guessing they may still be up their collecting dust with a lot of other junk. Want to have a look?"

* * *

The hardware store attic was dank and strewn with decapitated mannequins, old store signs and metal shelving, boxes of old lead plumbing joints, and unlabeled boxes stacked to the ceiling—decades of junk and forgotten inventory.

"We need to clean this place out. Maybe I'll donate all of this junk to the church for a yard sale. I need to score some brownie points with the Lord. Bound to be some valuable stuff up here," Cyril said.

After getting his bearings using a flashlight, Cyril pointed to several wooden trunks, all about the size of an army footlocker. Each was dusty gray with rusted hinges.

"Thankfully, they ain't padlocked," Cyril said. "Here ya go." He handed Carter the flashlight. "Knock yourself out. You can use my office downstairs. It's too damn hot up here. Just be careful hauling that stuff down the steps. These old railings are loose. I don't need a lawsuit on my hands."

Cyril kept a small office in the back of the store. It had an oak desk and lamp, a few bookshelves, a small fridge, and a 1950s calendar of blondes in bathing suits. Tonic water and other mixers filled the fridge. A bottle of flavored vodka lay in the tiny freezer along with ice cubes.

Carter hauled down three of the lockers, set them on the floor, and poured himself a vodka over ice.

* * *

The footlockers mostly contained old leather-bound bank ledgers. The edges of the pages were brown and brittle, some torn and missing corners. Each page was numbered and, from what Carter could tell, showed a record of deposits and withdrawals. There were also stacks of smaller ledgers, each numbered by year with black ink. Carter perused a couple of volumes of each with the flashlight. The names, dates, and amounts were so evenly and neatly articulated that the author most certainly had received an "A" in penmanship. Carter laughed, contrasting the artistry of this impeccable cursive with his own indecipherable chicken scratch. He remembered how Mrs. Halprin, his second-grade teacher, had once examined his hands to see if they fully functioned. At a time when teachers tried to convert lefties to righties, Mrs. Halprin had tried the opposite with Carter, hoping that writing from the southern hemisphere would straighten out his letters. The left hemisphere proved as illegible as the right, so Mrs. Halprin allowed him to switch back and instructed Carter's parents to buy him a typewriter.

Carter had only a vague idea of when Luzia Rosa Douro might have transacted business with the bank. All he knew for certain was that the Navy cruiser her beloved was on was hit July 19, 1918. So, that's where he would start. He parsed the ledgers by date and found a few from that year. He flipped through the pages and ran his index finger down each line quickly. He found a long list and a transaction in July, but it didn't bear the last name Douro. He looked at the small ledgers, which seemed more interesting. Instead of cash balances listed by name, they contained lists of numbers followed by a name: *112 Marcus Louis Verderose; 113 D. Earlworth Scruggs; 114 Eli Bernard Burton; 115 Kathrine Mae Kinard.*

"Kinard! Of course," Carter said. He scrambled back through the ledgers looking for entries under that name. After about a half hour of eyestrain, he hit pay dirt. *Luzia R. Kinard.* "Has to be her," he said aloud.

The entry showed that Luzia Kinard had deposits of $434.65. Carter used his iPhone to do a Google search. In 2016 money, that was the equivalent of about $7,700, surely enough to live on for a while. *She must have had a job. Either that or Young Kinard was very generous. He must have wanted her badly.* On the line below the deposit entry was the number *137.* Carter grabbed the stack of smaller ledgers from 1918. "Here it is," he said. Next to *137* was the name again, *Luzia R. Kinard.* Beneath the name was an entry: *Citizenship papers; two necklaces; broach; sterling silver hairband; gold ruby ring.* "Found you, little missy."

* * *

"How'd ya make out?" Cyril asked as Carter finally emerged about two hours later. "Was it worth the sweat?"

"I found the fair maiden, Cyril. Thanks. She had a nice nest egg in the bank and, apparently, a safety-deposit box of some sort with valuables."

"Yeah, banks and some of the hotels or post offices used to rent safety boxes. We had a lot of transients through here back in the day. Lots of people staying in boarding houses locked their valuables at banks or the post office for safe keeping."

"Cyril, I'm curious about something. What happens to unclaimed valuables?"

"As long as the safety-deposit box rent is paid, I suppose the stuff just sits there. Don't really know. If a box is abandoned, I suspect the bank, post office, or whoever rents the box sells it unclaimed, just like they do with storage containers. You've seen the TV shows, right? The ones where these scavengers bid on storage lockers. My guess is that if there was unclaimed stuff from the old bank, it was probably sold or auctioned. That was a long time ago, Carter. No tellin' where it wound up."

"I'm not even sure the items under the name I'm investigating were left unclaimed," Carter said. "But this proves that the woman who went missing was here, and probably for some time. Thanks again, Cyril. I put all the stuff back upstairs, and I helped myself to your vodka."

* * *

Carter called Rose seconds after he stepped on Mason Way. He felt invigorated by his find, the way he had when he began as a news reporter and had scooped other media. What he discovered in those arcane records wasn't exactly a *gotcha,* but it did buttress with hard evidence Rose's anecdotal accounts of her great aunt's presence in Cape Charles.

"Rose, what you heard about Luzia seems to be the truth. I found some old bank records from 1918. Luzia was definitely here. And she definitely had a connection to the Colonial Savings and Loan that burned. She had a pretty big stash of money in the bank and some valuables in a safety-deposit box."

"Very cool, Carter. Anything interesting in the box?"

"The ledger listed a ring, Rose. A gold and ruby ring."

"Wow! Just like my mom said. That Douglas Kinard fellow gave her his ring. Had to be!"

"Yes, and get this: She used his last name on the bank and safety-deposit box accounts. Hard to say why, but I'm guessing it's because the bank knew the Kinard family. In fact, I found a few other accounts under that last name. I'm guessing Luzia probably figured she would be better taken care of and her money and possessions would be more secure as a Kinard. Or maybe someone in the Kinard family arranged all of this for her."

"You're quite the snoop, a regular Horatio Caine."

"The *CSI* actor? Okay, I can live with that. And who does that make you, Samantha Stevens from *Bewitched?*"

"Now you're really dating yourself, Carter. How old are you, anyway?"

"You'll have to cast me under your spell to find out."

"Maybe I already have, sweet boy. Maybe you're doing my bidding."

"Your wish is my command. Just spare me the whips and chains."

"Okay, kinky boy, no whips. But I make no promises about chains. Call me tonight."

CHAPTER 16

SATURDAY NIGHTS AT Gil Netters in the summer almost always devolved into a bacchanalia—a sweaty, grinding orgy of drunken bodies squeezed three rows deep by the bar and gyrating to R&B and classic rock records spun by deejays. The sidewalk outside the bar entrance was always packed as well with cigarette smokers or those just needing a few minutes of fresh air before plunging back into steamy waves of body heat beyond the door. On this August night, at the epicenter of the volcanic mass, danced a gangly woman with a bony face and legs as thin as a healthy person's arms. Locals called her Thin Lizzy, but her given moniker was Luciana Alto. She was French, in her late thirties, and had married a NATO officer from her country who worked as a liaison with the US Atlantic Fleet in Norfolk.

Lizzy was a dancer, musician, and teacher. Besides English, she was fluent in three Romance languages and taught them in high school. She and her husband had bought a vacation home in Cape Charles and spent most weekends and summers there. After a few years, her husband had returned to France without her. No one knew why they had divorced, but there were plenty of rumors. Lizzy's husband had spent one month a year in Europe. And while away, she came to Cape Charles alone to play. Rumor was that she was sleeping with the town's top cop; others said it was the top cop's wife. Regardless, everyone loved Lizzy, even Gil.

Lizzy sat on the left end of the political spectrum, an advocate for migrant workers picking crops on the Shore. She was a vegan with bronze skin and a crown of brown waves that dipped to the middle of her back. She wore thick-rimmed glasses that magnified her hazel eyes and had dimples that punctuated a permanent smile. Best of all, her mild French accent intensified with each mojito.

Carter watched Lizzy at work. Her spindly arms and legs spasmed like one of those inflatable tubemen in front of car lots and tax-return offices. She twirled like a ballerina and hopped like a punk rocker, a mishmash of elegance, hot anger, and free spirit.

She must be wild in bed, Carter thought.

Just at that moment, the band started playing Lizzy's favorite tune, Justin Timberlake's "SexyBack." She rushed toward Carter, grabbed his arm, and yanked him to the pulsing dance floor.

Gil looked up and nudged Lil with his elbow. "Looks like your boy is about to become a man."

* * *

The dance floor, no bigger than an average-sized living room, was a zoological study of the animal homo sapien. Short, fat male specimens clung to tall, thin females. Skinny, dark-skinned men bumped and grinded into the hips and glutei of pale, husky redheads with freckled noses and forearms as thick as A-Rod's baseball bat. Bubbly gay guys wore eyeliner and wished they were as pretty as their bestest-best friends, and lean farm girls with golden locks had eyes that refracted light like the cubic zirconia necklaces they wore at Christmas. Aged women who once upon a time looked just like those enviable twentysomething lasses, their cheerleader hips now contorted from hatching babies and their jawlines pulled groundward by gravity, cut it up on the dance floor.

There were real jocks at Gil's, guys who played college or high school ball. They mixed in with would-be jocks and jocks of Christmases past who imagined they might really have a chance to score with the Goldilocks girls flashing smiles at anyone who noticed their perfect skin and teeth. These young girls of summer wore Daisy Duke shorts high and tight. Those with significant cleavage displayed their hills and valleys proudly, like flags on the Fourth of July. Those less endowed wore their shorts even shorter to keep wandering eyes focused below the waist.

The prudish in Cape Charles—mostly married couples and the church crowd—avoided this lurid, indiscriminate assembly of raging endorphins, testosterone, and pheromones. But for Carter, this scene, hosted by his bestest-best friend, resurrected a nostalgia that transported him back in time to frat parties at Syracuse. The one big exception, Carter noted, was that the revelers at the Gil Netters campus spanned four decades, not merely four years of college kids. Four generations of debauchery harmoniously mingled with no more conflict than at a Sunday afternoon picnic.

"*Gil!*" Carter called and waved his arm, trying to get his friend's attention.

"What do you need, Sparky?"

"Tito's and tonic, mostly Tito's."

"What, no white wine, wussy boy?"

"Just vodka. A tall one, please."

Gil quickly poured and handed Carter a drink. "Good thing you're decent looking, because you're no dancer, Sparky. Looked like you were having a seizure out their dancing with Thin Lizzy."

"Yeah, she's got some movement. Kinda scary, actually."

"Want to know what's scary, Sparky? Lizzy in bed. I heard she wore out our honorable police sergeant. He couldn't handle her. You know what they say?"

"I couldn't begin to guess. What do they say, Gil?"

"The sweetest meat is closest to the bone."

"Christ, Gil!" Lil smacked her boss on the back of the head. "That's disgusting, and it's mean. You're such a caveman, a real asshole."

"I prefer asshole, thank you very much. It's taken me years to earn that distinction, and I wear it proudly."

A barstool opened up, and Lil placed a glass down to hold it for Carter.

"Here ya go, sweetie. A front-row seat," she said. "Wave if you need anything—*anything*. And don't grow up to be like him." She pointed at Gil.

Carter flashed a smile and leaped onto the corner stool, best seat in the house, just feet from the dance floor. He watched wide-eyed, thinking the scene was way better than anything on Netflix or Hulu, his only other entertainment option for the night. The Shantilly and Oyster Reef, the town's two other bars, which had opened in the wake of Gil's, were no doubt romping; and there were likely a few folks in art galleries sipping wine and contemplating color and texture, depth, and dimension. But Gil Netters was center court, the main event in town, and by midnight most would converge here.

Guys in their sixties wearing tie-dyed or Grateful Dead T-shirts shuffled and swooned next to a group of bridesmaids from Virginia Beach in town for a wedding. The girls were bombed, sucking down rum and tequila drinks laced with an assortment of sugary reds, orange yellows, and blues. By Carter's estimate, half the place was stoned, the other half drunk, and the most wobbly in the crowd were hobbled by a combination of the two. Young girls took selfies. Strangers bought shots for strangers and hugged like reunited twins. Old guys with forearm tattoos from their biker days compared them to the calf and neck tattoos of hipsters.

The youngest among Gil Netters' eclectic swarm were born when Bill Clinton was president and Dave Matthews topped the charts. Some donned pierced navels, drove hybrids, and FaceTimed the bar scene to friends at home. The oldest had fought in Vietnam or protested it, drove muscle cars, and used their cells more as phones than video recorders or pocket computers. Normally, such generational chasms alienated oldies from the post pubescent. But Gil Netters was neutral ground, a Swiss détente, where race, age, gender, and sexual preferences mattered little, and where boozers and stoners, married and divorced, rich and impoverished simultaneously merged into a single mind on its way to losing consciousness.

"La-la land for misfits and morons," Gil would say as he stared from behind the bar at the boozy grins, flowing hair, ass-grabbing, crotch-grinding, bear-hugging hordes guzzling and slurping shots and mixed drinks like thirsty Texas cattle at a watering hole.

Carter watched a black dude break dance and then saw James, a white, cross-dressing delivery truck driver for Hen House Farms, standing and applauding. This night, James wore his Marilyn Monroe blond wig, lipstick the same ruby red as his Corvette, and a plaid dress with a brass lapel pin that said *Jamesetta*. Above it was another ornament: a black and gold life member NRA pin.

Carter had met James a couple of times before, once when he was sitting outside the bar smoking a cigar wearing his Hen House Farms work shirt, and another time during lunch at the pub. James' voice and opinions never changed, regardless of his gender mood. When he was attired as Jamesetta, he was simply seen by the locals as James in a dress wearing lipstick. No one cared, except when James once tried to use the women's restroom.

"James, you can't be using the ladies' room," Gil had admonished. "You freaked out a mother and daughter who saw you walking out of there. Come on, man."

"The courts say I can use the restroom according to my gender identity. Don't you watch the news? It's been all over TV. That transgender kid from Virginia, Gavin Grimm, won his case."

"Yeah, and my man Trump is gonna fix that real fast," Gil had huffed. "Just do me a favor, James, use the men's room. If you have a dick, which I am assuming you do since you fathered children, then you're a guy, at least for the purposes of this establishment. So, lift your skirt and use the urinal in the men's room."

Carter thought it odd that the cross-dresser James was ardently conservative and, apparently, the father of four. James bragged about his memberships in The John Birch Society and NRA. The bumper of his red Corvette donned decals of both organizations, along with a silhouette of a family holding hands.

When *James*, he drank IPA beer. When *Jamesetta*, mojitos. James might have been viewed as a nut elsewhere, but in Cape Charles he was considered just one of the gang, just a few more degrees slightly off-center than most. *Doesn't everyone stray a few degrees?* Carter thought. People here were just people, warts and all. Perhaps that simple acceptance was the binding force that glued together this strange little town by the Bay. It made perfect sense to Carter. Cape Charles is an outlier, an outpost away from the normal pace of strip malls, rush hour, soccer fields, and Walmarts. *People looking for normal don't come here.*

* * *

One of Carter's favorite eccentrics was Timothy John, a happy-go-lucky fatalist who had built a bunker in his basement and stuffed it with bottled water, canned goods, and plant seeds. Tonight, he made his way to the dance floor in his trademark tank top. He wore them almost year-round, so everyone called him "Tank Top." He lived perpetually convinced that a financial apocalypse loomed just hours away. The collapse would trigger street rioting, even in his sleepy hometown of Cape Charles. For protection from neighbors and outsourced marauders, Tank Top kept under his bed two semiautomatic rifles, a .38 Special, and a hand-launcher for explosives. A gas mask hung from a hook on his bedroom door.

Tank Top had an IQ of 143 and had earned a PhD in physics from Washington and Lee University. While finishing his doctoral dissertation, he took lysergic acid diethylamide to further expand his consciousness and add depth to his words. He had read Carlos Castaneda's *The Teachings of Don Juan* seven times. Peyote, prescribed in Castaneda's tale to enhance spiritual awareness, was hard to come by. And the hallucinogenic buds plucked from desert cacti tasted bitter, so acerbic in fact that chewing them induced vomiting. Being adaptive, Tank Top had opted for the synthetic instead of organic and binged on blotter acid for nearly three years in his quest to evolve into a shaman sorcerer. He had emerged from that experience disillusioned, seeing humans as little more than warring monkeys about to self-destruct. The least he could do was get the word out, so Tank Top had started blogging for preppy websites.

To earn money, Tank Top worked from home writing algorithms used by conservative groups to inflame right-leaning voters and track shopping habits. He would also add summer income by renting out his screened porch to college kids working at Gil Netters or the Oyster Reef or Shantilly's. There was one rule: No one was allowed in his basement under any circumstances. It was speculated that Tank Top kept stashes of ammo, two generators, canned beets, jerky, bottled water, and instant oatmeal—but no wheat products. Tank Top was gluten free pre-apocalypse, and, by God, he would remain so when the world collapsed.

Tank Top was a celebrity of sorts in town too. He was tapped each year to lead the Cape Charles Shuck-N-Suck parade, which he'd done in the morning on this very day. Shuck-N-Suck was celebrated with blaring fire trucks, locals wearing masks riding golf carts and tossing candy, kids darting into the street to chase clowns, and, best of all, Shriners doing figure-eights in their motorized go-cart cars.

Hours earlier, Carter had awakened early in the morning to witness the famed parade and Tank Top in action. With coffee mug in hand, he had begun his walk to Gil's and what would inevitably be a crowd of locals gathering to cheer on the promenade. Most of the historic streets in Cape Charles, Tyler Lane included, were a canopy of chestnut trees, sycamores, and pecan trees, some a century old. In their shadows were crepe myrtles, many senior citizens themselves, fully bloomed in a painter's palette of pinks, reds, and purples. Residents of the historic district coveted these shrubs, grooming and feeding them as if they were family members. Some of the oldest looked human, their torsos contorted and branches elbowing skyward.

They reminded Carter of the talking apple trees that chased off Dorothy and her entourage in *The Wizard of Oz*.

Carter had arrived to the parade just in time to see Tank Top riding point in the bed of the mayor's red Chevy Colorado pickup. He wore the same outfit he had donned almost every other year, and not too dissimilar to his regular attire: a foam cap that vaguely resembled a clam, oversized mirrored sunglasses, a Rudolph nose, and his signature tie-dyed tank top, frayed cutoff blue jeans, and yellow flip-flops. He smiled broadly, flashing a gap in his front teeth wide enough to slide a quarter through. And when he waved, he exposed armpits with more hair than was on his head.

"Tank Top oughta shave his armpits and make a wig," said Gil, who had sat with Carter in front of the pub mocking the festivities. "I love Tank Top, but he's out there."

"Seems pretty harmless to me."

"They all do until they snap," Gil had said. "I hear he's got some lethal stuff in his basement and even more extreme weaponry buried in metal boxes behind his house."

"Guess we better stay on his good side then," Carter had quipped.

Tank Top loved oysters, so much so he harvested his own. He would wade chest deep into the Bay during low tide, plucking the bivalves from the mud with his toes. He loved shellfish so much that he had even won a few clam-eating contests. This made him a natural poster child for Shuck-N-Suck, which celebrated the Eastern Shore's booming oyster and clam farming industry.

The parade culminated each year when a long flatbed trailer pulled by a green farm tractor rolled down Mason Way. On it were watermen shucking oysters and handing them on the half-shell to parade watchers bold enough to run into the street to fetch the slimy treat. No one had ever reported getting sick from the handouts, so the town health inspector never waved a red flag.

Standing on the corner, just a few yards from Gil and Carter, had been Major and his trusted canine colleague, Minor. When the oyster flatbed passed, Major had called out to Skip, one of his buddies on the flatbed shucking oysters for the crowd. Skip and Major regularly hunted waterfowl together in the fall. So, anytime Minor saw Skip, he knew he was going hunting—and nothing excited the Lab more.

Skip had given a shout-out to Major and Minor when rolling past. Minor's ears had perked and he'd bolted from his master's side, leaping onto the deck of the trailer in a miraculous athletic feat. No was hurt, and everyone who had witnessed the leaping Lab had laughed and applauded. Some had figured it was part of the show.

"Let 'em ride with me, Major," Skip had called, scratching his full beard and laughing. "I'll bring 'em to ya when the parade ends."

Everything had settled down until Minor did what male dogs do: He lifted his leg and sprayed one of the bushels of oysters.

* * *

Tank Top had recently introduced Carter to his best friend, Dude, an ex-Merchant Marine injured in a storm while at sea. Workers' comp paid Dude plenty, so his only paid gig was booking small-time rock bands into small-town venues and playing drums in cover bands. Dude looked like a Samurai warrior with a slight goatee and deep-set Asian eyes. He hobbled from his injury and could only hear out of one ear. Yet, if rock music played, he'd be among the first to start grooving and looking for a dance partner. He was high most of the time, which was abundantly evident by his brown-stained teeth and fingertips. His eyes were as glassy and as slick as the Bay on a windless day. When stoned, he grinned like a Cheshire cat.

Dude always remained remarkably coherent regardless of how much tetrahydrocannabinol he ingested—or how potent. Lately, he'd been smoking THC-enhanced marijuana harvested in a greenhouse outside of Colorado Springs. He desperately wanted to move to Colorado and be a marijuana tester for growers out there, the equivalent of a sommelier for wineries. But, alas, Dude was on probation for dealing weed and therefore restricted from leaving Virginia. So, with Tank Top's help, Dude imported the best stuff coming out of the West. He had packages mailed to a P.O. Box two towns away on the Shore.

"Smoke a bowl of this stuff and you'll be dancing the two-step with Alice in Wonderland," Dude had told Carter one evening as they stood outside of Gil Netters. "Four hundred an ounce and worth every dime." He had tried to hand Carter a tightly rolled duby tucked into a cigarette holder. "I can hook you up anytime."

"No thanks," Carter had said. "The stuff makes me paranoid and dumb. Every time I smoke it, I turn into a drooling mess."

"And the problem is?" Dude had quipped. "Drooling paranoia can be fun, if you let it."

"You'll have to teach me your secret sometime, Dude, but not tonight. I need to clear my calendar first and update my medical insurance before I enter your pot smoking academy."

Occasionally, a band Dude booked would let him play drums on a song or two. In fact, Gil claimed Dude only booked bands that indulged his sitting in. That was his version of a kickback. When flailing the skins, Dude would keep his head turned with his good ear pointed toward the bass player to help keep time. He loved banging away on Saturdays at Gil's, where he was revered. Locals would chant *Dude, Dude, Dude* to coax the band to let him jam. And that's exactly what was happening this Saturday night, many hours after the Shuck-N-Suck parade had ended, as Carter watched from his corner barstool.

The crowd started chanting, and a few thumped their fists on the bar. Dude happily complied, acting embarrassed. He took a bow and sat in as drummer for the Freddy Mac Lenders as they played a set of Otis Redding.

* * *

The band took a break after its second set, and the room quieted as sweaty patrons stepped to the sidewalk for fresh air or a smoke. Carter felt a tap on his shoulder—more like three finger jabs on his shoulder blade.

He whipped his head around, hoping one of the hot bridesmaids had noticed him, or, at worst, one of the bulky women with red hair was ready to collapse him into her cleavage. He saw neither. In fact, no one was behind him. He shrugged it off, drained the rest of his Tito's, and signaled Gil for another.

"How is it going, Sparky? You trolling or just watching everyone else have fun?"

"Just spectating. This is better than box seats at a Yankees game."

"Yeah, and you're striking out. Where's your girlfriend? The psychic chick? Home humping the old guy? Guess you can't compete with a limp-dick seventysomething."

"What can I say, Gil? Viagra changed everything. Old guys can keep up with us young bucks, thanks to Pfizer. Just look at this place. You got guys in their fifties grinding on girls in their twenties."

"Beautiful thing, ain't it, Sparky? Never thought of it that way, but I guess Viagra helps keep me in business. The old guys have money; they're the ones buying drinks. The young dipshits buy Miller Lite."

"I guess that's true. You sell booze, and Pfizer sells hope. Together, they add up to confidence, and there's a lot of that raging in here tonight."

"Where's yours, moron? It's Saturday night. You're single."

"Did I hear somebody talking about Viagra and getting laid?"

The voice from behind him sounded familiar—too familiar. Carter spun the barstool 180 degrees. When the rotation stopped, his face was inches from Kate Lee-Capps.

"Holy shit. I mean, this is crazy. It's you."

"Yes, Carter, it's me, and you're the crazy one. Remember? That's how we met." Kate giggled.

"So, who's your friend?" Gil chimed. His eyes locked on Kate's, and his grin was equally as broad. "Welcome to the Island of Misfit Toys."

"Gil, this is Dr. Kate Lee-Capps from Norfolk, my umm—"

"*Friend*. I'm his friend," Kate said, careful to keep her status as Carter's shrink under wraps.

"My condolences," Gil smirked. "I feel your pain. He's my friend too."

"Island of Misfit Toys, Gil? Do explain."

"Stick around, and you'll see what I mean."

* * *

Kate looked better than Carter had remembered. Her hair flowed over her shoulders. Her V-neck short-sleeve blouse accented her long, thin neck and cut arms. Her blue jeans hugged her hips and thighs and rode just above her ankle. There, she wore a gold ankle bracelet that matched her flat leather sandals and hoop earrings. She smelled like lavender.

"Without heels, we're on eye level," Carter said. He stood to give her a hug. "You look great, and it's great to see you."

"You too, Carter. I thought I might find you here."

"Not many options. There are only a couple of fishing holes in town, and most of the guppies congregate here late on Saturday nights."

"So, I'm a fish?" Kate laughed.

"More like a mermaid. And watch out for those," Carter said. He pointed to the gill nets draped over the windows. "Wouldn't want you to drown. So, the obvious question: What brings you to this little outpost?"

"My friend has a weekend place here, a condo over at the golf course community."

"Your friend a he or a she?"

"He. Name's Arnold. He's a physical therapist. Gives great back massages."

"Great back rubs, huh. That's hard to compete with."

"Oh, you're competing are you?"

"Like my friend Gil says, you can't win if you're not in the game."

"So, you're a player?"

"Maybe. I guess. Seriously, thanks again for helping me."

"I got the flowers and card. Nice touch. Thanks."

"I've thought about you and our conversation—a lot. I'm not sure I'm cured of harboring guilt, but I'm definitely not thinking about it as much . . . So, where is Arnold? I want to see his hands."

"Arnold played golf with some friends today. I think he got a little too much sun and had a couple too many bourbons. Nice night, so I decided to grab his golf cart to see if I could find you."

"Thank God for golf carts," Carter said. "Can I buy you a drink?"

"No, but in the cooler of my golf cart I have a very nice, very expensive bottle of Oregon pinot noir, compliments of Uncle Sid. Interested?"

* * *

Kate pulled the golf cart into the alleyway behind Carter's house and parked in the backyard.

"Safer here," Carter said. "More discreet too. Not many secrets in a small town. You gotta keep your eyes open and windows closed. Neighbors here aren't just nosy, they feel entitled to know each other's business. It's sort of a hobby. Come on in. I'll show you the place."

"Okay, but I can only stay a bit. Arnold—remember?"

Carter had done lots of work to the place—new kitchen countertops; remolded bathrooms up and down; plaster wall repairs; fresh paint throughout.

Bringing the old house back to respectability had proven therapeutic. The house, like Carter, sagged from the weight of too many storms. He had patched and smoothed each plaster crack as if putting a salve on some tear in his skin. The divorce, nebulous jobs, and now unemployment pelted him like hail stones on the hood of a car. He felt pocked and fearful of encountering more of life's bad weather. Meeting Rose had drawn him back into the weather, but he fought to keep his emotional investment in her at a minimum. *If only you could buy accident insurance for relationships,* he thought.

Kate loved the house, especially its hardwood floors, archways, and built-in walnut bookcases. She scanned Carter's small library while sipping her wine: Pat Conroy, Tobias Wolff, Jim Harrison, Ernest Hemingway, Mark Twain, Tom Wolfe, Pete Dexter, E.B. White, Gay Talese. Biographies on Muhammad Ali, William O. Douglas, Alan Greenspan, Thomas Jefferson, Albert Einstein . . .

"Not many female writers here," Kate said. "You have a problem with women authors? Maybe that's why your wife left. You ignore the female voice."

"Ouch. Low blow. I'm gonna need months of therapy to heal that wound. Know any decent psychologists?"

"Just one," Kate said. She toasted herself with a raised glass.

"Want to listen to some music?" Carter asked.

"You have any *female* artists?"

"I might have one or two CDs featuring *girls*. How about Alison Brown? Female banjo player. She does progressive stuff, kinda like jazz, but with a bluegrass and Irish folk flavor."

"Sounds like it'll go nice with this pinot—both very snooty."

They sat on Carter's brown leather sofa, close, but not too close. Kate kicked off her sandals, placed her feet on the coffee table, and pushed a *National Geographic* magazine out of the way with her heel.

"Do you mind?" she said. She winked and tilted her head like a B-movie actress.

"That's fine, as long as you cleaned between your toes." *And what beautiful toes they are. Straight and lean, just like the rest of your limbs.*

"So, Carter, how do you like living here in Mayberry? You having fun?"

"Good questions. I ask myself the same thing about every day. Some mornings I wake up and feel like I'm living the dream. I walk everywhere. No traffic. Quiet at night. Know all of my neighbors. Very peaceful. The post office is two blocks away, my bank three, beautiful sunsets, volleyball on the beach . . . it's great. But some days I think, *What in the hell am I doing here? This place is an outpost, a backwater. I'm going to morph into a monosyllabic townie.* I guess I feel disconnected here, like a bystander to the real world."

"Carter, did it ever occur to you that maybe the *real world* may not be all that great or real to begin with? What is it that you miss? Strip malls and Ruby Tuesday? Traffic cameras at intersections? Jet noise? Sirens?"

"I'd like to see a movie every once in a while or maybe take in a concert. I like being around interesting people."

"Then drive across the Bay and go see a movie or the symphony. It's fifty minutes away. A lot of people spend way more time than that commuting to work each day."

"You're right, Kate. I know that. But it's more of the feeling of being far away and isolated than actual distance. The action is over there; the people are over there. That twenty miles of water between Cape Charles and Virginia Beach makes it feel much more like an outpost here on the Shore. Living here changes you. I feel like I'm losing my edge. I used to wear Florsheim wingtips and Windsor knots. Now its Keen sandals and tank tops. Does any of this make sense?"

"I get it. Your world is small here so you're afraid of becoming small too; you're afraid of becoming a guber. But I think simple and mellow can add to your charm if you let them. Softer edges feel nice. Most people would kill to live in sandals and T-shirts. Just flow with the town's current, Carter. Don't fight it. See where it takes you."

"Good advice, doc. You should do this for a living."

The two sat silent for a bit, enjoying the CD and the vibe they felt from each other. It wasn't an awkward silence or nervous anticipation, but more like a relaxed contentedness.

"Do you mind?" Kate said as she swung her legs from the coffee table and over Carter's lap.

Carter set his wineglass on the table and reached for Kate's feet.

"Foot massage? I am, after all, competing with Arnold, aren't I?"

Just as Carter began kneading his knuckles into Kate's heel, just as she moaned, a knock rattled the front door.

Startled, Carter froze. He looked into Kate's eyes like a Labrador retriever awaiting a command from its handler.

"Well, I'd say you better answer it, and I probably should be going anyway. I'll leave through the back door while you answer the front."

Kate retracted her legs, grabbed her sandals, and stepped softly through the kitchen toward the exit. She blew Carter a kiss and vanished into the black night.

Was that even real? Carter thought.

* * *

"Rose. What a surprise. Come in." Carter forced a smile. "Wasn't expecting to see you tonight."

"That's what I gather. Two wineglasses and some pinot," she said.

She picked up the bottle from the coffee table and read the label. "Nice choice. Expensive. Special occasion or special guest?"

"Special friend, yes. A doctor actually. My doctor!"

"I heard. A tall, very pretty one. Where is she? Love to meet her. She upstairs, freshening up?"

"Doctor Capps had to leave. She's with her beau and just came by to check on me. It was a professional visit."

"A doctor who picks up patients at Gil Netters and makes house calls. I'll have to find one of those. You know, Carter, there is a fine line between obfuscation and lying. It's actually an art form. Anyway, it doesn't matter. I'm horny. Let's go to bed."

CHAPTER 17

AFTER COFFEE AND morning conversation with Rose, Carter's cell phone buzzed. He didn't recognize the number, but the voice was unmistakable.

"Carter, it's Cyril, from the hardware store. Got your number from Hattie Savage. Can you swing by? Got somethin' I think you'll want to see."

"Who was that?" Rose asked. She tossed her hair over her shoulder and smirked. "Your pretty lady doctor checking in on you?"

"Just Cyril, from the hardware store. Says he has something I should see. Wanna come?"

"Sure." Rose smiled and hiked her sleeping shorts to show her firm thighs.

Carter blushed.

"You're such a little boy. So cute." Rose leaned forward and pinched Carter on the cheek.

* * *

Cyril and Mac in their wicker rockers were perusing the morning newspaper and exchanging barbs over a sports story about a San Francisco

49ers quarterback kneeling on one knee during the national anthem. Apparently, the biracial quarterback was protesting because of a spate of African Americans shot recently by police.

"The NFL oughta throw his sorry ass out. We're talking about the national pastime here. If the guy wants to protest, fine," Cyril piped. "But let him do it on his own time, when he's not in uniform or on the gridiron. Kids were watching, for cryin' out loud. What kind of example does this set for them? It's a damn disgrace is what it is. People who hate this country need to get the hell out."

"Cyril, you sound just like Joe McCarthy in the 1950s. Anyone who speaks out is a commie. That's the trouble with you right wingers: You hate anyone not like you, and anyone who disagrees should be locked up. You're just like those crazy-ass ISIS people who chop people's heads off. Maybe you should wear a turban."

"Here's a napkin," Cyril said and handed it to Mac. "Wipe off the drool on your chin, and then use it to plug the hole in your bleeding heart."

"Well, well. At it again I see. Mornin', fellas," Carter interrupted. "I see you're both filled with compliments and compassion for each other on this wonderful morning. This is Rose Portman. I believe you've already met Mr. Cyril Brown, owner of this fine establishment."

"Hello again, ma'am," Cyril said and tipped an imaginary hat. "Come on inside back to my office, and I'll explain."

Cyril led the pair to the back of the store and sat behind his desk. He groaned from a sore back as he landed.

"After being up in the store attic with you the other day, I decided to have it cleaned out; lots of old furniture, lawn chairs, bicycles, rugs . . . all kinds of junk. There's a poor black family up the road from my house that maybe could use these old bedframes and end tables. One parent and four kids. What a shame. Nice kids too. Very polite. I see them go to church every Sunday. Their mother's gussied up like a mother hen with her chicks in tow. Cute as cute could be. The rest of the stuff goes to my church for a fundraiser coming up. I figured we could sell some of it. One man's trash is another's treasure, as they say.

"Anyway, I hired Hattie Savage's nephew, Jed, and his friend, that quiet kid, Elroy. They was haulin' stuff out, includin' a bunch of old storage boxes and chests filled with files, papers, and old business records, just like those ledgers you looked at the other day," Cyril said to Carter. "Some of the stuff goes back to the '20s. A lot of it was old invoices and order forms, catalogs, brochures, stuff from the hardware store. Junk and trash, mostly. Been up there decades. A fire hazard is what it is. There had to be sixty or so boxes of old papers and ledgers."

Cyril pointed to a box by his feet. "The boys was gettin' ready to toss this one to the dumpster out back when I walked by and just happened to lift the lid and look inside. I can't say exactly why I opened this particular box, but something told me to, so I did. And here is what I found sitting right on top."

Cyril handed Carter a leather book. It was tattered and moldy from years of freezing temperatures and sweltering heat inhaled and exhaled with changing seasons. It was about the size of a catechism, the small ones Catholics hand out to third graders to study up on for confirmation. There was no lettering on the cover, and the glue binding it together had long lost its hold. Inside were a few loose letters, postcards, and a few dozen pages filled on both sides with writing.

"Looks like some kind of scrapbook or journal, maybe both," Rose said. She stood between Cyril and Carter as Carter thumbed carefully through the brittle pages. The ink on some of them was faded and barely visible. Other pages were stuck together.

"The words look to be written in Spanish, maybe Italian," Rose said. She leaned her face in for a closer look.

"Looky here," Cyril said. He flipped to the inside of the binder's front cover and pointed to what appeared to be a smudge of ink. He reached into his desk drawer and handed Rose a magnifying glass with an ivory handle. "This 'ull help," he said.

Rose moved the magnifying glass in and out a few times and then stopped when the inky smudges revealed themselves: *Luzia Rosa Douro. 1918.*

"*It's her!* My great aunt! Can you believe this, Carter?"

Rose gave Carter a kiss and Cyril a shoulder hug. "You're a lucky man, son," Cyril said and winked at Carter. "*Lucky* that I ain't twenty-five years younger. You take this with you, young lady." Cyril handed her the binder with a wink. "If this Luzia person is your great aunt, then this rightfully belongs to you anyway, as I see it. Family's important. Always remember that."

Rose gave Cyril another hug on his shoulders, careful not to tempt the playful old bird by pressing her breast on him. Churchgoer and do-gooder or not, men will be boys when it comes to ladies.

"Cyril, may I ask you something?"

"Yes, my dear, what is it?

"You said something made you look into that one box out of the dozens and dozens being hauled to the trash. Could you be more specific?"

"Not sure what you're getting at, Miss Rose."

"I mean, what prompted you at that very moment to flip open that box? It seems uncanny."

Cyril slumped slightly in his desk chair. He grimaced at first and then rubbed his tall forehead. "Mind if I pour myself a Scotch? It's almost eleven. Would you care to join me?"

"It's a bit early for me," Rose said, "but you go ahead."

"Me too," chimed Carter. He leaned on an old wooden filing cabinet while Rose propped herself on the edge of Cyril's desk.

Cyril took a few sips of Scotch on ice, stared at the glass a few seconds as if focusing, and then peered deeply into Rose's eyes, his baby-blues clear and fixed.

"Miss Rose, not everything that happens in this town is easy to explain. I've lived here pretty much my entire life, 'cept for when I went to college, and I can tell you the oddities are just part of life here."

"Oddities? Interesting choice of words," Rose said.

"Things happen, some would say strange things, but not necessarily bad."

"Things?" Rose responded like a prosecutor beginning an assault on a sworn witness.

"Look, I'm a religious man, a deacon at the First Episcopalian Church of Cape Charles. I believe Jesus died on the cross. I believe in the afterlife. Some people think I am a mean, heartless son of a bitch because of my politics. That may be so. I ain't apologizing for believing in right and wrong. Problem with liberals is that many are godless. And without God as a moral compass, their thinking is wrong and destructive. They invent things to take the place of religion."

"We know which side of the political spectrum you sit. Hell, the whole town knows, Cyril," Carter interjected. "You got Trump signs all over your store. You're a church deacon. But what's the connection here to what Rose is asking?"

"Well, some things that I have experienced fall outside of the realm of my beliefs. I can't explain them, but they exist. I try to ignore them, or at least not dwell on them. Which means I don't discuss them—ever, with anyone."

"You've come too far to quit now," Rose said. "What is it, Cyril? What was it that made you open that box?"

"The lady," Cyril said, almost in a whisper. "The one who passes through here sometimes. I've seen her in the store from time to time over the years, just wandering in the aisles. She'll be there a few seconds, maybe a little longer, look at me, smile, and then vanish."

"A *lady*?" Rose asked.

"Yes, a young woman best I can tell. Pretty too. Looks like she's in a long dress and always carrying a bag of some sort. She wears her hair up."

"What happens when you see her?" Carter asked.

"Usually nothing. It happens so fast that sometimes I'm not sure it happened at all. The mind can play tricks on you, 'specially when you get to be my age and have had a few drinks."

"Any other manifestations?" Rose asked.

"Official sounding word, Miss Rose. Glad I went to college." Cyril grinned. The Scotch was starting to soothe him. "Sometimes, usually after we close and are cleaning up, items fall off the shelf, almost like someone bumped into them. Happens all the time during the day with regular customers. The aisles are narrow and we have stuff piled everywhere, as you can see. We're kinda messy here. But sometimes stuff just flies from the shelves for no reason. Just last month, a tray of PVC pipe joints got knocked down and spread all over the floor. One morning when we opened up, we found key blanks by our key-making machine spread all over the counter. Another time, the hip waders we sell watermen were turned inside out . . . Lots of weird stuff like that. Been going on for decades."

"How do you know it's not kids just playing tricks?" Carter asked.

"We got surveillance cameras, that's why. When we look at the recordings, we don't see a damn thing. Now how in the hell do you explain that?" Cyril huffed.

Rose and Carter exchanged glances and grins.

"What about the box you opened?" Rose asked.

Cyril downed the remainder of his Scotch and poured another. He walked to the office door and closed it slightly, peering out to make sure his employees and Mac were outside of earshot.

"Now this is between us, okay. Goes no further."

"Agreed," Rose said as Carter nodded. "Doctor-patient confidentiality." She smiled.

"Well, I wasn't completely straight with you about the box. I was closing the store and heading back to the office to cut off the lights. Those boys, Jed and Elroy, had actually just left. I heard some noise, like boxes being dragged across the floor upstairs. I called to see if it was the boys. I grabbed a flashlight, went up top for a look around. Sometimes cats sneak up there. Even found a litter of strays up there one year. I looked around, didn't see anything. Then I saw this goddamn box skid toward me." Cyril kicked the box by his feet. "I looked up and there was the lady, just staring. I blinked my eyes and she was gone, just like that, just like always."

"Holy shit," Carter said. "I'll take that Scotch now."

* * *

Rose clutched the little leather book close to her chest as she and Carter headed to the coffee shop. She seemed to glow. She stepped gracefully with her chin up and nose to the wind like a thoroughbred heading to the starting gate of a derby.

"Cyril is a nice man," Rose said. "His story is astounding, absolutely textbook material. This could be a PhD dissertation: physical manifestations, recurring apparitions, evidence of anomalies."

"No wonder Cyril gets hammered every day," Carter said. "No wonder drinking is the national pastime in this crazy little hamlet."

"I have a theory about Cyril," Rose said. "I think it may explain his stridence. He is, I think, overcompensating because he's actually a softhearted person. Cyril doesn't want to appear as weak or flaky. He probably detests kooky Californians because he fears becoming one, in a manner of speaking. Cyril, like lots of strict conservatives, is comfortable in a world with one god, and a firm set of rules that, essentially, demonize those who challenge order. Experiencing a ghost so convincingly falls outside of Cyril's neat little world of crystal-clear boundaries. Ambiguity bothers him. It's messy, unsettling."

"I think it has as much to do with the culture here," Carter said.

Carter spoke about how Cape Charles, like most of the lower Eastern Shore, remains very insular. He almost sounded like a textbook. "Things change a lot slower here. Folks are more set in their ways because there is less of an outside influence stirring things up. Those who challenge belief systems are ostracized, essentially voted off the island like in some tawdry TV survival show. It's like when archeologists discover tribes of people deep in the Congo. Isolated tribes live like they had centuries ago. When time is frozen, change is frozen out.

"I think that's why so many of the true locals here, families that go back generations, don't like people like me moving in," Carter continued. "We bring new perspectives, religions, and political beliefs, which represent change. They see that as a threat. Remember what Darwin said?"

"What's that, Carter?"

"Darwin said that survival isn't based on being the smartest or the strongest. It's based on the ability to adapt to change."

"Whoa! How very scholarly, Carter. I'm impressed."

"Thanks . . . I think. But now you explain something to me, Rose. Why is this ghost—possibly your great aunt Luzia—living in a hardware store? And don't tell me it's a coincidence."

"It's the woo-woo again. That spirit, whomever or whatever she is, lives here because she has a connection. There seems to be something about this place that either encourages retention in the afterlife or enables living mortals to perceive it. And I doubt *she* lives just in the hardware store. Single-domiciled spirits may be a misconception."

Rose explained her theory, one that she and Malcolm had explored. "Spirits may not be stationary. It could be that they inhabit or frequent lots of places, just like the living. It could be that they migrate."

"So, the same spirit poking people and showing herself at Gil Netters could be hanging out from time to time in Cyril's hardware store. But why, Rose? Why not move on? And why is it that only certain people, like Jessep Greyson, experience these anomalies?"

"More people experience them than you might think, Carter. Many more would if they weren't inhibited by conventional thinking. This place has a unique way of drawing down those barriers. You have to open the curtain to see who is on stage."

* * *

Carter and Rose sat in the coffee shop shoulder to shoulder for the next hour continuing their discussion, which drifted from Kierkegaard existentialism to the lure of Harry Potter. *What's real and what's imagined? What's literal and what's symbolic? What's orthodox and what's parable?* They agreed that wars have been fought over such questions for centuries and without resolve. ISIS exists because of that conflict. American evangelicals despise agnostics for much the same reasons, both camps seeing peaceful coexistence as unattainable.

"We're all a bunch of insecure savages," Rose said.

The two nuzzled as they examined the crumbling pages of Luzia Rosa Douro's writings, pointing to certain words they could decipher or interpret. They also perused the woman's letters, which were not in envelopes or addressed. The writing in them was the same as in the rest of the diary.

"It's Portuguese. Gotta be," Rose said. "I studied Latin and Spanish, and I can make out some of this. I recognize a lot of these words in Spanish, but it seems like they're used differently here. The word *doce* means *twelve* in Spanish, but here, in this sentence, it seems to be saying something else. We need an interpreter."

"Fat chance of finding one around here," Carter said. "Wait a minute! I take that back. Thin Lizzy! Someone told me she's fluent in Romance languages. She's a teacher. And I think she's French. We were dancing at Gil's last—"

"Dancing with a woman named Thin Lizzy? My perception of you is starting to change, Carter Rossi. You're a bit of a playboy. You had me fooled."

"It's Luciana, actually. And it was just a dance. I barely know her."

"Wait a minute. I sense something," Rose said.

At that moment—that very second in fact—a teaspoon flew off the table just as Luciana walked into the coffee shop, silk scarf flowing from her long thin neck, sunglasses the size of a billboard, lipstick as red as Dorothy's ruby slippers.

"What in the hell?" Carter stood as the spoon skidded across the floor.

A waitress wiping the next table picked it up nonchalantly. "Happens all the time," she said. "It's just the woo-woo. I'll bring you another."

"Carter, sweet man. So nice to see you." Thin Lizzy leaned over and kissed him—on the lips.

"Ah, Rose. This is Luciana."

"Just call me Lizzy. Everyone does."

CHAPTER 18

AT THE COFFEE shop hours earlier, Rose had invited Lizzy and Carter to the *Topp Kat* for grilled shrimp, kale salad, and a buttery summer chardonnay from Chatham Vineyards a few miles up the road. Rose was a closet wine connoisseur and had even studied oenology and viticulture as an undergrad at Cornell. She had wanted to be a sommelier—a master sommelier—someone with a wine palate so evolved that she could not only discern with a few swishes of juice the varietal and origin of a wine, but from which cutting of grapes it was harvested and precisely what year.

Attaining that imprimatur had been far too demanding, a skill that was 75 percent learned but 25 percent inherited through DNA. Very few, in fact only a few dozen worldwide, possessed the almost freakish ability to taste the soils from which grapevines drew their sustenance. With that acknowledgment of her wine-tasting mediocrity, Rose Portman had switched majors and studied psychology.

"Welcome aboard the *Topp Kat,* my leased home on the sea."

"Very nice," Lizzy said. "Much more interesting than renting some duplex."

"Agreed. Wine?"

The two women seemed to bond instantly. They ignored Carter, who sat in a deck chair thumbing through a *Vanity Fair* while the ladies sipped their golden steel-barreled chard, peeled crunchy jumbo shrimp, and talked about their favorite museums in Paris and London. Both had a crush on Hugh Grant and gushed about the Louvre. Carter felt like a dolt. The most interesting Francophile experience he had had was eating at a French restaurant in Disney World and spending a weekend in Quebec with his ex-wife, his now lesbian ex-wife. *I guess that's kinda French,* he thought and chuckled.

At the coffee shop, Rose and Carter had explained their quest to Lizzy and showed her the writings they had obtained from Cyril. Lizzy had affirmed immediately that Luzia Douro's words were in Portuguese and that she would happily interpret.

"I usually teach Spanish, French, and some Italian, but Portuguese is still very much within my grasp," Lizzy had said. "This will be fun."

Lizzy had taken the writings home, studied them, made notes, and then gussied up for dinner with her new friends. She was excited to see the bachelor Carter again, but more intrigued by the pretty woman Rose Portman.

"You look Portuguese," she told Rose. "Your skin is so beautiful. Dark, but not brown. And your hair—lush sandy blond. God to have hair like that, so thick and wavy. Those eyelashes are to kill for. And your lips are so full."

Is she hitting on Rose? Carter thought. He noticed Lizzy's nipples harden through her thin white V-neck. *For Christ's sake.*

* * *

They were on their third bottle of Chatham by the time Lizzy started sharing her notes and thoughts about Luzia Rosa Douro. Lizzy explained that she had read everything written, including the letters, and then tried to imagine Luzia in the context of Cape Charles in 1918. Lizzy knew more than a little bit about the town's history. In addition to teaching Romance languages, she was a history buff and admitted to being enamored with the 1920s, '30s, and '40s. She adored the actresses Gloria Swanson and Marion Davies.

"That's one reason I moved over here when my husband left me," Lizzy confessed. "I love these old houses. Sometimes, at night, I walk the town trying to imagine this place when it was booming. I walk by the old Palace Theatre and its marquee. I try and imagine how people dressed going to the movies, what they ate, the kind of books they read and music they listened to. I imagine what it was like seeing people from the big cities come and go through the ferry boat and train stations. It must have been magical. Sometimes in the summer, when I walk the streets alone at two or three in the morning, I can see things."

"What kinds of things?" Rose asked.

"You know, things that used to be here back then."

"You see people, Lizzy?"

"People and cars, and animals . . . the old houses lit. Figures rocking in chairs on porches."

"Aren't you frightened?" Carter asked.

"No. The opposite really, Carter. It's comforting. It's like I'm walking in another world but without ever really leaving this one."

"Do the people on these walks ever say anything?" Rose asked.

"Not in words, Rose, but more like expressions. I see them speaking to each other, but I don't hear words. They mostly don't seem to see me. It's like I'm invisible. But, sometimes, one of them will look at me and smile."

"Almost sounds like you're dreaming," Carter said.

"Sort of, but I know I'm awake. I can feel the sidewalk on my feet or the wind from the harbor. Sometimes I'll hear the foghorn of a ferry, or music from an open kitchen window, usually swing music or a piano concerto. It's very soothing."

Rose refreshed Lizzy's wineglass and her own. She ignored Carter. "How long do your walks last?"

"That's the weird thing," Lizzy said. "The walks themselves sometimes take an hour, depends on how far I go. But when I check the time when I get back to my apartment, only a few minutes since the time I left had passed. Very weird! Did you guys ever see the movie *Field of Dreams* with Kevin Costner? You know, the 'build it and they will come' movie. There is that scene where the Costner character, while walking the streets, meets the old doctor, who had died years earlier. They just walk and chat as if both are living in the past. It's very dreamy, but very real. You just quickly drift back in time almost without noticing."

"Wow!" Carter said. "How cool would that be? Maybe I could meet Shoeless Joe Jackson."

"If I could drift back in time I'd want to meet someone other than a crooked baseball player," Rose needled.

"And who might that be, Miss Hoity-Toity?"

"My great aunt, Carter. Who else?"

"Let's see if I can help you with that," Lizzy said. She reached for her notes.

* * *

For the next hour, Lizzy acted as narrator, reading sentences Luzia Douro had written presumably nearly a hundred years ago and filling in gaps with speculation. Like a detective, Lizzy was building a case. She created dots and then connected them with shreds of fact intertwined with circumstance. She started by telling Carter and Rose what they already knew, that Luzia was in Cape Charles waiting for her lover, Douglas Kinard III. She wrote of their fleeting affair in France, her trip across the Atlantic escorted by Navy ships, entry into the New York Harbor, and train ride to the Eastern Shore. The ocean voyage was frightening as seamen stood watch on each deck peering through binoculars for U-boat periscopes hunting for targets. Luzia felt overjoyed and relieved to have finally arrived in Cape Charles, where she stayed in a boarding home owned by the Kinard family.

"There are several beautiful passages where Luzia writes about her golden ruby ring. She wore it on a necklace so it would remain close to her heart. Listen to this line: *Meu lindo anel de ouro. Eu uso isso no meu coracao.* The rough translation is 'My beautiful golden ring. I wear it on my heart.' "

"The ring!" Carter about leaped from his chair. "The ring was in the bank security box, probably in the vault. She went back for the ring."

"I was thinking the same thing, Carter," Rose said. "That ring was her only tangible connection to Douglas. It's all she had of him, a symbol of the promise he made to her. It's why she kept it locked away in the safest place she could find. I'll bet my great aunt checked on that ring constantly. I'll bet when the bank caught fire, she ran in to fetch that ring."

Lizzy gave Rose a hug, both women dabbing each other's tears with napkins, both laughing a perfect blend of joy and sorrow. Carter felt left out.

"What about Kinard's family?" he interrupted. "Any mention of them, Lizzy?"

"No, Luzia never mentions meeting members of Douglas' family, only that she was treated well by the staff who ran the house. 'A ajuda me tratou bem.' "

"Not surprised," Rose said. "The snobby Kinards probably just ignored what they saw as a problem, or maybe they didn't know she existed at all. Douglas may have arranged all of this secretly."

Based upon dates on letters and entries, Luzia had remained in Cape Charles for nearly two years, Lizzy continued. She showed Carter and Rose the most recent date she had found: February 13, 1920. In that entry, she wrote about a friend she had met at work, that she had adopted a stray cat she named Mateus, and that she gravely missed her sister and family in Portugal.

"Mateus. Interesting name," Rose piped. "That's the name of a popular Portuguese rosé wine."

Lizzy said that she had looked for any reference to Navy Ensign Douglas Kinard arriving, but found none.

"That's because he was dead," Rose said. "He was killed aboard the USS San Diego. The Germans torpedoed it when it was in the New York Harbor. Carter and I think the San Diego may have literally crossed paths in the New York Harbor with the passenger ship Luzia was on before it was sunk. How ironic is that?"

"That's extraordinary," Lizzy said. Her eyes glistened as they peered into Rose's pulsing pupils.

"Do you think Luzia knew that Douglas had been killed?" Carter asked.

"Like I said, I didn't see any references to that in her letters or diary," Lizzy said. "But I can tell you this: Douglas' death was publicized. I called a friend of mine at the library in town and asked them to do an obituary search. Sure enough, there were tons of stories about the attack on the Navy ship. It was big news. A few days later, the men killed—I think there were four of them—were identified and articles were written about them. My library friend found a long obituary and picture of Douglas Kinard in the *Norfolk Morning Star* newspaper, the *Portsmouth Ledger*, and a local newspaper called the *Cape Charles Gazette*. They called Douglas a hero, named immediate family members as survivors and said—get this— that he was engaged to be married to Sylvia Mae Hoffler, daughter of a wealthy German businessman who owned a fleet of barges that delivered timber to the railroad."

"That two-timing prick was engaged to someone else!" Rose leaped from her deck chair and heaved her wineglass over the side. "That bastard!"

Lizzy stood and gave her newfound friend a consoling hug. She placed Rose's head on her shoulder and caressed her thick, sandy locks. Carter broke in.

"Ladies, question: If Douglas' death was plastered all over the newspapers, then why didn't Luzia just leave? Why stay here?"

"Christ, Carter! It's obvious. Because she didn't know," Rose said.

"How could she not know? You said it was in all the local papers. The Kinards were well known and even owned a place here. It would have been big news: Local rich kid killed in submarine attack on American shore."

"She didn't know, Carter, because she didn't speak or read English," Rose said. "*Remember?* She's Portuguese. I doubt she could have had a conversation with anyone. Why would she even bother to look at a newspaper she couldn't read? Duh! I thought you were a hotshot journalist. No wonder you got into financing."

Carter sat and took a long draw on his chardonnay. "Don't vent on me. I didn't kill the guy. I didn't cheat on Luzia. Christ! I guess when one guy screws up, we all do."

Lizzy's cork popped like a fifty-year-old bottle of champagne. "Men are selfish pigs. Given the choice between their dicks and the truth, they always choose their dicks. Women are dying all over the world because of breast cancer, but there's no cure. But when men's dicks go limp, guess what, the drug companies fix that. *Alakazam*: Viagra! That poor woman."

Carter had to admit that young Douglas had been a bit of a cad. "But maybe, just maybe, his intentions were honorable," Carter said. "Maybe his plan was to return to Norfolk, tell his parents that the engagement to Miss Hoffler was off, and introduce them to his beautiful Luzia."

"Interesting defense," Rose piped. "But, either way, Douglas either lied to my great aunt or, at the very least, omitted the truth about his situation. Guilty!"

"Yes, guilty as a rat in a cheese shop," Lizzy added.

After a couple of trips to the restroom and some bottled water, tempers cooled and empathy replaced vitriol. All agreed that Luzia was a victim, either by design or by happenstance, and the trio drifted back to puzzling together what might have become of the beautiful Portuguese woman alone in America and stranded in Cape Charles.

Lizzy imagined Luzia walking the streets on cool nights, thinking about home, avoiding strangers, keeping her doors locked, and sitting on her porch stroking Mateus, always wondering when she would hear from Douglas. Waiting for six months, maybe even a year seemed reasonable. But nearly two years without word? Most, even hopeless romantics, would have abandoned hope.

"Why wait? Why not head home or at least to a city where she could have met people who spoke her language?" Carter asked.

"Maybe she liked it here," Rose said. "Maybe it was as simple as that. Or maybe she never gave up hope that Douglas would return. Remember, the war ended in November 1918. Maybe Luzia figured Douglas had remained deployed. Maybe she figured they needed him for a while to help put things back together over there. Hope is a strong drug. It gives you a hangover for a long time. It's hard to shake off."

After hashing out a few similar scenarios, the trio ended their discussion where it started, trying to decide once and for all what happened to Luzia Rosa Douro, the invisible woman. Answering this would require one more trip to see the Wizard of Oz—Cyril Brown.

CHAPTER 19

CYRIL AND BEST buddy Mac were well into their routine of bad-mouthing each other and the opposing political parties when the trio approached. Coffee had stirred the cobwebs in their heads from the night before, but it hadn't loosened them. They all had had at least two glasses of wine over their limits and barely slept as their conversations about Luzia Douro formed shapes in their brains.

Rose had dreamed that night of seeing her great aunt standing on a ferry boat bound for Norfolk, waving to those on shore, smiling. She had screamed to her great aunt, who seemed oblivious. Luzia just evenly waved her hand like a wobble figurine attached to a dashboard.

Lizzy had rested on Rose's couch, leg raised on pillows, imagining walking the streets of Cape Charles arm in arm with Luzia, speaking in Portuguese about music, fashion, and art, smiling at neighbors sipping sweet tea on their porches, and gossiping about those frequenting the houses of ill repute scattered in dark corners of town and sightings of well-heeled industrialists cruising on Mason Way in their gold or burgundy Fords.

Carter had slept more soundly than the two women. His main thought was what Luzia must have looked like and whether she was as hot as her great niece, Rose.

* * *

"Mornin' gents," Carter said. "More titillating doom and gloom today, I see." He squatted to read the headlines Mac and Cyril no doubt were sparring over. "TRUMP SAYS 'LOCK HER UP' " read the largest on the front page.

"You shouldn't use that word around ladies, son," Mac said and scowled at Carter.

"What word?" Carter replied, dumbfounded.

"You know, the *T* word," Mac whispered. "*Tits*. It's disrespectful."

"That's not what he said, you old fool." Cyril chuckled. "He said titillating. *Titillating*. Just keep your yap shut and stick to what you know, which ain't much."

"Abraham Lincoln would be so proud," Carter quipped. He looked at Rose and Lizzy, who were giggling.

"Lincoln? Overrated!" Cyril barked. "Warren Harding—now there was a great Republican."

"There he goes again with this Harding crap," Mac said. "What about Harding's mistresses and the Teapot Dome Scandal? Congress damn near threw him out of office."

"Fake news!" Cyril said.

"Mr. Brown, sorry to interrupt your lofty repertoire, but may we have a word with you? It won't take long."

"Sure, Miss Rose. What can I do ya for?"

"First of all, thank you so much for the materials you provided to us. They've been extremely helpful in helping us figure out what might have happened to my great aunt. But, it seems we've hit a dead end—no pun intended. We think my great aunt died here in Cape Charles, and maybe even in the fire at the old bank, you know, where the pub is now. Or maybe she didn't die there. We just don't know. We can't find any record, other than those old bank ledgers Carter found in your attic."

"Right, I'm following you. So, what do you need from me?"

"Well, where would someone without family be buried? Are there places with unmarked graves or where the town put people who were homeless or unidentifiable?"

"Good question," Cyril said. He scratched his chin. "You know, cemeteries are scattered all over the Shore. Lots of families buried their own right on their farms or in their yards. There are lots of private cemeteries too. And churches used to chip in to take care of their own when someone died and was without family or money. I wonder, what religion do you think your great aunt was?"

"Most definitely Roman Catholic. We even have priests on my mother's side of the family. One relative used to carve crucifixes for churches in Portugal and Italy. Palo Douro, I think his name was."

"Well then, I'd suggest speaking with Father Ricardo at Saint Mary's," Cyril said.

"Which church is that?" Carter asked. "This town has almost as many churches as it does stray cats. There seems to be one on every corner."

"Yeah, we got loads of each." Cyril laughed. "Lots of sinners and cats here, I guess. Plenty of job security for soul savers. We got Methodist, three or four Baptists, Catholic, Episcopalian, Lutheran, Eastern Orthodox, even a couple of those whack-a-do New Age ones. No mosques though, thank goodness. Yeah, I'd say there's one church for about every eighty people, including children, who live in town."

"Lots of sinners here is right," Mac chimed. "The biggest one is sittin' right here. Cyril reads the Bible each night because he's looking for loopholes. Don't get near him in a lightning storm is all I can say."

Cyril snickered and gave his buddy a high-five. "Touché, you old goat." Then he turned to Rose. "Like I was saying, Miss Rose, go see Padre Ricardo. Maybe he can help. But don't say that I sent you. He'll slam the door in your face and probably call in an exorcist."

* * *

Saint Mary's was just six blocks from where Carter, Rose, and Lizzy stood. On the walk over they agreed that Rose would do the talking, and that they definitely would *not* say that Cyril had sent them.

Father Ricardo, a short, round man with heavy cheeks and stumpy legs, was watering flowers in vases on the church steps. He turned and flashed a smile that lifted his cheeks almost to the corners of his eyes. Rose extended her hand and the priest turned off the hose nozzle then wiped his damp hand on his khakis.

Rose introduced the entourage and quickly explained their quest. Carter thought she would have made a fine newspaper journalist by the way she condensed the story of Luzia into a few sentences.

Then the priest led them inside, down the long church aisle flanked by stained-glass renditions of the stages of Christ's crucifixion and resurrection. The main altar was small but ornate, with a life-sized carved rendering of Jesus hanging spread-eagle, nails in his palms and feet, his head bloodied by a crown of thorns.

"Rose, I want you to see something up close." Father Ricardo walked her up the two steps and onto the altar, then to the wall behind it holding the crucifix with a bloodied corpse.

"Extraordinary," Rose said. "It looks so real. It's beautiful, purely from an artistic perspective. The pain in the man's face seems palpable. The detail is exquisite—so lifelike. It gives me chills."

Rose looked over her shoulder and saw Carter sitting casually in the front pew, legs crossed and arms folded. Lizzy, however, was at the altar steps. She was kneeling with her palms pressed together as she stared into the bloodied face of her Savior.

"Closer," the priest beckoned as Rose approached the foot of the cross, its feet the size of her own, the spikes through them the size of her thumb.

"Look at the base of the cross. Do you see letters? Read them out loud so your friends can hear."

"*Presente de Luzia Rosa Douro.* Oh my God!"

"Indeed," the priest said. He smiled again, and his blue eyes beamed with the intensity of headlights. "Your great aunt obtained this for the church *dopo la morte, capire?*"

"*Sí.* Yes, Father."

"There is a signature by the artist. See it?" the priest asked. "Look right here." He pointed to a small mark near Christ's feet.

Criado por Palo Douro.

"My God . . . again. That says created by Palo Douro. Had to be Auntie Rosa's relative."

"Her brother, your great uncle," said the priest.

Carter approached the cross to get a look for himself. Lizzy, still kneeling, blessed herself, closed her eyes, and began to pray.

"This happened long before my time, but as I understand it, Miss Luzia came to Saint Mary's often," Father Ricardo said. "Some of our parishioners spoke Italian, and Luzia spoke Portuguese. The languages were close enough to understand each other. Apparently, Luzia was childless and unwed. But, she was engaged to someone in the war and living in a boarding house here waiting for him. The man never came for her, but Luzia kept her faith that he would. She prayed almost every day and thought that, perhaps, if she made a more substantial gesture to God and the church, her fiancé would return to her. So, she wrote her brother and commissioned this magnificent carving."

"Father, you said, in Italian, that she made the gift in memoriam. So, she was gone by the time it arrived?"

"Yes, my dear. Luzia had died, apparently in a fire. The church buried her at a small gravesite over by Oyster. There used to be a Catholic church there too. But it washed away in the Labor Day hurricane of 1935. Not much left there now. Most of the grave markers are gone. I'm afraid Oyster, and a lot of these small coastal towns, will suffer the same fate someday. God is punishing us for ruining our planet, I fear."

* * *

Rose sat on the front steps of Saint Mary's. She felt stuffed with feeling and needed a few minutes to absorb all the emotional calories the morning had delivered. It was a flood of information that washed over her like a storm tide. She needed to catch her breath and get oxygen to her brain. The priest handed her a cup of coffee and carried a mug of his own. Lizzy and Carter took the cue and left to give their friend and the padre some quiet time.

"May I join you?"

"Sure, Father. Thank you."

"A bit overwhelming, isn't it?"

"Yes, a lot to absorb, for sure. I'm feeling sad for Luzia but happy to know that at least she had someone here to talk to and that she wasn't entirely alone."

"People are often more resilient than we give them credit for," the priest said. "They find ways to find strength."

"Luzia must have had a strong constitution, Father. Truth is, we think that Luzia's supposed fiancé had no intention of marrying her. And we know that he was killed and that Luzia was supposed to rendezvous with him here, in Cape Charles. She waited for him, almost two years best we can tell, living here in the dark and under false pretenses. And, Father, I think she's still here."

"How so?" the priest said.

"Father, I'm a parapsychologist, a scientist trying to establish protocols to prove—or disprove—afterlife and the paranormal. As such, I hold open the possibility that we continue to exist in some form after we die. Perhaps that existence is internal only, meaning that the deceased live only in our imaginations. Or perhaps those manifestations we see or sense are some form of energy, or thought, or perception. I can't know for sure—no one does. But whatever is going on, I sense that my great aunt dwells in this place. Does any of that make sense?"

"Perfect sense, my dear. There are aspects of our conscious lives that we do not fully comprehend. I get that and embrace it. Do I believe we exist in some form after death? You bet. If I didn't, I wouldn't be in this line of work. It's why I am a priest. It's why I believe in a power far greater than us. The concept of life after death is the taproot of nearly all religions. Without that bedrock faith beneath our feet, we have no incentive to lead good lives."

The sky rumbled to the south and Rose looked up, spotting gray stacks rolling in over the Bay.

"Thunderstorms. That time of year I guess," she said.

The priest looked skyward and nodded.

"Father, sounds like we're searching for the same thing, but from opposite ends of the spectrum. You rely on blind faith in your religious dogma as validation that we live after death. I, on the other hand, place faith only in those things backed by what's tangible or can be verified. Faith is anathema in my world. Forgive me, Father, but accepting something as fact without proof seems like the lazy way out."

Father Ricardo lightly patted Rose on the shoulder. He gave a light sigh, like Yoda trying to figure out how to coach the stubborn, young Luke Skywalker.

"Rose, I hear this a lot—the science versus faith paradox. I've read many texts about it. I consult my conscience and Bible about this all the time. What I have concluded, after four decades of being a priest, is that the faith world and science world are more compatible than dissimilar. The difference is how we *perceive* what we experience."

Thunder boomed as clouds eclipsed the remaining rays of the noon sun, and humidity drew beads of sweat to the surface of the priest's forehead. "Living here has been a delight," he said, "but I'm really not sure how people endured before air conditioning."

Father Ricardo sipped his coffee and quieted himself, not wanting to proselytize. Rose was clearly beyond his persuasive reach, with an intellect likely more developed than his own. She was more colleague than subordinate.

"My dear, as a professional you at least acknowledge the possibility of life after death, correct?" Father Ricardo asked.

"Yes, that's correct. In some form, not necessarily physical."

"Okay then, you also try and verify paranormal events to give them credence, correct?"

"Yes sir, in general terms."

"In religion, we acknowledge that certain events cannot be fully explained, like the resurrection of Christ or the aspiration of Mary Magdalene. We simply suggest that if you believe these things to be true, then they are true. That's essentially what the Bible teaches: Belief and prayer create our reality. Those beliefs live in our mind and conscious. Religion—church—provides affirmation of those beliefs. It provides a venue for people to experience their faith."

"Sounds like a fancy way of promoting group think, Father."

"It is group think, precisely. And those in my business see that as validation, not as weakness. Remember, Rose, there is strength in numbers."

"Yes, but it seems you're selling afterlife insurance policies. I don't mean to be disrespectful, Father, but organized religion presents fairy tales as fact. I mean, come on now, walking on water, healing lepers, a virgin mother impregnated by an angel, Adam and Eve—*really?*"

"How can you be so sure those things aren't real? You base your beliefs on proof. So, where is your proof, Rose? How is a belief that Christ rose from the dead different from a secular person, such as yourself, believing that they heard a voice or saw a spirit? It's really just a matter of context. The afterlife only lives as concept if you believe in it. Those who channel spirits only do so because they *believe* they have some ability to connect with those who are dead. Conventional religions like mine, at their essence, legitimize those beliefs. They say it's okay to believe in spirits and that afterlife is the promise of God. We are, you see, essentially operating from the same premise, Rose. In my world, we simply accept as fact what you're trying to prove or mock. The way I see it, we believers are a step ahead of you. We've arrived at the spiritual place you're struggling to find."

"So, padre, just like the Cowardly Lion in *The Wizard of Oz,* you *do* believe in ghosts."

The priest giggled at Rose's jest. "Well, we have a different name for them, but yes."

"Okay, Father, then allow me this question: Do you believe the dead are among us? Do you believe the spirit of my great aunt Luzia resides in Cape Charles? Because I do. I think Luzia is still here. I don't think she ascended to some mystical heaven or perished in hell. I think she's still waiting for Douglas. I think she helped us find you. I think she wanders these streets and buildings waiting, and that makes me sad."

"If you believe that then it is real, because it lives in your mind, Rose. You may not be able to prove it or see it, but it's real to you. You feel it, sense it. That's what Catholics call faith."

"I have faith in my beliefs, Father, I do. But as a scientist I need more than wishful thinking. I need explanations. I want to stand up and scream to atheists and agnostics and faithless people that *'You're wrong, and I can prove it.'* I want to believe, desperately, that things we intuit, feel, or see that aren't quantifiable are in fact substantive. I want to believe that there is more to life than dying and then darkness. What a horrible scenario! Frightening, really."

"Maybe that is hell," Father Ricardo said. "Ever consider that?"

"Very convenient argument, Father. If you flip that around, what you're saying is that those who don't believe in life after death are living in hell, or destined for it. How insidious."

"You've got some anger inside you, Rose. But that comes from the frustration of walking in the dark. You're gonna get lost from time to time."

"As a child, I wanted to believe in Santa Claus, and it gave me great joy when I did. But, it turned out to be a lie. Religion—*all of them*—is at best a well-intentioned deception, just like Jolly Saint Nick. It's group rationalization intended to make us feel hopeful and to control how we behave. But in the end, it can't be taken as literal, which means it's more fiction than fact. I prefer fact."

"Well, Rose, you're obviously very scholarly and make arguments that are beyond my pay grade. I'm a small-town priest, a foot soldier charged with providing hope and comfort to those seeking it. I pray that I've provided at least a tinge of that for you today. If not, well, it's still been a delight to meet the great niece of the wonderful woman who so richly endowed our church. Fate has brought us to this doorstep."

Father Ricardo stuck out his hand to shake. "Go find your great aunt, and if you do, please send her my regards."

"Your regards? Sounds like you know her."

"In a manner of speaking, I do."

"How so, Father? Be honest. Have you seen my great aunt?"

The priest again grinned broadly, eyes blazing blue, cheeks flush pink like a schoolboy about to tell a dirty joke.

"I try to keep our chapel open a few hours every night, Rose. I stop in to see if there are any lost souls who come in darkness needing counsel or comfort." Father Ricardo cleared his throat. "On a few occasions, I have seen—how should I say—images of a young woman sitting in a pew, alone, just staring at the crucifix, not moving, not saying a word, just smiling and gazing. She appears, seemingly from nowhere, and vanishes as quickly. Is that real or imagined? And does it really matter? You tell me, Rose. Either way, you'd better get inside. That storm is almost here, and you know what they say about God and lightning bolts."

CHAPTER 20

GIL NETTERS FILLED up nearly as quickly as the rain flooded the street. Tourists and locals poured into the pub to escape the torrent and grab a bite or a brew while waiting it out. Classic rock played while thunder clanged like cymbals in a high school marching band.

"Good thing we got here a few minutes ago or we'd be standing," Carter said to Lizzy, both comfortable and dry on their barstools. Lil, serving drinks, gave Carter a hard stare.

"What can I get ya for?" she said to Carter, ignoring Lizzy.

"I'll have a Bell's Oberon draft, and Lizzy will have a mojito."

"How appropriate," Lil huffed. She reached for the cheapest rum on the shelf and ginger beer.

"What's up with her?" Lizzy said as she brushed back her hair.

"Moody, I guess."

"Moody? What are you implying, Carter?"

"What? Nothin', Lizzy. Just saying that Lil is acting moody."

"*Hormones!* You guys blame everything on hormones. You'd understand if you were a woman; but you're not, so you can't."

"Jesus, Lizzy. I didn't say a thing about hormones."

"No, but your implication was clear. You'd better apologize."

"For what? All I did was order a drink. Lil's the one with an attitude, and, if I'm not mistaken, it was directed at you."

"I sense something deeper going on. Anyway, just drop it, Carter. Men just don't get it."

"Okay. Consider it dropped. So, pretty wild stuff at the church. Blew me away!"

"I felt something in there, Carter. Something strong. Can't explain it, really. But staring at the cross was overwhelming."

"You religious, Lizzy?"

"No. Haven't been a regular at church since freshman year in high school. Just seemed like a lot of hocus-pocus to me. But I'm not so sure of myself anymore. The longer I live in Cape Charles, the more I experience—"

"What, Lizzy? Experience what?"

"Like I told you, I see things, that's all. And I hear things sometimes too."

A flash lit the windows at Gil Netters, followed by exploding thunder. The lights flashed off and then quickly back on. Power outages from summer storms were common.

"That one was close," Carter said. He looked toward the windows by the pub entrance. "And look who just walked in."

Gil slipped off a dripping rain jacket and headed right to his friend.

"Well, well, well. It's Sparky, with a girl. Who'da thunk it? How are you, Lizzy? So nice to see you. What are you doing with this moron?"

"Lunch. He's buying," Lizzy said with a sly grin.

"So, you two are together? A date I presume."

"Yes, but no. Dammit, Gil, we're conducting business."

"Yeah, funny business no doubt." Gil winked at Lizzy.

"Actually, Gil, we've had quite an interesting couple of days exploring the supernatural."

"Well, you're obviously in the right place for that activity. Ground zero in woo-woo land. You been hanging out with the Ouija board lady and her nutty professor friend?"

"She's a parapsychologist, Gil," Carter said. "A PhD. She doesn't mess with Ouija boards. She's a scholar."

"Well, I guess that makes me a doctor of mixology. I've spent a lifetime serving and studying mixed-up morons and drunks."

"I know it's easy to poke fun at the paranormal, but this is actually quite serious stuff, Gil," Lizzy said.

"No offense intended, Lizzy. I was just having some fun with my best buddy here." Gil leaned in and kissed Carter on the cheek. "I love this guy."

"Dammit, Gil, would you stop that?"

"Carter, you're so uptight. Nothing wrong with displays of affection, even between two men," Lizzy said.

"You tell 'em, Liz. The guy is a homophobe."

"Am not!" Carter huffed. "My ex-wife is a lesbian."

* * *

The rain stopped and the lunch crowd fanned back out to work and the beach. Gil helped Lil clean up the bar and get the cash register straight. Lizzy headed for home, deep in thought and more lightheaded than normal from three mojitos. Her limit was four. Carter sat alone, checking text messages and emails on his iPhone while finishing his beer. No calls or messages. He felt alone.

He really liked Rose—a lot. Beautiful, sensual, and smart. Intense too. Maybe a little bit too much. She excited him, for sure. But he didn't relax around her, not the way he melted into a placidity around his shrink. Kate Lee-Capps was equally as smart, attractive, and interesting. But whereas being with Kate was like sailing on a mountain lake on a calm day, carousing with Rose was like riding the Bay when whipped by thirty-knot winds.

"How's it going, Sparky, seriously?"

Gil sat next to his buddy with a plate of fries and a BLT sandwich.

"Better get rid of that," Carter said as he pointed to the lettuce on the sandwich. "Might be good for you. You could go into anaphylactic shock."

"Yeah, I know. Happened once ten years ago when I ate some broccoli. Never again."

"Gil, let me ask you something. And I'm being serious. This ghost stuff around the bar, how real is it?"

Gil looked right and then left to make sure no one was in earshot.

"It's real, and it's been getting realer since that chick you're dating came to town. My people are freaking out. Last night, Lil was cleaning glasses behind the bar, looked up, and saw whatever the hell it is walking into the vault and just standing there, staring at the floor. The place was closed and the door locked. Lil about shit herself.

"Then two nights ago, again after we closed, I'm walking around checking tables to make sure everything is cleaned up for the night. I go through the vault area and feel something jab my shoulder, like somebody poking me with a finger. I turn, and there's nothing there. Fifteen minutes later, I'm cutting off the lights in the kitchen and I feel it again. This time, I spin and see something—someone—walk into the vault. Looked like a hologram. It was that Gina ghost. Same description. Younger woman nicely dressed with a fancy hat. She's just standing, looks down at the floor. I look away, adjusting my eyes, look back, and it's gone."

"Damn, Gil. I mean *goddamn*! You know, when I was in here Saturday night, something jabbed me in the shoulder blade. I turned, and no one was there. I'd had a few Tito's by then and didn't think much of it at the time. But now that you mention it—"

"Weird, Sparky. Very weird. Some of the help in the kitchen's been experiencing more stuff too. Frier swears that he saw a spoon stirring a pot of sauce, but no one was holding it. He said the sink faucets have been turning on—themselves. I called in a plumber to check it out, but nothing was broken."

"I may know what's going on," Carter said.

He told his friend about how he confirmed the whereabouts back in 1918 of Luzia Rosa Douro. He told him about Cyril Brown's records, the diary, and the crucifix at Saint Mary's. He kept his promise to Cyril, not sharing what the hardware store owner had seen.

"The one piece of this thing we can't pin down is how she died," Carter said. "We know she had a connection to this building, that she kept her savings here, and had a safety-deposit box when it was a bank. We even know what was in the box. And, we know the building burned and was nearly destroyed when Luzia lived in Cape Charles. That's where the blood trail ends. I can only speculate that maybe she died in that fire. But why? Why would she have been here when everyone else cleared out?

Makes no sense."

"Not sure how much I can help you fill in those blanks, Sparky. I don't know much about what happened or what caused the fire. If this ghost we call Gina is lurking, I can't imagine what she, or it, wants. I just wish it would find whatever the hell it is and leave."

"Gil, I need a favor. I'm wondering if you'd let a few of us spend the night here, after closing. We know someone who seems to have a special talent when it comes to this type of stuff."

"And just who might that be?" Gil asked. "Glinda, the Good Witch of the South?"

"No, someone more real: Jessep Greyson."

"Crazy Jessep. Are you shitting me? He hasn't stepped foot in Cape Charles since the day the first gay couple moved to town. That was fifteen years ago. Rumor is he never leaves his farm. He's one eccentric cat."

"I know, I met him, and I'm not sure he'll come. But I'd like to invite him and Lizzy and Rose too."

"That's a lot of woo-woo to have in one place at one time. I'd better make sure my fire extinguishers are all fully charged and that the sprinkler system works. Could get hot in here. And I'll see if I can get a number for Max von Sydow."

"Who?"

"You know, the guy who played the priest in *The Exorcist*."

"If someone pukes green vomit all over your walls, I promise to clean it up before you open in the morning. Deal?"

"Deal, Sparky. But not a word to Lil or the staff, especially Frier. In fact, not a word to anyone. I don't want this getting out. Nobody will ever set foot in here again."

CHAPTER 21

ROSE AND CARTER had dinner together. He grilled kabobs on his back deck, and she brought a bottle of white Burgundy, already chilled. They ate in silence, enjoying Noam Pikelny's newest CD and older stuff from the Flecktones. Carter loved progressive banjo music.

Rose seemed unsettled, but not melancholy. She smiled politely and complimented Carter's cooking and music. For dessert, they walked to the beach. The sun was setting, and the sky was a blue canvas awaiting nature's paintbrush.

"Should be pretty tonight," Carter said. He reached for Rose's hand, and they locked pinky fingers. Their strides were evenly matched. They walked almost as if they were one.

"I really like you, Rose," Carter said. He leaned in with a kiss.

"Me too. You're a cool guy. Different than I expected when we first met."

"How so?"

"You're shy. I thought you were more of a player. I think your shyness makes you attractive to other women. Or maybe . . . I don't know. Maybe you're just cute in that Chandler Bing sort of way—kind of goofy-sincere."

"*Goofy cute* . . . Okay. Where does that rank? Just above *funny sweet* and below *awkward charming*? Babies are cute. I was hoping for something more: *macho stud.*"

"Sorry, sweet man, but macho you're not. Your hands are too soft."

Carter blushed. *She thinks I'm a wuss. Maybe I am.*

The sun dipped into the Bay, a pulsing fireball fading from yellow to orange in its daily curtain call, then casting purple shadows as it submerged. The wind picked up at the very moment of transition, just as always. Deadrises and charter boats scurried to beat the darkness to shore at full throttle, the throaty roars of their four-stroke engines echoing over the water. Tourists standing on the beach applauded the day's graceful exit.

"Spectacular," Rose said.

"Yep, sure is. Best sunsets in the state, maybe on the East Coast," Carter said with pride of ownership. "Those sunsets keep a lot of people here, and a lot more coming back. Magical."

"I can see how this place gets into your soul," Rose said. "Life is so connected to nature here, and simple. But there's substance here just beneath the surface. It's sort of like a chocolate lava cake. It looks plain, but when you bite into it, the thing erupts. Deceptive, very deceptive."

"You can get as many calories, or as little, out of this place as you want," Carter said. "You can be a recluse, like Jessep Greyson, or you can be a gadfly like Hattie Savage and know everyone in town on a first-name basis. There's the artsy crowd, survivalists, potheads, churchgoers, draft dodgers, retired Navy Seals, stock exchange executives, professional athletes, you name it."

"I haven't been here long, but I definitely feel that, Carter. I get it. Lots beneath the surface—literally. The stuff with the crater and magnetic fields is real. Exactly what effect it has on people here is harder to say. But I'm more and more convinced that sensory perceptions are amped up here, at least for some. Probably more than I suspect. Woo-woo runs deep in Cape Charles."

* * *

On the walk back to Carter's, Rose shared parts of the conversation she'd had with Father Ricardo. She confided what the priest said he saw: the ghostly woman who appears and vanishes. She talked about the corollaries between faith-based spiritualism and her more clinical approach.

Carter shared what Gil had told him that afternoon: the increasing frequent appearances of a vapory female figure at the pub. Then he made the offer.

"Gil has agreed to let us spend the night in the pub, after closing."

"Who is *us?*"

"You, me, Lizzy, and Jessep Greyson."

"Jessep? Interesting," Rose said. *"Very."*

"I'm not sure it will resolve anything, but it seems that Jessep, and maybe Lizzy, have more evolved abilities to witness anomalies than us— or certainly me. I've never seen a ghost or heard one. The closest I have ever come to a premonition was guessing which would be the fastest checkout lane at the Food Dog."

"Stick around this place a few years, and I bet you'll begin to *experience* the unexplained," Rose said. "You'll be a witness just when you least expect it."

"Honestly, Rose, I'm still not convinced how real all of this hocus-pocus is. But I will admit this much: People, like Gil, like Jessep, like Lizzy, like Cyril, who think they see *things*, really believe their eyes. Maybe that makes it real."

"How very noble of you, Carter Rossi. A man with an open mind, and of few words. Now, that's *sexy*. What are you doing the rest of the night, macho man?"

"*Sexy!* Guess I've been promoted from *cute*."

* * *

Rose decided it best to meet with Jessep to pitch Carter's sleepover idea. Carter offered to drive her, but Rose declined an escort. They settled on a night in the middle of the week for the gathering because business at Gil's was slow then.

"It's Monday. So, two nights from now. We have to work fast," Rose said as she lay beside Carter. "I'll get Jessep on board tomorrow. You reach out to Lizzy."

Carter wasted no time. He texted Lizzy, who immediately replied, *I'm in.* She'd have to get someone to let her dog out, but that wouldn't be a problem. She'd get a neighbor or one of the kids on the street to do it. Her bulldog had an overactive bladder and needed to pee every three hours.

Figure on being at Gil Netters from two until sunup, Carter texted. *Don't worry about food or beverages. We'll raid the kitchen.*

* * *

Carter spent the day repairing hairline cracks in the plaster in his upstairs bathroom and guest bedroom. Floor joists and the other ninety-year-old-plus timber that made up the skeleton of his house had expanded in the summer heat and tugged and stretched the walls and floors. Wall cracks seemed to have developed overnight. He quickly ran out of spackling and hoofed over to the hardware store.

"Hey, Carter. What can I do ya for?" asked Cyril, more chipper than normal.

"Fixin' wall cracks. Always something, right? These old houses are more of a hobby than a home."

"Yes sir. And these old houses keep me in business," Cyril said.

"Where's your sidekick?" Carter asked.

"You mean Mac? I sent him to get a hearing aid. Told him I'd pay what Medicare didn't cover. Can't hardly have a conversation with him anymore 'cause he only hears every other word. Been like that since the war, but it's getting worse lately, a lot worse. The old coot is makin' a damn fool of himself."

"You're a good guy, Cyril, taking care of your friend like that. I know the story: You pay all his medical bills and even help with his rent. Hattie told me."

"Damn her. Can't keep her mouth shut. She's ruining my reputation. I don't want to lose it now. Besides, I owe old Mac. He saved my ass more than once when we served in Nam. In fact, one reason he can't hear is because he took mortar fire pulling me from a burning Jeep. I was out, I mean lights-out unconscious. Mac was riding in an infantry truck in front of me. He grabbed me by my armpits and dragged me off the road. Just as he did, another mortar hit. Mac did a summersault in the air from the impact, but the shrapnel missed him somehow. So, I figured I owed him. Been paying off that debt ever since."

"Quite a story, Cyril."

"Yeah, I wish they would have just given him a medal. It would have saved me lots of grief. I think that knock in the head he took from the mortar explains why he's a flaming liberal."

"Well, I only half believe you, Cyril. Somewhere inside you is a heart, whether you want to claim it or not. By the way, thanks for all of your help with the Luzia Douro matter."

"No problem. But remember, lips sealed. What I said is strictly between us. Got it?"

"Yes sir. Now, where's the spackling again?"

* * *

Jessep Greyson tipped his homburg and lifted Rose's right wrist to his lips. He had been delighted when she called to speak with him and even more so when she'd asked to stop by. In preparation for the visit, Jessep had scrubbed the axle grease from beneath his fingernails, shaved with a new razorblade, and flossed. He had plucked a few hairs from his nose and even trimmed his eyebrows.

"We've got a visitor coming, so be on your best behavior," he had said to his chocolate Labrador. "With any luck, you'll be sleeping in the hall tonight."

The ceiling fan whirred as a breeze tunneled through the windows facing the water. The old cottage was just twenty or so yards from the dock, which was less than a quarter mile from where the creek merged into the Bay. In the summer, winds prevailed from the southwest, cooling five to ten degrees as they passed over the great Chesapeake. In the fall and winter, the estuary served as an insulator, holding heat that warmed dry winds pouncing from the northwest.

"I apologize if it's too warm for you, Rose. I believe in living fully within the seasons, and air conditioning is unnatural. It prevents full acclimation and dampens appreciation for cooler months."

"How do you stay comfortable at night? I'd imagine sleeping in the heat would be difficult."

"I sleep naked with the windows open, as God intended." Jessep smiled and peered into Rose's pupils, probing for sparks of titillation.

He poured Rose a glass of port and joined her on his couch. She looked even more alluring than she had at their first meeting. Her hair was down and her sleeveless T-shirt exposed the definition in her shoulders. Her denim skirt rode high up her thighs, which were as cut and rock hard as her arms. Most impressive were her ankles. You could always tell by the girth of a woman's ankles how heavy she might become. Jessep called that the "ankle theory." Rose's ankles and feet were slender, no wider than her fist—a passing grade.

"So, to what do I owe this wonderful surprise on this fine day?"

"Jessep, I've come to ask a favor, a rather awkward one."

"Your wish is my command, fair lady."

"Wonderful. But indulge me while I give you some background first."

Rose provided Jessep all the details—*all*—even those she had been sworn not to disclose. Jessep listened intently, showing not one ounce of dismissiveness or judgment. These were serious matters. He stared into her eyes the entire time she spoke, not longingly or with seductive intent. Rather, he wanted to understand, like a first-year law student trying to wrap his mind around vague legal concepts. When Rose finished, Jessep gently took the glass from her hand and stepped to the bar to pour a second round.

"Fascinating accounting of your travails," he said. "Very detailed; very compelling. It's obvious that some force, or being, with some connection to you lingers in these parts. I agree with your assumption that this entity could be, and very likely is, your long-lost relative. There is no other apparent explanation. You have verification—a priest, Mr. Brown, bar staff. What's missing, obviously, is a personal encounter. You need to experience this for yourself. Such matters cannot be legitimized secondhand."

"That's why I'm here—mainly. We want to try and make contact with my great aunt, and we think that someone with your elevated sensory perceptions might bring that to fruition. You said when we were here before that you have experienced apparitions on this farm—frequently. I believe you. And I'd like to borrow that ability. I'd like for you to spend an evening with us at Gil Netters. I'm hoping that with your help, we'll have a communal encounter."

"Forgive me, my lady, but may I ask with whom would we be communing?"

"The two of us, plus Carter Rossi, whom you've met, and a woman with heightened sensitivities. Her name is Luciana Alto, but she goes by Lizzy."

"Ah yes, Lizzy. She speaks multiple languages, as I understand it. I know of her. Her ex-husband was an acquaintance. He turkey hunted on my farm a few times with two Navy Seal friends of mine. Nice fella as I recall. Ladies' man too. Spent the night here with a young concubine. No surprise when he and Luciana divorced. The old chap sent me a postcard from France signed by him and his mistress."

"Men. That one sounds like a selfish bastard to me," Rose huffed. "Are men even capable of being monogamous?"

"Honestly, my dear, it's quite unnatural."

Rose stiffened and sat up straight. Her eyes widened. "Do explain, Mr. Greyson."

"Rose, it's biological. Male homo sapiens were engineered to spread their seed among as many females as possible, and until death. That's why we have an unending supply. It's survival instinct in the raw. We as individuals don't live forever, but through propagation our DNA can. Philandering provides eternal life. It is one of the cruelest, yet most delightful dichotomies of nature."

"No doubt a man came up with that stream of logic. An excuse for cheating proffered as scientific inevitability. Impressive, *insidious*, but impressive. But if I thought you truly believed that bunk, I'd leave right now. So, indulge me. Let me at least believe you're not a complete Neanderthal."

"No, just slightly more evolved." Jessep smiled. "But, yes, for the sake of civility and mutual admiration, let's move on. So, your friend Carter will be joining us. Nice chap, but mediocre poet. I've studied the work he gave me and have a few suggestions. I hope he takes criticism constructively. His word choice is clever in parts. But the poem lacks continuity and feels like a shallow pool in places."

"You mean it's superficial?"

"Your word, my dear, not mine."

"You can provide constructive criticism when we're all cozily sitting around Gil Netters awaiting my great aunt. I'm sure Carter will be receptive."

* * *

As the afternoon waned, Rose felt herself adjust to the heat and relax with quiet conversation. *Jessep is Jeffersonian*, she thought. *Gentlemanly, well read, and curious.* She'd never known a man who preferred Walt Whitman over the NFL, but who could timber his own trees, shaw a horse, rebuild a tractor motor, and drop a deer with a bow and arrow from fifty yards. *Man's man. Total man.*

"Would you be so kind as to join me for dinner, Miss Rose? I'll be serving fresh rock fish, snap beans, and white corn. Please accept."

You had me at "Would you." "Thank you, Jessep. I'd be delighted."

"Excellent! Well then, let's go get dinner."

"Get?"

"Yes ma'am. The snap beans are in that field, and the corn is over there," Jessep said and pointed.

"And the rock fish."

"The tide is in. So, with some luck we should be able to hook a cod right off the point. It's a ten-minute boat ride down the creek. Boat's at the dock ready to go."

CHAPTER 22

A NIGHT PASSED, and Carter had not heard one word from Rose, despite texting her three times and calling twice. He stopped by the *Topp Kat*, and she wasn't there. Nor was her car. She hadn't been by Saint Mary's, and Gil hadn't seen her at the pub.

"Another fish off the hook," Gil quipped to his friend.

Carter reasoned that Rose had either left town or was at Jessep's. He boiled at both scenarios. *Or maybe she and Lizzy . . . no, no way.*

Carter thought about driving to Jessep's but didn't want to appear as the smitten, pathetic would-be boyfriend. Technically, he wasn't. They'd slept together a few times, and the sex was as hot and salty as a California sulfur spring. But that didn't make them an item. So, Carter did what Carter does: He let it go.

He certainly wasn't going to duel with Jessep Greyson to defend his honor. Carter had none to defend. He'd act nonchalant, indifferent, even dismissive. Acting hurt would only validate what Rose had probably already concluded: Carter Rossi is a *nice guy*, but not *the guy*.

I knew it when she called me cute. Guess I'm gonna need more couch time with Dr. Kate.

Carter and Lizzy met at the appointed time at Gil Netters. It was almost two, and the place was empty, except for its owner, who stood behind the bar closing out the cash register.

"Well, well. If it ain't Sparky and the beautiful Miss Lizzy. So, you're going through with this madness I take it."

"That's the plan—if Rose shows up that is," Carter said.

Gil thought about further chiding his friend about yet another failed relationship, but figured the wounds were too fresh to salt. Besides, he didn't want to embarrass Lizzy, just in case she had a thing for pathetic Carter.

"Supposed to get another thunderstorm tonight," Gil said. "Should be a nice mood setter for your little quest. You guys going to do some satanic ritual?"

"Oh Gil, come on now. You know better than that. This is for real," Lizzy admonished. "You know it is. We're here because of what you told us."

"Okay, Lizzy. I get it. Just seems a bit extreme to me. No one knows for sure if what we saw or heard is imagined or real."

"Precisely," Lizzy said. "Maybe they're one and the same."

"We're gonna have a long night, Sparky. Want some coffee?"

"We're? What do you mean *we're*?"

"I figured I'd stick around awhile. Free entertainment. Stories to tell the drunks and morons. Who knows? Maybe the ghost lady Gina has a thing for me. I wouldn't want you to steal her away; but I'm guessing the odds of you taking another man's woman are slim to none. Usually works the other way around for you." Gil couldn't resist.

"Stop being so mean to Carter, Gil. He's a nice guy," Lizzy said. "A bit of a chauvinist, but aren't all men?"

"Loaded question, Lizzy."

Just then the front door swung. Jessep Greyson held it open for Rose, who immediately approached Carter and gave him a hug.

"I'm sorry, Carter," she whispered as her chin rested on his shoulder. "You're so sweet. I should have called."

Carter stepped back, smiled, and said only, "Glad you and Jessep could make it. I think our double date is being crashed. Gil says he wants to hang here with us tonight."

"Do you mind?" Gil asked. "I think Gina the ghost may have the hots for me. I could be an asset."

Rose and Lizzy hugged and rolled their eyes. "It's your bar and your ghost, Gil," Rose said. "Who are we to evict the owner? Gil, this is Jessep Greyson."

"How do you do, sir?" Jessep removed his hat and shook hands with Gil across the bar.

"You're a legend," Gil said. "I've heard lots about you over the years. Glad we could finally meet, although under peculiar circumstances."

"Peculiarity makes life interesting," Jessep said. "It's to be embraced, never shunned."

"Well, you've landed in the right cabbage patch then, my friend. I know of no other place more peculiar than this bar and its patrons."

"So," Carter piped. "When do we start?"

The group agreed it would be best to remain together at the bar. From there they could see the booths and tables in the vault and beyond. An entrance to the kitchen was in plain view. Gil decided to have a beer. Carter, Lizzy, Jessep, and Rose had Cokes on ice.

For the first hour the five ghost hunters chatted lightly and joked. By three thirty, boredom had set in. Just as Gil had said, thunder started its march across the Bay toward the Peninsula. The wind picked up, and rain started pelting the cathedral windows by the pub's front door. The lights flickered once, twice, and then the pub went dark.

"Christ! Here we go, Sparky," Gil said. "Load the guns and empty your bladders."

At first, the gentle taps sounded like more rain. Then, all five heard the tapping grow louder.

Rose grabbed Jessep's hand. Lizzy pressed against Carter, and Gil stood, his eyes scanning the pub like searchlights in a prison yard.

Bang, bang. There it was again. Jessep stood, undaunted by the darkness or noise.

"I believe it's coming from the door," he said. Calmly, he strode toward it. He unlocked the turn bolt. "Well, looky what we have here."

He pushed open the door and there stood Jed and Elroy, Hattie Savage's nephew and his friend.

Just then, the lights flickered back on.

"Mind if we join ya?" Jed asked from the doorway, soaked. "Me and Roy here figured you might need some help tacklin' that ghost if it shows up. Plus, I gotta write a report for English class 'bout something I did over the summer. I figured nobody could top this."

"You wanted peculiar. Well you got it," Gil said to Jessep. Then he turned to the boys. "No one was supposed to know about this. How'd you boys find out?"

"Aunt Hattie. She said there was gonna be a *say-ounce* at the pub."

"*Say-ounce*. Oh, you mean *séance*." Gil laughed. He looked at Carter and mouthed *moron*. "You'd better do that English paper. Sounds like you'll need the extra credit."

"Sorry to disappoint, boys," Rose said, "but nothing exciting has happened yet. We're just sitting here . . . waiting quietly, until a few minutes ago."

"*L-like de-deer* hunting," Roy said. "Sittin' and waitin' for one to come by."

"Something like that, yes," Rose said.

"Hear that?" Jed piped. "Sounded like a door slam."

Heads turned in every direction. Gil checked the bathrooms and kitchen. "Nothing here," he called. Another door slammed, followed by thunder.

"This is gettin' good, Roy," Jed said. Roy stiffened.

The pub door opened slowly, first just a crack and then the width of a body. "Hey there, y'all, anybody home?"

"Aunt Hattie. What you doin' here?" Jed called.

"Guess I could ask the same of you boys. Stopped by to make sure you people don't hurt property values with all of this ghost stuff. Any luck?"

"Well, if it isn't the town gossip. Pull up a barstool, Hattie. What are you drinking?" Gil asked.

"Dark 'n' Stormy. What else?" Hattie smiled.

Gil walked around the bar and poured the ginger beer and rum over ice. "Sparky, I thought this was supposed to be kept quiet."

"Me too," Carter said. "And I'll have a Dark 'n' Stormy too, since you're pouring."

"Me three," added Rose.

"Okay. Drinks on me," Gil said. "Boys, you can have the ginger beer."

"You should know by now that nothin' stays a secret 'round here more than a few minutes," Hattie piped. "Lizzy here asked her neighbor to let her dog out in the middle of the night. Her neighbor is my cousin, on my mother's side. She thought that sounded suspicious, so she told me."

"And how'd you know we'd be here?" Carter asked.

"I checked with Cyril at the hardware store," Hattie said. "He told me about the goings-on. I figured there was a connection, so I told Jed and Roy here to keep an eye on Lizzy. They said she'd been hanging around with you, and that you've been hanging around with Rose, who's been spotted staying with my cousin Jessep here. Hello there, cuz. You hooked yourself a nice one." Hattie winked.

"That's a big reason I no longer come to town," Jessep said. "People here track your every move like a bloodhound on the trail of a fugitive."

"Jessep always had a way with words—and the ladies," Hattie said. "Charmer, a real charmer."

I guess that makes me a loser, a real loser, Carter thought. He could see Gil smirking and shaking his head. *He's gonna bust my balls relentlessly when this ends.*

A knock rattled the door. This time three people filed in. Smitty the cop, Cyril Brown, and Lil the barmaid. Apparently, Smitty and Lil had been hooking up. Six more people showed up after them, then another dozen. By four in the morning, the bar was packed with at least fifty locals hoping to see Gina the ghost, or at least witness the séance. It would go down in Cape Charles lore.

Smitty told Gil he could serve drinks as long as the door was locked and it was considered a private party. Gil had just one drink on the menu: Dark 'n' Stormy.

"We'll call it Gina's Going Away Party, because we all hope she's gone and never comes back," Gil said.

"Works for me," Smitty said. "By the way, Gil, you can't charge for drinks at a private event. Guess you'll be hiking prices this week to make up the difference."

Gil poured himself a shot. "Goddamn ghosts."

* * *

The party raged until sunrise, which seemed appropriate. Throughout the night, the crowd had grown and become more raucous. James came dressed as Jamesetta, donning his best Marilyn Monroe wig. Tank Top forgot about the apocalypse that night, wondering, if only for a few seconds, whether it would actually descend. Benny Frier and Cousin Nate told ghost stories and argued about the details of hauntings on their family farm.

Thin Lizzy decided to harness the townspeople's energy to, perhaps, liberate the spirit of Luzia Douro from Gil Netters and Cape Charles. She needed to remind the crowd that's why they were there. She stood on top of the bar and led the chorus in the Beatles song "Lucy in the Sky with Diamonds." Dude, the drummer, joined her. Gil found the tune on the pub iPad and played it twenty times that night. The townies hooted and mangled the song. No one cared, and few knew what the song was about anyway. It was weird but cheerful, like the town. They substituted *Luzia* for Lucy.

> *Picture yourself in a boat on a river*
> *With tangerine trees and marmalade skies*
> *Somebody calls you, you answer quite slowly*
> *A girl with kaleidoscope eyes*
>
> *Cellophane flowers of yellow and green*
> *Towering over your head*
> *Look for the girl with the sun in her eyes*
> *And she's gone*
>
> *Luzia in the sky with diamonds . . .*
> *Luzia in the sky with diamonds . . .*
> *Luzia in the sky with diamonds . . .*

* * *

Carter and Lil stayed to help Gil clean up and watch him lick his financial wounds as he counted the gallons of rum and ginger beer he'd given away. Before she left with Jessep, Rose pulled Carter by the hand into a booth in the vault.

"Carter, I'm sorry. I didn't mean to hurt you. It's just that Jessep and I, well, there is something special there."

"Spare me, Rose. We weren't dating anyway. We were just acquaintances with privileges. I had a good time and, presumably, you did too. I wish you and Jessep the best. Maybe you two can start a ghostbusters company, since you both seem so convinced this stuff is real."

One good insult deserves another, Rose thought. "Here." Rose reached into her handbag and handed Carter back the poem he'd written. It was marked up in red pen, words and stanzas crossed out and rewritten.

"Jessep was going to share this with you, but considering . . . He asked me to give it to you. He says it needs more substance. Hope you take it constructively."

"Nothing like a little insult to spice up my injury. Maybe I should challenge the son of a bitch to a duel," Carter said.

"Don't, Carter. Trust me. You'd lose."

Carter hobbled over to the bar to pick up glasses and handed them to Gil, who was standing over the sink washing them.

"You cost me a bundle tonight, Sparky. All because you had the hots for some wacky witch. Worst part is, she dumped you for a guy even stranger than you. Honestly, I almost feel sorry for you . . . almost."

CHAPTER 23

CARTER ROCKED ON his front porch, cupping the warmth of his coffee mug. His Syracuse University hoodie made his arms equally as toasty. Months ago, the soupy Gulf air of summer had retreated from the brittle north winds swooping down the Bay from Canada. Carter inhaled the crispness through his nose and felt his lungs cool.

Better than caffeine, he thought.

The flocks of summer tourists, who had inhabited Cape Charles like noisy geese, had migrated back to suburbia. The golf carts they had rented were now bedded down for the winter, batteries unplugged. Most of the art galleries and knick-knack shops on Mason Way that existed for them were shuttered or open weekends only.

Carter felt oddly content as he swayed in his rocker, watching the last leaves on the giant sycamore drift to the ground, their chlorophyll long drained. *Beautiful, but messy, just like Rose,* he thought.

Carter felt strong and happy, as if he were in a state of emotional remission. Since college, he had always felt a need to be in a relationship or moving toward one. The same with friends. They provided validation. What Cape Charles had taught Carter, the antiseptic it provided, was that you find happiness within—not through others. Happiness was not a dependency, like narcotics or booze. Rocking on the porch, working on his house relaxed Carter's mind and soul.

He realized that the tranquility of floating on this earth solo clashed with the visceral nature of human beings needing others. Humans are social animals—*or are they?* For Carter, tranquility had finally conquered its nemesis. Carter looked to his right and contentedly accepted that one of his rocking chairs sat empty, and he felt relieved. The pressure to be with someone—to make them happy, to meet their expectations, to impress—had been swept south with the soggy air of summer. For once, Carter's priority was *Carter*, just as Kate Lee-Capps had prompted when she consoled him back in the spring.

Smart woman, he thought. *Beautiful woman.*

The summer had been exhilarating. By exploring the town, its past, its woo-woo, Carter had become one of its eclectic fixtures—maybe not quite an oddball like Tank Top and some others, but a townie for sure. Hattie had been right. If folks aren't gossiping about you in Cape Charles, then you're not trying hard enough. *Maybe Tennyson was right too. Maybe having loved and lost is better than not having loved at all.*

Carter thought about his college sweetheart and that magical night in North Carolina's Blue Ridge. He thought about Sophie and the good times and other women who had come and gone. On the caboose of his thought train rode Rose Portman, the summer fling who had flung. She seemed so perfect at first, luring him like a shark to bloody bait and then cutting him loose to float on life's tides, weak and wounded. Beautiful, sophisticated but dangerously self-absorbed. Rose used men, and when their Old Spice turned stale, she tossed them overboard like chum.

The pre-Cape Charles Carter might have carried those scars of rejection for years. But he felt stronger now, more confident, less emotionally dependent. Rose's dismissiveness said more about her than him. He got that now, and, as a result, he could breathe again. Life felt refreshing, like Canadian air. He thought about the note Rose had left in his mailbox a few days after the Luzia crescendo at Gil Netters. Her cutting words had left barely a nick.

Carter,

You're a sweet man and an affectionate lover. You'll make some woman very happy, but, unfortunately, not this one. Our minds are more in sync than our souls, and, my dear Carter, my spirit is more restless than yours. Trust me, I need someone stronger than me; I would have made you miserable. You are too giving, and I am too taking. Find a gentle soul to match your own.

Stay in touch, my sweet. Let's remain friends and share a bottle of pinot gris at Gil's from time to time. Thanks for an enchanting summer.

Rose

When he learned a few days later after the letter that Rose had moved in with Jessep Greyson, he laughed.

Poor Jessep. He may be a man's man, and his soul may have survived the Civil War, but I doubt it'll endure Rose.

Carter hadn't ventured into Gil Netters or the hardware store or much of anywhere in town, but not because he feared bumping into Rose. It was because Trump had won the election, and Carter couldn't bear to face Gil, Cyril, or the other jubilant neocons toasting a man swept into office on a platform of intolerance and mania. He thought of Thin Lizzy, who visited a few days after the election and cried for her Hispanic friends fearing deportation.

"The haters won," Lizzy had said.

Carter had always strived to see the good in people and avoided talking politics or religion. Now, he couldn't seem to escape it. Trump's victory roiled the world and eclipsed the sunshine in Carter's beloved Cape Charles. In the president-elect, Carter saw only hysterical darkness, a Lord Voldemort crushing Harry Potter.

One day they'll carry this maniac out of the White House in a straitjacket, Carter thought.

Discussion about Gina the ghost and Cape Charles' woo-woo were about the only barroom topics that trumped Trump's unseemly and highly suspicious win. Townsfolk who thought they saw or heard strange things, or who had kept their sightings a secret, were no longer closeted. It was suddenly in vogue to be paranormal. Hattie, Mac, and Lizzy were right—Cape Charles had nearly as many wandering spirits as stray cats. And, perhaps, the magnetic field from the asteroid enabled these powers, as Rose and Professor Dunbar had theorized.

As for Gina the ghost, there had been no encores at Gil Netters, Bay Hardware, or Saint Mary's. Carter speculated that Luzia had moved on, unleashed by the will of the masses shooing her away in drunken revelry. Or maybe she had fled the lunacy of drunkards shouting her name in the middle of the night. On the other hand, maybe Luzia had stuck around Cape Charles because it was peaceful and she liked the view.

To Carter's delight, Gil, ever so much the businessman, had conjured a scheme to capitalize on his homegrown anomaly. He had posted on his Facebook page that on one night every August, Gil Netters would host a Gina Going Away Party. It would commence at two in the morning and last until sunrise. The annual event would be preceded by a small parade that would start at Saint Mary's and amble the full length of Mason Way under the escort of Sergeant Smitty of the Cape Charles Police Department. Once in the bar, the locals would exorcise spirits by chanting, over and over, "Luzia in the sky with diamonds—BE GONE."

Some strictly religious types in town thought such a spectacle blasphemous. But Father Ricardo took a more progressive view. "Better to believe in some form of afterlife than be an atheist," he told Lizzy and others. In a Facebook post, the priest said he would be honored to bless the parade of believers.

Lizzy and Carter remained friends, and she stopped by his place every couple of weeks to say hi and share some wine. Though Carter seemed upbeat, she was concerned that he hadn't been on a date since the Rose debacle. She sensed Carter's heart weeping, though he wore a constant smile. Carter had shown Lizzy the Dear John letter, and she had grown animated after reading it, contorting as if on the dance floor.

"Carter, she wasn't right for you; Rose isn't right for anyone. I saw Jessep at the Food Dog, and he said Rose is driving him nuts. He called her 'dark, pushy, and selfish.' Says she likes to argue. Count your blessings, Carter. That could have been you."

"I dodged a bullet, no, make that a torpedo," Carter said. "Trust me, Lizzy, I'm over her. In fact, I'm over everybody. I'm in a good place."

Lizzy had taken a job at a local community college teaching Romance languages and had registered a business called Woo-Woo Tours. Her plan was to drive tourists around old Cape Charles in a golf cart at midnight to point out buildings or abodes with spiritual inhabitants. Lizzy had also found love. She was three months pregnant and the dad was a Portuguese exchange student she'd met at the college.

"It's a girl, Carter. I know it," Lizzy said, rubbing her belly. "I'm going to name her Lucy."

* * *

As the fall air hardened into winter, Carter became even more reclusive. He listened to baroque music, developed a penchant for novels set in the 1920s, and turned his basement into a wine cellar. He even started wearing cardigans and socks. Gil called from time to time and invited his pal for a drink and to Christmas dinner. Carter politely declined. Gil shrugged off Carter's rebuff—but not Jill.

"He's just humiliated, that's all," Gil told his wife. "Hell, everyone in town knows he got dumped. Hattie told me she even sent Carter a sympathy card. The boy is just lying low."

"Carter needs tending to. He needs companionship," Jill chided. "Dammit, Gil! Carter's your best friend and my ex-brother-in-law. It's time for you to step up and be a buddy. Guys are such animals. No empathy. You need to get him out of the house."

"Carter knows I'm here for him. Besides, I've reached out and he seems fine. Leave him alone, Jill. Guys process stuff differently. We don't need to hug everything out. We're solitary creatures, like an old stag in the woods. When Carter gets tired of whacking off and watching Netflix, he'll emerge. Trust me."

"Gil, you reach out to Carter or I'm going to invite my sister Sophie and her lover to come live with us for a month next summer. You understand me, mister?"

"Yes, dear. Anything but Sophie and her liberal goofball girlfriend, please. Come to think of it, Carter is acting weird. Last time I saw him he was dressed like Mr. Rogers . . . *Hmm.* Don't worry about Carter. I know what to do."

Gil found the telephone number he was looking for on an Internet directory and left a heartfelt voicemail message. "Please call me back as soon as you can," he pleaded. "It concerns a mutual friend who needs our help."

A few days later, Gil called Carter.

"Sparky, I'm knocking off early. Meet me at seven. Show up, or I'll send Jill to drag your sorry ass over here. And if that doesn't work, I'll send your ex-wife. Dinner is on me, and please don't wear that nerdy sweater."

Right on time, Carter strode back into his old haunt. Gil came around from behind the bar and kissed his buddy on the cheek. With his hand on his back, he pushed Carter to a booth in the vault.

"Sit down, you bleeding-heart wuss. I know the Trump thing pisses you off, but get over it. You need some Kleenex to soak up your tears?"

"Only to wipe the slime you left on my face. I told you to stop that kissy Godfather crap."

"Calm down, Sparky. Jill's worried about you. Should I be?"

"I'm good, Gil, really. Just been lying low, relaxing, working on the house. Trying not to vomit every time I see Trump's face on TV. It's nice here this time of year. Calm. I'm more relaxed than I've ever been."

"Good to hear. I thought you were home boo-hooing about voodoo Rose."

"Summer fling; that's all it was, Gil. Rose is high maintenance. I hear she's making Jessep miserable. She caused a lot of chaos around here."

"True, but it was fun chaos, Sparky, you have to admit. You got laid and have more crazy Cape Charles stories to tell. Sounds like a win-win to me."

"I guess I'm part of the folklore now."

"Yep. People are gossiping about you and this ghost stuff. It's been good for business. The Gina Going Away parties are gonna be a hit. People are talking about it all over Facebook. I'm even having *Gina Be Gone* T-shirts made. I guess I owe you one, Sparky."

"You owe me for a lot more than one for putting up with your shit all these years."

"Maybe so, but as we both know, my shit doesn't stink."

"So, I'm guessing Jill ordered you to buy me dinner."

"So, you're telepathic. Good guess. Sit tight, Sparky. I'll be right back."

Gil left and about five minutes later, Carter felt someone—or something—poke his back, right on the shoulder blade—just like before—just like what Gil had experienced. Carter froze, afraid to look over his shoulder.

"Hey, handsome, Gil called me. He tells me you're in serious need of therapy."

Carter felt a hand massage his shoulder. Standing over him, her face nearly touching his, was Dr. Kate Lee-Capps holding a bottle of Oregon pinot noir, the dimple on her left cheek as deep as the Chesapeake crater. She set the bottle on the table.

Kate smiled, kissed Carter's forehead, and stroked his hair. Carter pulled her onto his lap and kissed her back . . . hard, without hesitation, and on the lips.

"I wasn't expecting that," Kate said, almost breathless.

Carter winked and pulled her closer. "Me neither."

"Well then, here's to being bold," Kate said, hoisting the wine bottle. "Compliments of Gil!"

ACKNOWLEDGMENTS

Books are born through encouragement. And for that, I have plenty of folks to thank. First off, to Cheryl Ross, a meticulous editor and dear colleague who nitpicked me until I bled. Next, my business partner, John Koehler, a creative wizard and all-around good guy. There's not a more honest book publisher out there. To Shari Stauch, the consummate author advocate. To Jana Sasser, an author with a Southern voice as thick as beeswax and as sweet as Tupelo honey. Thanks for egging me on. To my readers, Kristin and Kellie, who let just enough air out of my balloon to keep me humble but afloat. To Gene, Chip, Roger, Lou, Warren, Malcolm, Gina, Ben, and a gaggle of neighbors and drinking pals in Cape Charles—you stoked, albeit unwittingly, the embers of this book. I've never laughed so hard.

CPSIA information can be obtained
at www.ICGtesting.com
Printed in the USA
LVOW11*1550291117
558023LV00007B/76/P